AZURE CANYON

reek

× Azure
Peak

Falls

× Phantom
Peak

Drowned Man's Canyon and Environs

THE
EXPEDITIONERS

THE
EXPEDI

MᶜMM

MᶜSWEENEY'S MᶜMULLENS

www.mcsweeneys.net

McSweeney's McMullens and colophon are copyright © 2012, McSweeney's & McMullens
Manufactured by Thomson-Shore in Dexter, Michigan, USA — 587AF524 — January 2013 (second printing)
ISBN: 978-1-938073-06-9

IONERS

and the Treasure of Drowned Man's Canyon

by S. S. Taylor

illustrated by Katherine Roy

For my own explorers of the world—
Judson, Abe, and Cora

Prologue

The old wooden puzzle was kept on the top shelf of the closet in my parents' bedroom, a treasured family artifact that we were allowed to play with only when Dad was around. It featured a map of the world, with the continents and countries outlined in gold and silver ink, the capital cities marked by little golden stars, the oceans and seas painted a deep, turquoisey blue. It smelled, even many years after it was made by my great-grandfather, of varnish and paint and wood.

Dad said that he had always dreamed of traveling the world, and he told us about how he used to take it apart and put it back together, saying the names of the countries, imagining himself sailing across oceans to visit them. That puzzle was the world as he knew it.

And then, when he was ten, they told him that it was a lie.

He became a student at the Academy for the Exploratory

Sciences and studied all the new maps, the ones drawn with real ink on thick, beautiful paper, that included all of the New Lands that were added to the gold and blue and silver map he'd played with. He'd loved the puzzle, though, and he kept it for us.

"Did people really think there were only seven continents?" I would ask him skeptically when I played with it, picking the pieces up one by one, feeling the smooth wooden edges of Africa or North America. "Did people really not know about Deloia and the New North Polar Sea or Mount Anamata? Did people really think this map was right?"

"Be careful, Kit," Dad used to say. "We Explorers have always been redrawing the maps. That map was no less correct when it was made than the ones made by Ortelius or Mercator. A map of the world isn't a fixed thing. We know only what we can see."

I was fascinated by that old puzzle and I was fascinated by the idea that one day, Dad and everyone he knew had woken up and found that everything was completely changed, that where everyone had always thought one country or continent ended was not an end at all, but a beginning of something new and strange and unexplored.

One

Amerigo Vespucci and I had gone out to try to find some flour when the Explorer with the clockwork hand caught up to me in an alley behind the market stalls.

I was going as fast as I could, striding along, trying to stay warm in the damp spring air and trying to keep away from the watchful eyes of the agents. The parrot, whom we called "Pucci," was riding on my shoulder, mumbling nonsense words into my ear as we went. He could be a pest, talking away in his scratchy voice and shrieking when you least expected it, and sometimes he was aggressive. I'd tried to leave him behind, but he'd snuck out of the house, and now he was laughing and mocking me from my shoulder.

"I wish I knew what you find so funny about life," I told him.

Ever since I'd arrived at the markets, I'd had the feeling that someone was watching me. It wasn't anything specific; I was used to the constant surveillance of the agents who were posted everywhere, especially in public places. But there was something else, too, a sense that I was being tracked stealthily through the streets and alleys, as though I were a rabbit followed by a hungry fox.

There had been a three-month shortage of flour because of a drought out west and the uprisings in the new Simerian territories, and we'd heard a rumor that one of the off-market grocers had gotten a shipment in from somewhere. The off-market stalls sprung up in most towns and cities when there was a major shortage, and the government looked the other way until the regular supermarkets were stocked again. Lately it had seemed like the stalls were always there, hawking days-old meat, crates of oranges, dramleaf cut with grass or herbs, and other exotic products from the New Lands, sold by the traders and merchants who didn't like the price the government was willing to pay. There was a big picture of President Hildreth up on the side of one of the buildings, and I watched as a man walking by looked up at it and then spat on the ground.

I stopped to look at a stack of cages on one of the tables. Pairs of pale green birds sat listlessly inside. Argentine Lovebirds, read a sign underneath. I felt Pucci tense up on my shoulder. He was a Fazian black knight parrot my brother, Zander, had rescued from a cat a couple of months ago. The black knights were a species known for its intelligence and ability to be trained to complete tasks, and a lot of people had brought them back as pets after they'd been discovered during the exploration of Fazia. Pucci, like a lot of the birds, had had his legs and feet removed and replaced with metal talons that could hold smoke bombs and other weapons used in crowd control in the new territories. We didn't know where he'd come from or how he'd ended up in the clutches of a stray cat in our yard. But despite his bad temper and unpredictability, we'd grown attached to him. He already knew a lot of words, and Zander was trying to teach him more. As I felt him tense up on my shoulder, I knew what he was going to do.

"Pucci, don't—" But I was too late. He hopped over to the poor, staring lovebirds and chortled something in his strange voice. Whatever it was, it caused the whole row of them to start flapping wildly and squawking, rocking the flimsy cages.

"Get that thing away from my lovebirds!" the old woman standing by their cage yelled at me. I whistled and, thankfully, Pucci sailed back onto my shoulder, chuckling at the awful screams the lovebirds were making.

"That was just mean," I told him, and he cackled evilly.

"Get it here! Juboodan whizrat fur," a man called from one of the stalls. "Warmest fur you'll ever wear!" I wandered over and looked at the pile of thin, pale brown pelts stacked on his table.

"That's not whizrat," I said, loud enough for a white-haired woman looking through the pile to hear. "It doesn't have the undercoat. And whizrat fur is reddish. That looks like woodchuck or nutria."

The man scowled and made a rude gesture as the woman dropped the furs and walked on. I shrugged. "It's not whizrat," I told him.

The voices of the market hawkers echoed around me, boasting and selling. I kept going, my head down, looking over the items for sale, the lines already forming for cooking oil and sugar. People were shoving each other for their places in line.

It was still new to me, the *rawness* of the markets. We hadn't had to deal with the shortages before Dad's death. As an Explorer of the Realm, he'd gotten deliveries of all the hard-to-find goods coming in from the territories and colonies. But the deliveries had been drastically cut six months ago, and now my brother and sister and I waited with everyone else. I checked my watch. It was still early and if I took a shortcut through the alley and got in line ahead of the crowds, I might have a chance of a pound or two of the flour.

I was halfway down the alley when the man caught up to me. I sensed him before I heard him running behind me, but there wasn't anything I could do. Suddenly he was pushing my face into the brick wall and jamming something against the small of my back. I'd been mugged in the marketplace once before, and I knew what a pistol against my back felt like. I didn't think this was a pistol, though; it wasn't the right shape. Pucci squawked and rose into the air, alighting on a nearby windowsill. I couldn't help but think that if it had been Zander, the parrot might have tried to protect him or raise the alarm.

"Quiet," the man growled.

I could smell the dramleaf on his breath. He was a chewer, like a lot of the population had been since one of the early Explorers had found dramleaf in the Deloian hills. The scent was sweet and spicy, like the clove oranges my mother had made for us at Christmas.

She had died when I was four and this was one of the only things I remembered about her.

"Don't call for help, son," he said, his mouth pressed against my right ear. "I'll have to hurt you if you scream." He had an accent—German, maybe, or Eastern European—but it was faint, like it had been some time since he'd lived there.

My right cheek stung where it had been scraped on the brick, and I could smell his strong body odor. It had been a while since he'd had a bath, too. I was scared, but I forced myself to breathe and focus on what I could see of my attacker. He took his right hand off the back of my head and rested it on the brick in front of me. It was a clockwork prosthesis, a shining brass and Gryluminum fabrication, everything articulated so that it would move just like a real hand. A lot of Explorers who had lost limbs or body parts on their expeditions had them replaced with the clockwork fabrications. I could hear all the little gears and mechanisms in the prosthesis click and whir as he moved his hand. I recognized the knife utilities set into the fingernails.

His jacket sleeve, made of some kind of reptile hide, rode up a bit and I could see where the prosthetic met his forearm and, a little bit higher, on his skin, a small red tattoo of two overlapping globes.

"I don't have any money, but you can have the copper in my coat pocket," I whispered, trying to show him I wasn't going to scream. We were all alone in the alley. No one would hear me over the noise of the market. There wasn't any point.

"No," he said, "I don't need copper. Turn around. Slowly now."

I felt the pressure on my kidneys ease up, and I turned around as slowly as I could, buying myself some time. My glasses had slipped down on my nose and I pushed them up so I could see him.

His jacket, along with his broad-brimmed hat, was made of Krakoan alligator hide. I recognized the shiny hide now, with its odd colors that always reminded me of an oil slick on a puddle. Dad had had a similar hat, complete with the razor-sharp thorns that studded the brim and turned it into a weapon when thrown.

This man was wearing the government-issue leather Explorer's leggings that Dad had worn, too. They were made of tough cowhide and were covered with cargo pockets. The government gave every Explorer a black cowhide jacket, but Dad had preferred to wear a vest he'd made himself from Krakoan alligator and other hides he'd found on his travels. The sleeves of this Explorer's jacket were studded with various metal gadgets embedded in the leather, just the way Dad's vest had been.

Explorers had made a science out of customizing their jackets and vests with the little gadgets. One might be a knife that could be shot from the sleeve by pressing a button. Another might be a chronometer, protected by a bubble of reinforced glass, or an instant umbrella that would form a shelter over the wearer at the first sign of a tropical storm. Dad had broken his leg on an expedition a couple of years ago, and he'd had a little cane that shot out of his vest when he needed it.

"Look down," the Explorer growled.

I did as he said and saw that I'd been right. It wasn't a pistol that had been jammed against my back, but rather a rectangular object,

wrapped in greasy brown paper and a metal cord. He was offering it to me. My hands were shaking but I managed to take it from him. It was heavy, about the weight and shape of a printed book.

"What's your name?" he asked.

"Christopher," I whispered. "Christopher West."

"How old are you?"

"Thirteen."

"Your dad was right. You don't look much like him."

I looked up at him in surprise. What did he mean? Had he known Dad? "I look... look like my mother," I stammered. "The way our mother looked."

"He said that. But he said your name is Kit."

"That's what people call me."

He watched me for a minute. He was sunburned and skinny, with sharp cheekbones, a week or so of beard growth, and tired-looking, wolflike green eyes underneath the brim of his hat. He had the look about him that the Explorers always had when they were just back from an expedition. Dad always said that no matter how many baths you'd had, it was like you were covered with the dust of the other place for a couple of weeks after you returned.

"This is from your dad, from Alex," he said finally, in a rough, low voice.

I stared at him. I knew I'd never seen him before, but I tried to remember what he looked like in case I needed the knowledge later. His hair was very blond, bleached by the sun and long enough to peek out from under his hat and hang over the collar of his jacket. He held the arm with the clockwork hand awkwardly at his side, as though he was still getting used to the feel of the prosthetic. Some gadget on his jacket started clicking and beeping in a low, insistent way and he turned to check both ends of the alley before flashing me a quick, grim smile.

"Sorry about the scrape," he mumbled and then he was gone, leaving behind the faint smell of dramleaf and something else, too, a scent I decided was the scent of unfamiliar dust.

The words were out before I remembered there was no one to hear them. "But he's dead," I called into the sudden emptiness of the alley. "He disappeared in Fazia six months ago…"

Pucci lighted on my shoulder again, clucking and murmuring to make sure I was okay. His metal feet were cold against my skin. I looked down the length of the alley, but the man was gone and the only thing I could hear was the sound of the marketplace beyond. I wasn't more than twenty steps from a hundred other human beings, but I'd never felt so alone or missed Dad as much as I did standing in that cold alley, my own voice echoing off the walls around me.

Two

Forty-five minutes later I was walking home over the causeway to Oceania Island, three pounds of flour and the man's package tucked into an old backpack of Dad's I'd brought along. I'd been tempted to open it up on the spot, but I knew that agents were everywhere. Instead, I'd tucked it into the pack, underneath an old sweater, and walked to the final grocer, where I'd known I was going to be lucky as soon as I saw a line forming outside. I'd managed to trade all the scrap copper in my pocket for three pounds of flour and hadn't had to spend any of the Allied Dollars I'd brought.

Oceania Island had been built for the families of Explorers and merchants twenty years ago, a giant mound of earth poured right into the gray Atlantic. It was close to New York, and to the ports where the merchants did their work and from which the Explorers left to travel the world.

The Coast Road wound along the perimeter of the island, the beach on one side, and on the other the big houses of the merchants and traders. They had gotten rich after the New Lands had been discovered, and they'd started shipping back the lumber and food and coffee and jewels and animals. The Explorers lived at the northern, sheltered end of the island, where the houses were smaller and boats could be safely kept.

A lot of the big houses were empty now. I kept spotting newly abandoned ones every time I walked the road. They were hard to heat, and now that the uprisings and protests were making it hard to get any of the products out, a lot of the merchant families couldn't afford Oceania Island anymore.

Our own house was at the end of a short driveway off the Coast Road. It had been built in what Dad jokingly called "the Classic Style," with lacy trim and wraparound porches that looked out over the sea. The wind and sea air battered the houses on the island, and without paint or materials for repairs, it was now a moldy gray color. The woodsmoke curling out of the chimney in the early spring air reminded me that we'd almost run out of the firewood Zander had foraged from the mainland after the coal had run out. But it was May, and if it warmed up soon, we'd be okay until the next winter.

The shipments of firewood and coal for Explorers and their families were another thing that had stopped when Dad had disappeared. After the government had come to tell us he was gone, we'd kept expecting someone to come and take care of us. But no one had. It was just as well; I'd heard stories about the government's orphanages.

Pucci was flying in his funny way ahead of me, flapping a little faster than a normal bird would to make up for the extra weight of his metal legs. His body was iridescent black and his head shimmering silver, like the knight's helmet that had given his species its name.

"We'll just have to hope it warms up soon, Pucci," I told him as he swooped down and landed on my shoulder. We approached the big oak trees that marked the start of our yard. There had once been six of them, transplanted from the mainland, which was why our house was called "Six Oaks," but a storm a few years ago had reduced their number to five. The trees always made me think of Dad. He had loved them and had been so happy when they'd thrived, against the odds, in the salty air and poor soil of the island.

He'd been standing out by the oaks the last time we'd seen him, the SteamTaxi chugging impatiently as he'd hugged us and told us to be good while he was on the expedition. "Maybe next time I go to Fazia, you can come with me," he'd told us, trying to smile. "Remember, you're the Expeditioners." It was what he'd called us when we were little, but he hadn't used the nickname for a long time. The taxi had been loaded with all of his gear, and I remember thinking that he seemed off, edgy, his eyes darting around the yard as though he was waiting for someone to show up. He'd hugged me hard and I could still remember the feeling of my face pressed into his neck, the smell and feel of his Explorer's vest, the sense I'd had that he was afraid of something.

21

A chilly sea breeze pricked the raw skin on my cheek. Later, I couldn't put my finger on what made me stop and hide the package. A buzz of apprehension in my belly, I guess, or maybe it was the way Pucci started plucking nervously at my hair. In any case, I looked around me to make sure no one was watching, opened the pack, and found the secret compartment that Dad had sewn into it. The opening was hidden along a seam; you had to know it was there and wedge a fingernail under one corner in order to open the large pouch that would be invisible once I closed it up again. I took the parcel out of my pack and, even though I knew it was risky, ripped a corner of the paper so I could see what it was. It seemed to be a leather-bound book, and as curious as I was, I replaced the paper and dropped it into the hidden compartment, pressing it closed again. Dad had insulated the compartment so that you couldn't feel the shape of what was inside, and I tested it before putting it on again. Sure enough, the pack appeared to hold the flour and my sweater. Nothing more.

As I rounded the corner of the yard, I saw the shiny black SteamDirigible tethered to the posts at the end of our driveway, and I was glad I'd listened to my sixth sense or whatever it was. Maybe it had been my nose; now I could smell the faint woodsmokiness that the dirigibles gave off.

It was brand-new, which would have tipped me off that it belonged to the government even if it hadn't had the red BNDL logo imprinted on its side. The fancy steam-powered dirigibles were amazing things: egg-shaped, lightweight Gryluminum balloons with gondolas below, and sealed, superefficient steam engines that allowed them to travel nearly as fast as gliders. There were a few giant commercial SteamAirships around, but most of the dirigibles were owned by the military and the government. Dad had used them on some of his expeditions but we'd never owned one. They were dangerous, of course, with the engines so close to the cells of lifting gas. There had been a couple of big accidents involving Explorers out on expeditions, but the factories kept churning them out.

The framework of the dirigible—the "balloon" part of the aircraft that held the gas cells—was about the size of a large elephant. The gondola below was about half that size and shiny black like the rest of the craft. It was studded with polished brass rivets and had crystal-clear windows through which I could see red leather upholstery and more brass and polished wood on the instrument panels. The two men and one woman talking to Zander and our sister, M.K., had come out here in style.

They were all wearing the black leather uniforms of agents from the Bureau of Newly Discovered Lands, the blazers reinforced with Gryluminum plates on the lapels and decorated with a ruby red BNDL logo. The woman had her silver hair wrapped into elaborate braids on top of her head and a military-issue Gryluminum chain-mail cape, decorated with a little military insignia marking her as a veteran of service in the new territories. She must have lost her left eye, because she had a clockwork eyepiece set into the socket.

"I got the flour," I called out as I approached the group, trying to look innocent. What was going on? Had a BNDL agent seen me talking to the man with the clockwork hand? Zander turned when he

heard my voice, and I could see he was worried.

People always said how much Zander looked like Dad. At fourteen, he was only eighteen months older than me, but a good head taller and fifty pounds heavier. He already fit into Dad's clothes. His too-long blond curly hair had sticks and leaves caught in it, and his blue eyes, exactly the same color and shape as Dad's, narrowed at me, telling me to be careful.

Pucci rose up into the air and found a perch high in a tree, out of sight of the agents, so he could keep an eye on Zander and protect him if needed. Zander had sat up with Pucci all night after he'd rescued the parrot from the cat, making sure Pucci was okay and feeding him sugar water with an eye dropper. Zander had tucked him into his sweater to keep him warm, and Pucci had spent nearly a week like that, nestled up against Zander's heartbeat. Zander would always come first with Pucci. Actually, Zander came first with any animal or bird. They knew somehow that he liked them better than people, that he'd rather be out in the woods training a dog or a bird than anywhere else.

Our sister was standing next to him, glaring at the three agents. At ten, M.K. looked a lot like Dad, too, with her blue eyes and light hair. But hers was straight and tucked under a mechanic's cap, and she had a pair of lightweight brass-riveted welding goggles pushed up on top of the cap. In her raggedy mechanic's jumpsuit, holding a wrench that she had customized for adjusting steam engines, she looked like a very small inventor, which was in fact what she was—one of the best inventors of the New Modern Age, Dad always said.

I was the odd one out, with our mother's dark brown hair and navy eyes that had needed glasses since I was six. I was slighter than Zander, and I'd been waiting for a year for the growth spurt he'd had at twelve.

"This is your brother, Christopher?" the taller of the male agents asked Zander.

"I'm Kit," I told him. He didn't try to shake my hand.

The female agent handed me a piece of thick paper printed with a photograph of the man with the clockwork hand. "Have you seen this man?" she asked. I made a show of taking the paper and adjusting my glasses to study it carefully. He wasn't wearing his hat in the picture, but I knew it was him. It looked like a standard Explorer Card photo. Dad had had one. The name had been blacked out, but I saw that someone had made some notations at the bottom of the page: "STK" and "KA."

"Have you seen him?"

"No, I don't think so," I said, pretending to study the man's face some more. "Nope. I wasn't out there very long. Just looking for flour. I was lucky to find some at that stall at the end of the row."

The agents glared. The government didn't like to be reminded of the food shortages.

"You're sure?" the tall one asked me. He was a big Archy, with longish hair and a flowing dark mustache I bet he was pretty proud of. The muscles in his arms and shoulders seemed about ready to burst out of his uniform. "We have reason to believe he may have been trying to contact your father."

"Wouldn't have much luck with that, would he?" M.K. snorted. Zander and I glanced at her, trying to warn her with our eyes. M.K.'s mouth was always getting her into trouble.

"I'm sure," I said firmly, handing the paper back. I tried to seem relaxed, but my heart was beating like a steam hammer.

"What happened to your face?" the female agent asked, noticing the scrape on my cheek.

"Oh, this?" I gambled, hoping the mention of the shortages would get their minds off of the man. "I got knocked down in line waiting for the flour." Underneath the military insignia on her cape, there was a slim, embroidered badge that read "Agent Euphronia Wolff."

They all watched me for a minute and then one of the agents nodded in the direction of the dirigible. The passenger-side door of the gondola opened and a man stepped out and walked slowly over to us. He wore a BNDL uniform, the sleeves dotted with a few discreet gadgets, and a Gryluminum top hat, shiny silver like Agent Wolff's cape.

"This is Mr. Francis Foley, the director of the Bureau of Newly Discovered Lands. He—" one of the agents started, but I interrupted him, my gaze locked onto Francis Foley.

"We know who he is," I said. I wouldn't ever forget his thin face and small dark eyes, with their oddly long eyelashes. His mouth was somehow too large for his face and it gave him a sharky look. His teeth were very white.

Foley cleared his throat. "Yes," he said. "I had the unfortunate task of notifying the family that Alexander West was killed during his expedition to Fazia."

"Was it *unfortunate* that you had to steal all of Dad's maps and books and things, too?" M.K. asked. "Was it *unfortunate* that you had to be a complete bas—"

"Quiet, little girl!" hissed Agent Wolff, her eyepiece clicking and turning to look at M.K. "Mr. Foley is a very important man."

Foley's right eye twitched. "Your father was an Explorer of the Realm registered with the Bureau of Newly Discovered Lands. His work belonged to us. It was essential to national security that we secure his papers after his death."

"The hell it was!" M.K. shouted, taking a step toward him. The wrench gleamed in her hand and I felt the agents tense up, ready to act. She came up only to their elbows, but they looked scared.

"M.K.," Zander said in his calmest voice, reaching out with his free hand and pushing her behind him.

"He lied," she protested. "Kit said. Didn't you, Kit? You looked at the maps. There's no way Dad was where they said he was."

Foley's small eyes turned to me, and I felt his interest in the way he studied me before he said, "Is that right? Are you an expert on maps… Kit?"

"She's exaggerating," I said. "I was just doing some work on a map of Dad's route in Fazia."

There was an awkward silence and then Francis Foley said, "Now, if I could just see your backpack, young man…"

"But why? It's only got flour in it." I felt panic rise in my throat. These guys were serious. They might know to look for a hidden compartment.

"The man we're seeking is very… motivated," Foley said. "He may have hidden something in your backpack without you knowing. Explosives, for example. It's for your own safety." One of the agents took the pack from me and searched it thoroughly—though not quite thoroughly enough—before handing it back.

"Just a sweater and the flour," he told Foley. I tried not to let them see how relieved I was.

They all stood there for a moment, watching Foley. He seemed to be thinking. Finally he said, "We'll be going now, but I expect you'll let me know if you hear from this man."

"Of course," I told him.

"Yes, well… Hail President Hildreth!" They all made the salute, and we imitated them halfheartedly. They turned away and climbed into the dirigible. We heard the engine and the blowers start up, and we all watched as it rose slowly above our house, a dark storm cloud trailing gray smoke against the blue sky, and then disappeared across the water toward the city.

Three

"What was that about?" Zander asked once the dirigible had disappeared from sight. Pucci, sensing it was safe, flew down and landed on Zander's shoulder.

"I don't know, but I hate those damn agents," M.K. said, picking up a small rock from the driveway and chucking it at one of the oak trees. It made a dull thud and a red squirrel jumped down from an upper branch and sat there for a minute looking dazed. "*Run, run,*" Pucci squawked at it, cackling. "*Run for your life!*" The squirrel ran around the side of the house.

I looked around nervously, though I knew no one could hear us. "The thing is," I whispered, "I *did* see that man."

"What?" M.K. wheeled around. "Who was he?"

"I thought you looked nervous," Zander said. "What happened?"

I scanned the road again, completely paranoid now. "Inside.

I wouldn't put it past them to leave someone behind to spy on us."

They followed me into the house and through the front hallway. The house hadn't warmed up yet, and I shivered as we stepped into Dad's study.

"He was an Explorer. He had a clockwork hand. I thought he was going to mug me," I told them once we were inside. "But instead he gave me this and said it was from Dad." I took the package out of the backpack, unwrapping it completely, and held it up for them to see. "*The New Modern Age of Exploration* by R. Delorme Mountmorris."

"A book?" M.K. asked. It was cold without a fire in the fireplace, and she took a bearskin Dad had brought back from Grygia off one of the couches and wrapped it around her shoulders.

The room was filled with candlesticks and statues and carved masks and odd-looking animal skins and hides from Dad's travels. There were a few photographs on the walls of places that Dad had visited. As an Explorer, he'd been allowed to use a camera on his expeditions, though the government had controlled how much film he got and which pictures could be developed. I looked up at the photograph of him at the summit of Mount Anamata, grinning and holding his arms out as though he were holding up the sky.

It was a strange-looking room, I suppose, with Dad's collections and bits and pieces of gadgets and utilities scattered all around. I loved it, though, because it reminded me of him.

Even though I knew there was no way Francis Foley could hear us, I pressed a button on the wall and the government-issued radio squawked to life. "…*restored peace in the Fazian capital*," a radio announcer was saying. "*Government agents were able to secure the square before significant casualties occurred.*"

"Hah!" M.K. said. "I wonder how many Fazians died before they 'restored peace'?"

"*Peace!*" Pucci squawked. "*Ha, ha! Restore Peace!*"

The announcer went on. "*President Hildreth announced an additional one thousand BNDL peacekeepers would be deployed to mountainous regions of Deloia in order to secure the Raproot mines in the territory of Deltan. Spokesperson…*"

"They can't hear us." Zander reached up to shut off the radio. "Well, are you going to tell us?"

I told them about the man with the clockwork hand and put the book down on the special table in the center of the room. The table had clips for holding the big paper maps that Dad had used for his explorations and that he had made based on his travels. He'd been an expert cartographer, one of the best of the New Modern Age Explorers who had had to learn to make paper maps again after the Muller Machines were all shut down. He had made incredible maps of all of the new places discovered by the Explorers of the Realm. He'd also made maps for us, made-up maps of storybook places, and treasure maps that led us to chocolates or coins hidden in the woods behind our house. He'd made maps with disappearing ink and maps that were hidden inside other maps and once, for M.K.'s birthday, a secret map that you had to peel away from a dummy map on top and that led to her present, a new soldering iron.

The wall above the table had once been covered with frames holding his maps, their delicate blue and red and green and black lines forming amazing patterns. But Francis Foley and his agents had taken them all the night they'd come to tell us Dad had disappeared, and now the wall was scarred by the unfaded rectangles on the wallpaper where they'd once hung.

I lifted the heavy leather cover. Printed books had started to be made again after the Muller Machines were outlawed, but they were still pretty scarce and I had read the ones Dad had in his library over and over. I'd never seen this one.

"It's about the New Modern Age of Exploration," I told them, skimming the introduction. "Just the usual stuff about Arnoz and the Muller Machines and the Explorers of the Realm and BNDL."

It was history that everyone knew, the first part about the Muller Computing Machines. They had kept track of numbers, stored information, and made maps of the world, of the countries of the Allied Nations, and the Indorustan Empire. They did other things too, connected you to networks of other machines and showed you pictures of faraway places. The idea for the machines had been brought to George Washington by a spy in 1791. The plans had been developed by a man named J. H. Muller, an engineer in the Hessian army who hadn't been able to get the Hessians to build the machines. But in 1880, the Americans finally had. There had been a lot written about how, without the machines, America might not have won the war over Britain and then the rest of Europe. Without the military weapons controlled by the Muller Machines, the United States and its Allied Nations might not have been able to force the Indorustan Empire into a stalemate in 1970, bringing the long years of war between the two superpowers to a halt. The Muller Machines had become so much a part of everyone's lives that people trusted them completely. Once the gasoline from Texas ran out, there wasn't much to be had and only a very few people approved by the government could fly on airplanes or own cars. No one traveled or explored the world. Everyone believed the Muller Machines that there wasn't anything left to explore.

You could take "vacations" on the Muller Machines, and see photographs of all kinds of amazing places, even feel the heat of the sun, or the chill of the snow, from the machines. Dad said that people would take time off from work, even put on their bathing suits or ski clothes in their living rooms, never realizing how ridiculous it was.

And then the machines were hacked. Over the course of three months, a series of coordinated attacks on the networks and the power stations that kept them running brought it all down and the "century of the Muller Machines" came to an end. No mail, no power, no trade. It had happened when Dad was eight, and for a couple of years there was no heat, no money, and very little food. Martial law was declared, but things were so bad that the government was overthrown the first winter, and when the new government came in, President Barbado outlawed the Muller Machines and anything that had been run by them, including the power stations. Engineers returned to what had worked in that distant past: steam and clockwork engines, old-fashioned to be sure, but safe as could be.

"Here's the stuff about the New Lands," I said, reading aloud.

"*Little did the citizens of the world know that in the midst of a crisis of epic proportions, a light of hope and possibility was shining high on a cold and forbidding mountain.*"

"The book says that?" M.K. asked. "That's really corny."

"No, that's what I think. Of course that's what the book says." I crossed my eyes at her and went on.

R. Delorme Mountmorris detailed how one day, a couple of years after the failure of the Muller Machines, a young biologist and explorer named Harrison Arnoz, who had been living in a remote region of Eastern Europe near the Indorustan border, studying bear populations, discovered that where the "official" maps showed absolutely nothing, there was in fact an entire mountain range, new species of animals, and a group of tree-dwelling people who had never had contact with the outside world. Only a few months after Arnoz told the world about this new region, called Grygia, a commercial cargo ship got lost north of Denmark and came upon a small sea, obscured by a glacier, that appeared not to be on any of the official digital maps. The ship's captain and crew had discovered the New North Polar Sea.

There was only one conclusion: the maps of the world were wrong.

Pretty soon the Explorers were heading out to discover what else had been hidden on the Muller Machine maps, and the discoveries from the New Lands started to trickle in: an ultra-strong metal in Grygia called Gryluminum that could be used to make fabric and armor; a breed of hearty, high-yield cattle in Deloia; disease-resistant bananas in Fazia. BNDL found itself in the position of governing the New Lands, and the American Newly Discovered Lands Corporation—or ANDLC—was started to run the mines and farms and factories and to send all the goods home. First President Barbado's government and then President Hildreth's had controlled everything very tightly, anxious to make sure that the United States and its allies owned all the new discoveries.

And that was when the Archaics—the "Archys"—had gotten going, making cars and airships and furnaces and dishwashers that were powered by steam and coal and clockwork gears, technologies that didn't require gasoline or electricity. Dad was an Archy and I guess we were, too.

There were also the Neotechnologists—or "Neos"—who dreamed of wind power and solar batteries and dressed in their strange, bright, fabricated outfits—plastics and rubbers and odd fabrics, flashing lights embedded in their bodies. But the government suspected them of building secret Muller Machines and kept them from experimenting too much. Only a handful of Neo inventors had successfully developed new technologies, like gliders and electric autos. A lot of Archys refused to use these strange, silent machines, but Dad had always said that he didn't care who had made his boat or plane, as long as it worked.

Mountmorris wrote all about it, about the new Explorers who went out to find the New Lands, about how they were celebrated for their discoveries, and about how, around the time M.K. was born, the new discoveries had trickled to a stop and the government had decided we'd found everything new there was to find.

The problem was that there wasn't enough of anything to go around.

And so the people in the territories and colonies we'd claimed had started fighting back. And just as we started eyeing the territories claimed by the Indorustans, they started eyeing ours, too.

It was pretty likely that the uprisings in Simeria were just the beginning.

"We know all this," M.K. said in an exasperated voice. "Why did Dad want us to see *this*?"

"I don't know," Zander said. "We don't even know who this guy *is.*" He seemed annoyed, and I thought it might be because the Explorer had given the book to me and not to him. Zander always talked about how he was the one who was going to follow in Dad's footsteps and go to the Academy for the Exploratory Sciences, how he was the one who was going to make a discovery and join the Expedition Society. I loved maps and understood them better than he did, but he didn't care about that.

"The thing that I never got," I said as I flipped through the pages of history, "is why it took so long for the New Lands to be discovered."

"Because of the Muller Machines," Zander said, still sounding annoyed. "They were wrong and people became so dependent on them that they didn't question the maps. People just went to the places that were on the maps. They didn't look for new places. The government didn't let them."

"But someone had to put the information into them, didn't they? The coordinates and everything." I had always wondered about this. Whenever I'd asked Dad, he'd just told me again about the Muller Machines and how the government hadn't let anyone travel freely or use gasoline for anything but an approved purpose. I'd never found his answers satisfying.

"I don't know, Kit," Zander said. "See if there's anything about Dad in there."

I opened the book to the table of contents and sure enough, there was a chapter entitled "Alexander West: Mountains and Mapmaking."

For the next half hour, we turned the pages of the book, reading about all of his famous expeditions and discoveries during the New Modern Age: his ascent of Mount Anamata, the tallest of the mountains in the New Lands; his discovery of St. Helena, a new volcanic island in the Caribbean; all of his scientific and mapping expeditions to the New Lands. I'd heard about all of it before, of course, but it was interesting reading someone else's account of Dad's bravery; he hadn't been one for bragging about his expeditions and had always made it sound like he'd lucked into whatever record it was he'd set. There were chapters about other Explorers too: Leo Nackley, Jacob Omboodo, Delilah Neville, and all the names we'd come to know.

The book was full of photographs of Dad with his best friend, Raleigh McAdam. In all of them he was wearing his Krakoan alligator hat, which had been made for him during an expedition to Krakoa, and his Explorer's vest, which he was never without. The vest had been as much a part of him as his right arm; it was made of patches of different hides: multi-colored Krakoan alligator, green Fazian anaconda, reddish-brown Juboodan whizrat, and other skins I couldn't remember the names of. But Dad, who didn't have most Archy Explorers' aversion to synthetics, had also included patches of Gryluminum and plastics, the Gryluminum forming a sort of breastplate over his heart and vital organs. The vest was lined with the soft, incredibly warm fur of the blue Arctic namwee, a weasel-like creature discovered around the New North Polar Sea. The namwee's fur had been discovered to be both extremely warm in cold climates and extremely cooling in warm ones.

And, of course, the vest was embedded with gadgets, its pockets filled with his expedition "utilities"—small brass gadget boxes the size of a pack of playing cards or a lighter that might transform into a knife or an inflatable sled at the touch of a button.

"Why," Zander asked, leaning over my shoulder, "would anyone risk his life to give you that? It's just a book."

"I don't know." I really didn't. It didn't make any sense to me. I flipped through the book and was reading about Leo Nackley, who had gone to school with Dad and had gone on some expeditions with him, too, when I noticed some symbols scrawled in the margin of the page, in the bright red India ink that Dad had always used in his mapmaking.

"What are those?" M.K. asked, pointing to them.

"Beats me." They looked like Native American symbols to me, little birds and feathers and animals and suns and moons and trees.

Dad had loved doodling when he was reading or writing, so it didn't seem strange that they were there. But there was something about the way they were arranged that made me look more closely.

They appeared to be random, but that was what seemed strange to me. If they were doodles, wouldn't Dad have arranged them in some sort of pattern? A bird, a feather, a frog, a turtle, a bird, a feather, a frog, a turtle? I hesitated. Maybe I was overthinking this. But when I looked again, I saw what was really bothering me. The symbols were grouped together like… well, like… words.

"What are you doing?" M.K. asked.

Ignoring her, I found an old magnifying glass on the mantel and used it to study the symbols in the thin, late-spring light coming through the library window. The glass wasn't bad: I could see the little turns Dad's pen had taken, where he'd made a false start or gone back to correct something. He'd been very careful, separating the symbols so it was clear where one word ended and another began. And suddenly I understood.

It was a code.

Four

"Remember the treasure hunts he used to set up for us?" I asked them, jumping up from the table. I got my leather-bound journal and a pen and sat down again.

"Of course," Zander said. "You think he left us a code?"

I didn't answer. I was already searching the little doodles.

The first thing to do was find a word I could use as a key, that is, a word I could identify because of its length or because of the repetition of a particular letter or letters. For example, a word like *Mississippi* was a good key. Say you'd created a code where a different letter stood in for each letter. If you saw *Tfjfjifyyf*, you could figure out that *T* stood in for *m* and *f* stood in for *i* and so forth, because there were no other words with that exact pattern of repetition.

But *Mississippi* was a dead giveaway. Anyone who knew anything about codes would recognize it. Dad—if in fact Dad had written the message—would have used something that only we would understand. And this code didn't replace letters with letters, it replaced them with symbols.

I pushed my glasses back up on my nose, wrote the whole thing out on a clean page in the journal, and started studying the combinations of symbols.

"I'm looking for the key," I told them.

"Maybe it's one of our names," M.K. suggested.

My name and Zander's wouldn't be much help, as they didn't contain any repetition of letters and weren't abnormally long or short. M.K.'s full name was Mary Kingsley, after a famous English explorer. That might help, because of the rarer combination of a four-letter word and an eight-letter one with only the repeated y, but I didn't see anything that fit.

And then suddenly I thought of Dad in the yard, saying goodbye.

"I think I've got it," I told them. "What did Dad call us? What did he say when he was leaving for Fazia?"

"The Expeditioners," they said together. *The Expeditioners*. That had to be it. I had to find a thirteen-symbol word.

I read over the symbols I'd copied and, sure enough, the sixth word formed by the symbols was thirteen symbols long, with the first symbol repeated in the fourth and then again in the eleventh place. So the little eagle symbol was *e*. I wrote that down. Then I wrote down the symbols for the rest of the letters included in the word.

Now I knew the symbols for *e*, *x*, *p*, *d*, *i*, *t*, *o*, *n*, *r* and *s*. Slowly, I started working the code, using the same process of elimination you use to solve a difficult crossword puzzle.

Zander and M.K. were absolutely silent while I worked. I wasn't sure how much time had passed, but when I finally looked up from my work, my stomach was rumbling with hunger. I didn't care, though. My heart racing, my skin prickling all over with the excitement you feel when something's about to happen, I read aloud the fragment of the message sitting in front of me:

CAN YOU CRACK THE CODE,
EXPEDITIONERS?

THE THIRD OLD OAK ON
THE RIGHT FLIPPED

Five

The three of us stared at the nonsensical words. What could they mean? The message was from Dad. There was no doubt about that. No one else knew that he'd called us the Expeditioners. But what was this about the third old oak—?

"The oak," Zander said, reading the words over my shoulder. "It has to be the—"

"Desk," I said.

M.K. rushed over to Dad's big desk, sitting in a corner of the room. It had been made from the wood of the sixth old oak in front of the house after it had fallen. Dad had built the desk himself and secured the drawers with his ingenious locks, difficult things with combinations that were hard to figure out. The BNDL agents had gone all through the house, looking for maps and documents, but they hadn't been able to get into the desk.

"The rest is easy," I told Zander and M.K. "The third old oak on the right is the third drawer down on the right." I tried it and of course it was locked, the seven brass rotating disks showing different letters. I spun them around. What was the combination that would open the lock?

I studied the coded message. THE THIRD OLD OAK ON THE RIGHT FLIPPED.

"Flipped?" Zander suggested. "*F-l-i-p-p-e-d.*"

Flipped? Could that be it? It was the only word left. I spun the disks so that they read *flipped* and tried the drawer. Still locked.

What could it be? I felt a flash of annoyance. We were so close.

Zander looked excited now, his blue eyes wide and curious, just like Dad's when he'd been on the scent of something. "M.K.," he said, "do you think you could get in, with your tools?"

"I could try," she said. "But I'd probably have to destroy the desk. His locks are unpickable. You know that."

Sitting behind the desk, I couldn't help but think of Dad, his smile, the way his eyes turned up at the corners when he joked with us about something or other. He'd loved riddles and word puzzles and codes and ciphers, and he'd sometimes leave little notes for us that we had to figure out.

The polished oak was smooth under my hand. *Flipped. Flipped.* Suddenly I had it. I had to flip *flipped.*

"I've got it," I told them.

I turned the disks so that they read *deppilf.*

The drawer opened.

Even all these years after he'd built the desk, the inside of the drawer smelled of wood, varnish, and sawdust. The drawer was fairly shallow; a rectangle of green velvet lay in the bottom, and when I lifted it up, I saw a piece of thick paper, facedown in the bottom of the drawer. I lifted it out, turned it over, and found myself staring at a large and beautiful map.

Six

To be precise, it was half a map. It had been neatly torn in half so that it ended abruptly on the left-hand side. The title, written in red ink at the bottom in Dad's handwriting, was cut off so that it read "*ed Man's Canyon and Environs.*"

"Is it one of his?" M.K. asked in a quiet voice.

"I think so," Zander said. "I think that's his handwriting."

"Of course it's his handwriting," I told them. Even if I hadn't recognized the handwriting I would have known that Dad had made the map. It was beautifully done, the graceful, wavelike contour lines describing the depth of the canyons and mesas, the words written in his distinctive, scrolling handwriting. The map was obviously of a desert region, probably in the American Southwest. I made note of a town called Azure City and crossed the room to search for it in the big atlas on the windowsill; I found it not far from the Grand

Canyon. So it was northern Arizona. The legend was missing; it must have been on the other side.

I took the map over to the window to look at it in the bright spring sunlight coming in the library windows. I looked through the magnifying glass and the tiny lines seemed nearer.

"We're missing part of it," I told Zander and M.K.

Pucci had been dozing up on the curtain rod, but now he flew down and perched on the windowsill, looking at the map and bobbing his head. "*Canyon,*" he squawked. "*Azure Canyon.*" We all looked at him. It was weird; I could never tell if Pucci was just repeating something he'd heard or actually talking. Zander said that black knight parrots had been known to put sentences together using words they knew, but he wasn't sure, either.

"He's right," I said. It was hard to tell without the rest of it, but the map seemed to focus on Azure Canyon. I knew that this part of Arizona was full of deep, winding canyons, carved out of the bedrock by rivers over thousands and thousands of years. Some of them were now dry or wet for only part of the year, and others—like the Grand Canyon—had rivers running through them still. By reading Dad's carefully drawn contour lines, I could tell that Azure Canyon was quite deep, dropping at least half a mile down into the earth—the thin lines crowded together to show the sheer drop of the canyon's walls. Like all of Dad's maps, this one was easy to read and beautiful. From the arrangement of the contour lines, it seemed like maybe another canyon branched off from Azure Canyon, but it must have been on the other half of the map.

51

I looked up at my brother and sister, who seemed as confused as I was. "But why was it hidden in the desk?" M.K. asked.

"And why did he cut it in half?" Zander ran his finger along the rough edge.

"How did he get the book to the man with the clockwork hand?" I asked the silent room.

None of us had any answers.

"Obviously he wanted us to find the map," I said. "But it was only by chance that he got it to me. What if I hadn't cut through the alley? What if someone else had been there?"

"That's a good point," Zander said. He thought for a moment. "You said he looked like he was just back from an expedition. Maybe he was... I don't know, traveling with Dad or something, and he brought the book back for us."

"Everyone who was traveling with Dad in Fazia died," M.K. said. "At least that's what they told us." We were all quiet, remembering the night Francis Foley had arrived, telling us that pieces of Dad's party's boats had been found in the Fazian River, in an area "unsuitable for human survival." We'd known exactly what that meant. If the Fazian crocodiles or piranhas hadn't gotten him, the cannibals had.

"Yeah, that's what they told us. But I've gone over and over the maps and there's no way they were in Bartoa when the government says they were. I told you that I don't believe it for a minute."

They both looked at me. "So what, you think Dad's alive?" Zander asked.

"No. If he was alive he would have let us know. But I don't think he died where the agents say he did."

"Because I think that…," Zander started, then trailed off, looking troubled. "Forget it."

We all fell into silence for a minute, remembering all the times Dad had complained about the government agents. He was always talking about how they asked so many questions about his expeditions and how he thought that they sometimes followed him, how no Explorer could go anywhere without BNDL's okay. Dad hadn't been a big fan of the government.

"What do you think it means, anyway?" M.K. whispered, as though they were listening in at this very moment. "Do you think Dad wants us to go to this canyon, wherever it is? Do you think *he* went there?"

"I have no idea," I told her. "I don't remember him ever talking about going to Arizona. He didn't go on any expeditions there or anything like that. Arizona was explored a long time ago. By the Spanish. He liked to go to the New Lands."

"I think he wants us to go to Arizona," Zander said. "I think that's what he's trying to tell us."

"Hold on a minute." It was just like Zander to start packing before we knew anything about the map. "What we need to do first is find out whether he ever went to Arizona and whether there's another half to the map."

"Who's this Mountmorris guy?" M.K. asked, picking up the book. "He seems to know a lot about him. Was he friends with Dad?"

I went over to the bookshelf and took down Dad's raggedy copy of *The Explorer's Yearbook,* which the BNDL agents hadn't found interesting enough to take with them. "Here he is." I read aloud from his entry, "'*Randolph Delorme Mountmorris. Author, historian, and collector. Notable for his books about the New Modern Age of Exploration and for his collections of animal specimens and artifacts from the New Lands.*' That's pretty much it. There's an address here too. In the city. On Fifth Avenue."

"He must have met Dad when he was writing the book," Zander said. "Maybe he could tell us about the map."

"I think we have to be careful…," I was starting to say when I heard the faint chug of an engine. "Did you guys hear something?"

Pucci cocked his head, listening, too.

We were all silent for a moment, and I was just about to say that I must have imagined it when we heard knocking from the hallway.

"*Knock, knock,*" Pucci cackled. "*Knock, knock.*" He hid himself behind the dingy curtains.

M.K. went to the window. "SteamCycles," she told us, standing behind the drapes so she couldn't be seen. "With BNDL logos on their sides. They're back!"

Seven

Z ander jumped up. "Hide it! Hide the map. I'll go."

I put the book and the map into the hidden compartment of the backpack and then, just for good measure, stuffed it behind the empty wood box next to the fireplace. It wasn't a great hiding place, but I thought it might buy us some time. M.K. and I hurried out into the hallway, where Zander was talking to Agent Wolff and the tall male agent with the flowing mustache. Agent Wolff had taken off her cape and we could see a holster containing a shiny silver pistol under one arm.

"Oh, there he is," she said, fixing her gaze on me. The eyepiece clicked a few times as it focused. "Agent DeRosa and I have gotten some new information from witnesses in the marketplace. There was a sighting of the man dressed in Explorer's gear. We know you were there, too. Are you sure you didn't see him?"

I froze. Should I lie? Should I say I had seen him? The agents were staring at me and finally I choked out, "No. I definitely didn't see that man."

I could see Zander's eyes widen in alarm. I knew he thought I'd made a mistake lying to them. I felt a hard nausea start in my stomach.

"Let's sit down somewhere," Agent DeRosa said, "so we can really... talk." He reached up to smooth his moustache and there was something sinister about the way he said *talk*.

I led the way into the dining room and lit a few of the candles in the candelabra over the table. We'd found some old packets of vegetable seeds in the attic and we had planted them in flowerpots and broken cups and bowls, thinking we could have a vegetable garden once it got warm. They must have been too old, because none of them had sprouted.

Agent DeRosa pushed a few cups of dirt out of the way and crammed himself into a chair. "Now, we want to know what—" Agent DeRosa started to say, just as one of the many mice that had moved into the house during the cold winter decided to make a break for it and ran across the dining-room floor.

Agent Wolff screamed as it ran over her foot and Pucci came flying in from the library, his metal talons unsheathed in front of him, ready to attack. I felt my stomach sink. We weren't sure what would happen if the government discovered we had been taking care of the parrot, but I had a feeling we were about to find out.

"It's okay, Pucci," Zander said desperately, and the parrot reversed direction and landed on his shoulder.

"*Danger!*" he squawked. "*Danger!*"

Agent Wolff stared at him. "Is that a modified Fazian black knight parrot?" she asked. "What are you doing with it? That thing is the property of BNDL."

"He's not a *thing*," Zander said in a low voice. "He's a bird, a bird who had his legs cut off by a butcher in one of your workshops and replaced with metal ones." He whispered something to Pucci, who squawked and went to sit quietly on the windowsill.

"We'll take it with us when we go," Agent Wolff said to Agent DeRosa. "Now, I've lost my train of…" She caught sight of M.K., standing there with a furious look on her face. "You, girl, go make some coffee," she said, waving a hand at her as though she were some kind of servant. I saw M.K.'s eyes narrow in anger.

Please, M.K., please just go do it, I thought, wishing I was telepathic. I knew my sister, and I knew how much she must hate the way Agent Wolff was talking to her, but she must have been really scared of the agents because she forced a little smile and said, "Okay."

Once she was gone, Agent DeRosa took a deep breath and said, "You know that lying to agents of the Bureau of Newly Discovered Lands is a federal offense, don't you? Do you know what they do to people who lie to BNDL?"

"I can guess," Zander said quietly.

Agent DeRosa stroked his mustache thoughtfully. "Well, they lock them up and—"

"No need to talk about that, Julian," Agent Wolff interrupted, with a sickly sweet smile. "I'm sure they have good imaginations.

Now tell us about the man."

"I don't know anything." My voice sounded shrill and scared, even to my own ears. I could feel the panic starting to rise in my throat and I started babbling, "I swear I don't…"

I didn't know what to do and I remembered something Dad had told me once, that if you didn't want to answer a question, you should answer with a question of your own.

"What did he do, anyway?" I asked them.

"That's none of your business," Agent Wolff said, her eyepiece boring into me. "What did he say to you?"

I might have broken down and said something really stupid if I hadn't, at that exact moment, seen M.K. come up quietly behind Agent DeRosa.

She was holding her wrench.

Agent DeRosa opened his mouth, but he didn't have time to say anything before M.K. brought the wrench down squarely on the back of his skull. His eyes rolled into his head and he slumped to the floor with a long, muffled thump.

I don't know what kind of training Agent Wolff had gotten from the Bureau of Newly Discovered Lands, but whatever it had been, she forgot it as she blinked at me for a long moment, then looked down at Agent DeRosa as though she couldn't quite believe he'd just been brained by the cute little girl with blond hair.

A moment was all M.K. needed. She hopped over behind Agent Wolff, and just as the agent started to stand, M.K. brought the wrench down on her head, too.

Agent Wolff didn't so much crash to the floor as slide out of her seat and fold into a heap of chain mail and leather.

We all stared at the two of them stretched out under the table.

"M.K.?" Zander asked finally, drawing out her name the way Dad had when he suspected her of something.

M.K. shrugged. Her little fish knife was tucked into the leather belt she'd wrapped around the waist of the mechanic's jumpsuit and there was a wicked gleam in her eye. Other than that, she looked like any other cute ten-year-old girl in need of a haircut.

I watched Agent Wolff's chest rise and fall in a steady rhythm.

"Are you crazy?" Zander asked her in a low whisper.

I pointed at the agents. "What are we going to do now, M.K.? We're going to be in really big trouble." I could feel the panic set in. There was no way to undo this, no way to go back to the moment before she had appeared with her wrench.

Agent Wolff let out a soft little snore.

"I had to," M.K. said. "They were going to take Pucci. And what about the map? You were about to tell them you saw the man, and they would have searched the house until they found the map." Her little chin was thrust out at me, her blue eyes calm and steady.

"I wasn't going to tell them," I protested weakly. I was almost shaking, still scared from the agents' questions, and completely rattled by the realization of what M.K. had just done. "What do you think they're going to do when they wake up?"

"I'm kind of thinking," Zander said slowly, "that it's going to be better if we're not *here* when they wake up."

I turned to look at him. His cheeks were red, like he'd been outside, and he was staring into the distance the way he always did when he had an idea.

"And where will we be?"

He was still staring. The agents kept snoring.

"Zander? Where will we be?"

"Arizona," Zander said thoughtfully. "Like I said, Dad must have wanted us to go there." He gestured to the agents. "And it does have the advantage of being all the way across the country."

I shook my head. "We don't even have the whole map."

"But the part we do have is of Arizona, right? Maybe the other half is there."

"Yeah, I'm sure it is. Luckily it's not like it's a huge state filled with *deserts* or anything." I looked down at the agents. "How long do you sleep when you've been hit on the head?"

M.K. shrugged. "It depends. An hour? Something like that."

"We need more time than that," Zander said. "Help me, Kit." He opened the door to the kitchen closet and dragged Agent DeRosa over to it. "Get his feet."

"Zander!"

"Come on. This will buy us some time."

And because I didn't have any better ideas, I helped him stash Agent DeRosa and then Agent Wolff into the closet. He shut the door and M.K. wedged a chair under the doorknob.

"We should probably get out of here," she said, picking up her wrench and wiping something off it onto her sleeve.

"And go to Arizona?" I paced around the kitchen, thinking out loud. "This is crazy. I wish we could find out if Dad ever even went there."

"Let's ask that guy. Mountmorris," Zander said. "We have his address, right?"

"But… I don't know. We don't know anything about him. That Explorer risked his life to get me the map. We can't just go around showing it to people."

"We won't say anything about where we got it."

I hesitated. What did Dad want us to do? It was frustrating, not having any idea.

"Uh, aren't you forgetting something?" M.K. asked us. "Say we did want to see this guy. How are we going to get into the city?"

We all stared at each other. We hadn't thought of that. It would take us a long time to walk. We'd be caught for sure. Dad had had a SteamCar, but it had been taken away by Foley and his agents.

Pucci, who was still on the windowsill, made a funny *put-chugga-chugga* sound, like an engine, in his throat. He liked to imitate sounds, rain falling or wind blowing or…

SteamCycles.

We all looked out the window. The agents had parked them right in the driveway. They were brand new, with Gryluminum frames and polished Gryluminum boilers and brass instrument panels. The wheel spokes shone in the late-morning sun.

"Hey," M.K said, "look at that."

"All right," I said, deciding. "M.K., do you want to go and check to make sure they're working and everything?"

She was already out the door.

"That's settled, then," Zander said, grinning. "I'll get some warm clothes for us. Kit, find that money Dad left for emergencies and make sure you've got the map."

Eight

R. Delorme Mountmorris lived in a five-story brick mansion on a quiet block facing Arnoz Park, surrounded by huge apartment buildings. It was a part of the city where a lot of merchants and government workers lived, and the security was especially tight. There were blue-uniformed security agents everywhere, and we were glad we'd ditched the SteamCycles in a not-so-fancy neighborhood on our way in. Three kids and a parrot standing on a street corner didn't seem to arouse their suspicions, but three kids and a parrot on BNDL SteamCycles definitely would have. Just to be sure, we saluted the big picture of President Hildreth mounted on a building across the street.

"I think there was a terrorist attack near here last week," I said, watching two agents carefully checking a trash can on the corner in front of Mr. Mountmorris's house. "Some guy who works for

Hildreth got blown up while he was out walking his dog."

"Simerians?" Zander asked. I was surprised. He never paid attention to the news unless the story was about Explorers or animals.

"That's what they said, anyway."

Two green-haired mail messengers raced by us on their SteamCycles, almost colliding on the turn. They were always competing with each other to see who could make deliveries faster, and lately there had been a lot of accidents. They were fun to watch, though. Most of the messengers were Neos, and they cut their hair in crazy Mohawk styles and dyed it all kinds of amazing colors.

As for us, we were dressed in our own clothes and worn-out pieces of Dad's exploring gear that we'd been able to find quickly. I was wearing an old pair of his alligator-skin leggings, a cactus-fiber T-shirt he'd brought me back from somewhere, a yak-fiber sweater lined in namwee fur, and a pair of tall brown cowhide boots with crampons hidden in the soles that Dad had made for me the winter before.

Zander was wearing Dad's hunting gear—warm yak-fiber leggings and a long-sleeved shirt painted to look like the Grygian forests. M.K. was wearing an old pair of Doolandian buffalo-hide leggings that I'd outgrown and a cactus-fiber field shirt of Dad's that she'd tucked into the leggings. She'd wrapped a long piece of buffalo rawhide around her waist, and into this makeshift belt she'd tucked her wicked little fish knife, her wrench, which she'd cleaned, and a few other tools. Zander and I had both brought a few tools, too, and I'd brought pens and paper for maps. I kept wishing we had

Explorer's vests like Dad's; his was in Fazia, though, wherever his body was, and I doubted we'd ever see it again. Both Zander and M.K. had on boots like mine.

We climbed the stone steps to a dark-green door with a heavy brass knocker in the shape of a frog. Zander lifted it and let it fall. Almost immediately the door opened and we found ourselves face to face with a bright red Mohawk hairstyle. Beneath it was a tall man dressed in a red synthetic jumpsuit, the sleeves decorated with the flashing purple lights that Neos liked to wear on their clothes and sometimes embedded in their skin. I'd always found the way Neos dressed kind of silly, but there wasn't anything silly about this man; he looked as though he wouldn't think twice about using the sharp edge of his Mohawk to cut someone's throat.

He looked past us as though he couldn't quite believe that there were three children and a parrot on the doorstep. Finding no one else behind us, he settled his eyes on us and said, "Yes?"

"We'd like to see Mr. Mountmorris, please," Zander said.

"I'm Mr. Mountmorris's secretary, Jec Banton. I'm sorry, but he's not available. Can I give him a message for you?"

Something about the way he said it made me think he wasn't going to give Mr. Mountmorris any message at all. Zander must have thought so, too, because he said, "We *have* to see him. Please."

"Absolutely not. He's a very busy man. He doesn't have time for... visitors."

He gave us a snide sort of look, and his voice was full of sarcasm. I didn't like him at all.

I don't know what gave me the courage, but I said, "Just tell him that the children of Alexander West are here to see him. If he doesn't want to see us, we'll go."

Jec Banton raised his eyebrows and disappeared inside the house, leaving us on the steps. A couple of minutes later, he was back, with a slightly surprised look on his face.

"Please come in," he said. He stepped aside and we followed him inside. Zander shrugged Pucci off his shoulder, and the parrot found a perch above the door, where I could hear him mumbling.

The heavy front door closed behind us and immediately I felt chilled. We were in a large, formal entryway. The floor was green marble and the walls were made of some kind of synthetic paneling that reminded me of iced-over glass. The floor gave off a faint green glow. Everything was clean and shiny and smelled of rubbing alcohol, like a doctor's office. A huge staircase of the same material as the walls curled away from us up to the second floor. There were no windows that I could see, and the light was very low. We could have been underground.

"This way," the secretary said, leading us through the foyer toward a door cut into the paneling. He opened it and showed us into a very large room that was, for all intents and purposes, a museum.

Each of the four walls was lined with glass display cases. There were also freestanding display cases in the middle of the room, and we looked around at them, trying to take it all in. One section of the wall was devoted to trophies: a huge moose head, an elk, a stuffed Grygian bear, a Derudan carnivorous hippo head, a lion head, and many others. There were weapons, too. Guns and rifles and bows and arrows, nestled into the glass display cabinets. More cases contained stuffed birds of many colors—macaws, birds of paradise, pheasants, and other species I couldn't name.

Yet another section of the room held wooden masks, fantastic things I knew to be from Africa and the South Pacific and the New Lands.

"Mr. Mountmorris is at his desk," Jec Banton said, shutting the door behind him and leaving us in the big room. We looked around, trying to find a desk, but all the glass created a sort of hall of mirrors, and we couldn't see a thing. It was even colder in here than in the hallway, and I found myself shivering, even in my warm sweater.

"Please come back this way," called a high voice from somewhere at the back of the room. We followed it, winding in and out of the display cabinets. "Over here," the voice said again, and we finally found him sitting behind an enormous wooden desk. The wall above him was adorned with many brass gear clocks, and they tocked along at different speeds, so that it was hard to keep track of the seconds. The desk was covered with glass paperweights, and each one contained a different species of frog—some green, some black, one red, one blue. They stared up at us from their glass prisons.

The man sitting above them reminded me of a larger version of the creatures on his desk. He was nearly bald, with just a thin, low crown of bright white hair above his ears and a few long pieces stretched across his scalp. His egg-like blue eyes seemed to be popping out of his head. They were bright and I had the feeling that he was watching everything we did. His right ear was pierced with many small lights—all shades of green—and they seemed to flash in response to his speech, as though they could hear him.

"What a marvelous surprise!" he said. "At last, I meet the children of the great Explorer Alexander West!"

Nine

He was the oddest-looking man I'd ever seen, a mixture of Archy and Neo in his shiny green suit and earlights and old-fashioned hair. I didn't know what to make of him.

"Now," he said, "before I ask you why you're here, I must know, what do you think of my collections?"

"They're incredible," said Zander, looking around. "I see a dodo bird—is that really a dodo? And a silver-billed grub warbler. A crimson night catcher. I've never seen a blue diver before. That *is* a blue diver, isn't it? I thought you couldn't have those stuffed anymore."

Suddenly, we were all talking at once. "That mask there is Navajo," I said, gawking at the wall. "Dad has a photograph of one." I gaped at these incredible things I'd only heard about. "And is that an original Dijkstra map of the world? No one knows where it is…"

M.K. was gaping, too. "You have an original Peterson steam engine," she said, staring. If it hadn't been inside a display case, she would have had it apart in about ten seconds.

"I am so glad to find an appreciative audience," said the man behind the desk. "I am Delorme Mountmorris. Sit down so we can talk."

We sat in the chairs facing his desk, the three of us lined up in order of descending age, first Zander, then me, then M.K.

There was a long silence during which he appeared to be studying us. Finally, he said, "I was so sorry to hear about your father. To what do I owe the pleasure of this unexpected visit?"

I took a deep breath and looked at Zander. He nodded and I said, "We read your book, and we were wondering... I mean... do you know if our father ever went to Arizona? On one of his expeditions?"

Mr. Mountmorris looked up quickly. "Arizona? Not that I can recall, but it's possible, I suppose. Why do you ask?"

I could feel my heart pounding. There was a sour taste in my mouth.

"Well," I started, unsure what to say. I was suddenly nervous, and I didn't want to show him the map.

"Show him," Zander said.

"Show me what?" Mr. Mountmorris said it casually, but he was sitting up very straight in his chair.

I hesitated. M.K. gestured to the backpack. I still wasn't sure it was the right thing to do, but I took the half map out of my backpack and spread it out on his desk. "We were wondering if you might know what this is. It was Dad's and we're just trying to get some information about it. You wrote about him, so…"

Mr. Mountmorris tapped his glasses down on his nose and studied it.

Have you ever seen someone who is very happy or very excited about something try to keep himself from *acting* happy and excited? That was what Mr. Mountmorris seemed to be doing. As he looked at the map, his hands were almost vibrating over it, as though he could barely stop himself from seizing it and hugging it to his body. But he kept himself very rigid, and after a couple of seconds, he sat straight up in his chair and said, in a calm voice, "This is very interesting. Very interesting indeed. May I ask where you found it?"

I tried to keep my voice even. "Uh… around. With some of Dad's things."

He smiled, making a little tent of his fingers in front of his face and studying each of our faces in turn. When he came to me, I felt the power of those protruding eyes; he seemed to stare right down into me and I didn't like it at all.

"Do you know what it is?" he asked finally.

"A map," I said. "Obviously." His eyes flickered with something, annoyance maybe. He looked at me as though I was two rather than thirteen, which was why I couldn't help myself—I showed off a little. "It appears to be of the American Southwest. From the topography, I can tell it's a high desert environment. One of the identified locations is Azure Canyon, which is located in Arizona—the northern part—up near the Grand Canyon. Azure Canyon was one of the early domestic discoveries of the New Modern Age. It is known for its blue pools and waterfalls, but otherwise it wasn't a particularly exciting discovery. No natural resources or anything like that. What I can't figure out is what the title is down at the bottom. It's something Man's Canyon, but I couldn't find any references to it. Do *you* know what it is?"

Mr. Mountmorris smiled and nodded as if to say *touché*, and then there was a long silence, as though he was deciding whether or not to tell us something. Finally, he stood up and walked over to one of the display cases. He looked down at something in the case for a few minutes before he started talking. The room was eerily quiet and it struck me that although we were in the middle of the city, we had not heard any sound from the street since we'd stepped into his house.

Mr. Mountmorris began. "In 1567, a group of Spanish conquistadores—the Spanish soldiers who had come to the New World looking for Aztec gold in what is now Mexico—decided to run off with a fortune in gold ingots and bars, unprocessed nuggets, statues, and jewelry—an incredible treasure in gold."

Ten

"They made it to a remote area of northern Arizona, where they were stricken with a mysterious illness and died. When their bodies were located, carefully buried in the desert, the gold was missing. The legend went that the Spaniards had been cared for by a group of Indians living nearby and had made a present of the gold to the Indians. The Indians were, shall we say, *questioned*. But the treasure did not appear."

As Mr. Mountmorris talked, I could almost see the wide, hot desert and the glimmer of gold coins. Zander and M.K. were leaning forward, listening intently to the story, and I could feel us all holding our breath as Mr. Mountmorris paused for a moment. I usually thought that Neos' body lights were kind of weird, but there was something soothing about the way his blinked and flashed as he talked.

"Nearly three hundred years later, around the time of the invention of the Muller Machines, a prospector named Dan Foley was looking for gold in the region. Gold was highly valued, and with the war with Britain on, well… it was much in demand. Lost in an unexplored canyon, starving and exhausted, Foley made a wrong step and fell through a camouflaged wooden floor into an underground chamber. Later, he said that he thought he would die in the chamber, until, in the distance, he saw the glint of gold. When he explored further, he said he saw piles of gold bars—stamped with Spanish words—gold statues, and jewelry, and a 'huge pile' of Spanish gold ingots in another chamber along a tunnel. There was so much debris in front of the treasure that he had no way of getting to it without tools. Motivated by the idea of the fortune, he fought his way out of the mine shaft. When he returned to Flagstaff, he told a… well, a lady friend… about his discovery and bought tools to excavate the old mine. He left Flagstaff to return to the mine on June 15, 1857."

For almost a whole minute, Mr. Mountmorris didn't speak.

Finally, my curiosity got the better of me. "Well? What happened?"

He turned to look at me. "He never returned," he said in a quiet voice. "It began to rain the next day. Very hard. The theory was that a flash flood tore into the remote canyon where he had seen the mine shaft and the gold. He wouldn't have stood a chance. He is presumed drowned, though his body never washed up. The canyon near where he thought he'd found the Spanish conquistadores' store of gold, and where he was lost, is now referred to as Drowned Man's Canyon."

"That must have been the title of the map," I said. "So what happened? Did anyone ever find the gold?"

Zander and M.K. and I waited for the answer.

"No," Mr. Mountmorris said finally. "Scores of men and women have gone looking for Dan Foley's treasure, but no one has ever found it." His eyes gleamed with a greedy delight. "But perhaps the great Explorer Alexander West knew where to find the treasure of Drowned Man's Canyon."

Eleven

We all stared at him for a moment. Golden treasure? Spanish conquistadores?

"I bankrolled an expedition out to Arizona many years ago, after I first heard the story of Drowned Man's Canyon. But my men had no luck, no luck at all." Mr. Mountmorris put his fingertips together again and watched the three of us, as though he was making a decision. "So your father never talked to you about going out to Arizona to look for the treasure?"

"No," I said. "At least, I don't remember if he did..."

I had the feeling again that Mr. Mountmorris was trying to keep himself from getting too excited. "Well, *think!*" he blurted out before regaining control of himself. "I mean, are you sure?"

Zander and I glanced at each other.

I tried to keep my voice neutral. "I'm sure he mentioned

Arizona," I said, "in the course of normal conversation. It *is* one of the fifty-six states, after all." I looked at the trapped frogs on his desk to avoid meeting his eyes; I was afraid he'd see how nervous I was all of a sudden. There was something about the way Mr. Mountmorris was acting that made me think we never should have shown him the map. Next to the frogs was a little collection of what looked like religious idols and a stone paperweight engraved with the words *For extraordinary services rendered as advisor to ANDLC.*

And then I noticed a framed newspaper clipping on the other side of the desk. It was a picture of Mr. Mountmorris and Francis Foley. They were at some sort of celebration, and they were shaking hands as they smiled into the camera.

Suddenly, my whole body went numb.

Zander must have seen something on my face because he glanced at me again before telling Mr. Mountmorris, "There are amazing varieties of hummingbirds in Arizona. He and I talked about birds all the time. If he'd been there, he would have mentioned it."

"You are sure?" Mr. Mountmorris asked. "Think carefully now. He never told you about a trip he had taken there? He never talked about the treasure?"

"No," I said, trying to keep my voice even. "I mean, he found that rare emerald in the cave in Acapurna, if you remember, but he never said anything about a golden treasure in Arizona."

"Hmm. Yes. Well."

There was another long silence. We waited for Mr. Mountmorris to speak.

Finally he did. "I wonder, what has happened to your dad's, er... effects. His books and maps and things? Perhaps the other half of the map is among them."

"BNDL came and took them," I said. "But there wasn't another half. I'm sure of that."

"You seem to know something about maps, young man. Kit, is that right?" Mr. Mountmorris watched me for a second with his pale eyes. I felt the way I imagine a fly feels before being caught by a frog.

"Uh... sort of."

"Well," Zander said, "we really should get going. We should get home."

"Yes," I said. "Thank you for telling us about Drowned Man's Canyon." I realized that the half map was still sitting on Mr. Mountmorris's desk, and I stepped forward to get it.

He was too quick for me, though, and he picked it up himself, folding it in half before offering it to me. I reached forward to take it and his hand slid back just a bit, just enough to put it out of reach. "You wouldn't... By any chance... Might you be interested in selling it?" he asked in a quiet, controlled voice. "I would be willing to pay quite a substantial sum. It's missing the relevant part, of course, the section including Drowned Man's Canyon. So its value to anyone but me would be... negligible."

Zander and I exchanged a worried look, and it was M.K. who put a hand on the knife at her waist and said, in a strong voice, "I don't think we want to sell it."

"Hmm. Well, if you *think of anything*, shall we say, or change your mind about selling it, you know where to find me." I took the map from him and instantly, as though he'd pressed a button, Jec Banton was back in the room, ready to usher us out.

"Goodbye," Mr. Mountmorris called out. "Goodbye, children." In a few minutes we were out on the street again. It was going to be a warm, springlike day, and the strong sun felt good on our faces. We stood there for a moment, warming ourselves up after being in that refrigerator of a house. As we crossed the street and entered the park, Pucci caught up to us and alighted on my shoulder. I turned around to look back at the house, and I could swear I saw Jec Banton watching us from one of the first-floor windows.

"I don't trust him," M.K. said.

"Neither do I," Zander said. "He was lying."

I glanced around to make sure no one else could hear me. "He's an advisor to ANDLC. Everyone knows that they work with BNDL. And did you see the photograph over his desk? He's friends with Francis Foley. We never should have shown him the map, Zander." I remembered Dad talking about how ANDLC might as well have been part of the government because they worked so closely with BNDL.

"Damn!" said M.K. "That lying, damned, no-good…"

I started to feel panic set in again. "If he works for BNDL, he's going to tell Francis Foley about the map. As far as he knows, those agents are with us right now. And they'll go to the house and find them. This is bad."

We were all silent for a minute, watching squirrels racing up and down the oak trees that lined the paths. We'd been alone in the little section of the park when we'd entered, but when I looked up, I saw a man sitting on a bench reading a newspaper. It seemed crazy, but I had the feeling he was watching us.

"Zander," I whispered, "I think we should get going."

"Okay," Zander said, following the direction of my eyes toward the man. He lowered his voice. "But I've been thinking and you're right. We can't just take off for the Southwest. We need to know whether Dad ever went to Arizona, whether he found this treasure, and whether the map might tell us where it is."

"How are we going to do that?" M.K. asked.

"I don't know exactly," Zander said. "I wish we could ask someone. Of course, it would be a risk, but..."

I knew exactly what he was thinking, and I hesitated for a minute, waiting to see if he was going to say it. But something was stopping him.

"What?" M.K. asked us. "Of course what?"

"What he means," I said after a moment, "is that it might be time for a visit to the Expedition Society."

Twelve

The outside of the big gray stone building looked just like any other city business or association headquarters; the only clue as to the nature of the organization inside was the red globes that decorated the top of each post on the wrought-iron fence along the sidewalk. There was a stone staircase and a small, discreet sign over the double black doors that read The Expedition Society.

We climbed the stairs and waited there for a moment nervously, looking around to make sure we hadn't been followed. The agents must have woken up by now. If they'd managed to get out of the closet, there would be agents looking for us at this very moment. Besides which, walking into the Expedition Society was a bit like walking into the lion's den.

"Zander," I whispered, "how are we going to get in?"

"Let's see what happens if we just walk inside," Zander said. "Dad always said that half of belonging is acting like you belong, right?"

"I think he was talking about our social lives, not dealing with the government," I hissed back.

Then a voice behind us said, "I'm trying to get through, if you don't *mind*."

We turned around to find a tall Archy boy about my age. He was wearing the BNDL-issue Explorer's uniform, the black cowhide leggings, and a jacket polished so well that I had to look twice to make sure it wasn't some kind of plastic. He had very black hair that was shiny from some sort of oil, and a snubby, freckled nose that made me think that he liked to hit people and tease small animals.

"Excuse us," said Zander, smiling at the boy. "We were just—"

"Whatever it is you're doing, don't do it in front of the door." The boy pushed past us, almost knocking M.K. over. Pucci flew up in the air, squawking loudly in anger. The boy swiped at the air, muttering, "Someone should get these birds away from the entrance," before pushing through the big doors and disappearing into the building. M.K. made a rude gesture to his back.

"Do you think…?" I hesitated, but Zander just ignored me. He called Pucci down and tucked him inside his sweater.

"Now stay there and be quiet," Zander whispered, and followed the boy through the doors. M.K. and I trailed after.

The doors shut behind us and we found ourselves inside the Expedition Society.

Dad had brought us in for lunch sometimes when we were small, but as his disillusion with the government had grown, so had his disillusion with the Expedition Society. I don't think he'd been for a year or more before his trip to Fazia.

The back of the Expedition Society was lined with dirigible ports and SteamCycle bays, and we watched as Explorers got out of dirigibles, still dressed in mud-spattered gear from wherever they'd been, and greeted each other. A tall woman dismounted from a shining IronSteed and walked around in circles for a minute to stretch her legs before passing through the big glass doors. I'd only ever seen a couple of IronSteeds, and I was still amazed by the huge mechanical horses used for backcountry travel and military campaigns. They were made of iron and Gryluminum and powered by small, self-contained steam engines.

The Society acted as a kind of home base for Explorers while they were in the city, and the third, fourth, and fifth floors were dormitories for any Explorer of the Realm—or any Explorer from another country or territory—who needed a place to stay. There were men and women wandering around, looking as though they'd just gotten back from the bush or the jungle. A couple of Neos, in red jumpsuits like the ones Mr. Mountmorris's secretary had been wearing, were laughing about something nearby. They reminded me of parrots with their bright, spiky hairstyles and garishly colored jumpsuits. I remembered Dad explaining that they wore the jumpsuits in honor of Pierre Neville, the first Neo inventor. We hadn't met many Neos—most of Dad's friends were Archys like him—and the three of us couldn't help staring.

The tall woman I'd seen before was dressed in a snowy white Arctic snowsuit lined with namwee fur. She ran up to an older man with a long white beard. "Mr. Mills, I'm Dolly Frost, exploration correspondent for the *Times*. I understand you're just back from Deloia City… "

"We've got to move fast," I whispered to them. "Mountmorris is probably calling Foley right now."

We headed for the Hall of Explorers, walking past a poster advertising ANDLC's new IronPonies, smaller, more versatile versions of the IronSteeds. Barring our way was a reception desk and a large woman in a leather trenchcoat and top hat standing behind it. Behind her was a large portrait of President Hildreth. The woman was holding a clipboard, and for the first time we saw the sign that read Members and Guests of Members Only.

She smiled in a cold, polite way and pushed her top hat back. "Excuse me, are you members?"

"We're just visiting," Zander said. "We…"

"They're with me, Annmarie," said a voice from behind us. We turned around to find a tall Neo girl of about my age standing there with a pair of high-tech plastic and metal flight goggles pushed up into her copper-colored curls. There were little lights embedded in the goggles and in her earlobes, too, and they blinked at us like extra pairs of eyes. She was wearing a royal blue jumpsuit made of a synthetic fabric that shimmered in the overhead lights and tall blue boots that were molded to her legs. Her flight jacket was made of the same material as her jumpsuit, with many pockets and tight sleeves that ended at her elbows. She had a tattoo of some sort of airplane or glider on her right forearm.

"Fine, thank you," said the woman in the top hat, writing something on her clipboard.

"Hail, President Hildreth," the girl said. I noticed that the index finger of her salute hand wasn't straight, the way it was supposed to be for the presidential salute, but bent at a ninety-degree angle.

We followed her into the great hall, too surprised to say anything. "You're welcome," she said, taking off for the other side of the room without another glance.

"Who was that?" I whispered to Zander.

"I don't know," he said. "But she saved us." He looked after her for a moment. "Now, let's go inside."

The Hall of Explorers was a huge space, well lit by the oil lamps that lined the walls and filled with tables and chairs made of exotic woods. Snaking all around the perimeter of the room were portraits of every member of the society since Harrison Arnoz, nearly a hundred in all.

The Expedition Society had been built the year after a group of Explorers discovered the ruins of the Great Temple of Lundland, near the Arctic Circle, and the Hall of Explorers had been modeled on the intricately carved ice temple. There were tall pillars of etched glass everywhere, and huge windows that looked out onto the city streets. In the very center of the room was an enormous, hand-painted wooden globe that slowly rotated on its axis by way of the clockwork mechanisms inside. It glittered with little gold stars to mark the places that Expedition Society members had discovered. All along the sides of the big room were tables laid out with coffee and tea and plates of exotic-looking food from the New Lands—juicy slices of Juboodan grubfruit, giant Maloisian cherries, sandwiches made with tender Fazian beef, and pitchers of lemonade made with rare Florida lemons. Apparently, the food shortages hadn't affected the Expedition Society. M.K. walked right over and swiped a couple of beef sandwiches. After hesitating a minute, Zander and I followed her. It had been a long time since we'd eaten anything like those sandwiches, and I felt a flash of guilt and resentment, thinking about how happy I'd been to get a pound of flour this morning at the markets.

It struck me that perhaps the mysterious man with the clockwork hand was a member of the Expedition Society, but as hard as I searched among the sunburned, weather-beaten faces in the room, I didn't see him.

"There's Dad's portrait—" Zander said. "It's right—" He stopped, and my eyes followed his to the wall above the fireplace, where I remembered seeing a portrait of Dad as a young man, painted upon his return from his successful ascent of Mount Anamata.

But the portrait was no longer there. In its place was a portrait of an elderly, gray-haired man I didn't recognize.

"It's not there," I whispered. "It's not there anymore."

Zander was staring at the space. "But why would they take it down? He was a member of the Society. Where is it?"

I searched the wall again to make sure it hadn't been moved.

"Let's see if we can find the Expedition Log," Zander said

quietly, "and then we'll go." I looked around the room, and it seemed to me that we had been noticed. A few people were looking our way, and the boy with the very black hair was watching us closely from across the room. He was standing next to a tall man with a long, flowing black mustache oiled with what looked like the same substance as had been used on his hair. The man was wearing high black boots and a tightly fitting Explorer's jacket like his son's, only his had many brass dials embedded in the sleeves. Now I knew why the boy looked familiar.

"That's Leo Nackley," I told Zander in a low voice. "He's a famous Explorer. That boy must be his son."

"Everybody's looking at us," M.K.said.

"Just follow me," Zander whispered.

But before we could get across the room, the black-haired boy approached us.

"Non-Explorers aren't allowed in here," he said.

"Are you an Explorer?" Zander asked the boy.

"Excuse me?" Anger flashed across the surface of his light blue eyes.

"I know your father is an Explorer of the Realm, but I thought kids could be members of the society only if they had accomplished something themselves. I keep up with these things, and you haven't done that."

"Who do you think you are?" The boy's voice was low and angry, full of unpleasant possibilities.

"Zander West," Zander said, sticking out his hand, which the boy ignored. "And as far as I can tell, I'm the same as you, the son of an Explorer. If you can be here, I don't see why I can't."

"West?" I could see something moving across his face, surprise and then something else—something hateful and dangerous. There was a long silence and then he said, "I know all about your father. He got himself killed in Fazia. My father says he was a coward and a traitor."

The front of Zander's sweater moved a little, and I could hear a low, angry chuckling sound. I hoped Pucci would stay hidden.

The three of us stared at the boy. "You can't get away with that," M.K. said in a choked voice. "I'll make you pay!" And in that moment, I really believed she would.

But Nackley's son just sneered and took off for the other side of the room, where his father was waiting.

"Zander…" I watched as the boy whispered something to Nackley, and they both turned to look at us. There was something about the older Nackley's blue eyes—even paler than his son's—that made me shiver as they settled on us. "You shouldn't have done that. If they haven't already called Francis Foley, they will now."

"Let's look at the Expedition Log quickly," Zander said, taking a deep breath. "Then we'd better get going. Pucci, stay in there and be quiet. We don't need any more problems."

Self-consciously, we crossed the room and found the huge leather-bound logbook on a table near the globe. It was open to the middle and when I looked down at the page, I saw the name *George Cruthers* and a list of the famous Explorer's trips around the globe, including his history-making crossing of the Bernal Sea. I flipped through the book, reading the well-known names out loud: "'*Jacob Omboodo, Rachel Banfield, Robert Tighley, Siddartha Meube, Harrison Arnoz...*' Zander! Here's Leo Nackley. This is incredible; it's everyone who's ever done anything important in the field of exploration."

"Where's Dad?" M.K. asked.

"He should be right here," Zander said, pushing me aside. "'*Walters... Womack...*' Hang on." He flipped back and forward through the pages, and then looked up at us.

"He's gone from here, too."

"And look at this," I said. We all looked down, where the torn edges showed where the page had been carefully removed. The thin ruff of white paper taunted us.

"What's going on here?" Zander said, to no one in particular. "*What* is going on?"

Thirteen

"**A**re you okay?"

We turned around to find the copper-haired girl standing in front of us again. She had taken off the goggles, and they were dangling from her right hand. I hadn't noticed it at first, what with the glittery jumpsuit and the flashing lights distracting me, but she was pretty. She was grinning at us in a good-humored way.

"Excuse me," Zander said.

"Are you okay?"

"Yes, we…," Zander started to say. He stopped and focused on her. "What makes you think we're not?"

She scratched her nose and shrugged. "Well, first of all, I had to get you in, and then you seemed surprised and dismayed about something up on the wall. Then you had a run-in with the awful

Lazlo Nackley. And now you seem surprised and dismayed about something in there." She pointed to the book. "So I just wanted to make sure you were all right."

Zander and I glanced at each other. We weren't sure how much we should tell this strange Neo girl. But there was something about her that made me trust her.

"My name's Kit," I told her. "Kit West. This is my brother, Zander, and my sister, M.K."

"West as in...?" Her eyes widened.

"Yes," I said. "We're his children and we came here to... to see his portrait, and his portrait's gone, and all of his entries are gone from the Expedition Log, and we... we don't know why."

She had strange, amber-colored eyes, with heavy, dark lashes. "Oh," she said in a low voice. "I'm so sorry. Didn't you know?"

"Know what?"

"Know that he was stripped of his membership in the Expedition Society?"

"No," Zander said. "We didn't know."

She seemed worried all of a sudden. "Look, everyone's looking at us. Nackley's raised the alarm, I think. Why don't we go over there and talk." She pointed to one of the little rooms off the hall. We nodded and followed her into the tiny conference room, settling into the comfortable chairs. On the wall was a painting of Mount Fuji in the mist.

"Why did they take away his membership?" I asked her, keeping my voice down and looking around for BNDL agents.

"I don't know. It was a while ago. I'm so sorry, by the way, about what happened to him. He was kind of a hero of mine." She looked up at us quickly with her strange eyes. I'd assumed her hair was dyed red, but close up I could see its rich color. "I remember my mother talking about it, but I never heard why. No one seemed to want to go into it."

"Is your mother an Explorer?" Zander asked her.

"Yes. I'm sorry. I should have…" She stuck out a hand. "I'm Sukey Neville. My mother is—"

"Delilah Neville," M.K. finished. "I have a picture of her on my wall. With her glider." Delilah Neville was probably the best-known Neo pilot and Explorer of the New Modern Age. She'd flown her combination-engine glider all over the world and tested lots of other Neo technology besides. People called her "Brave Delilah."

"I remember when your mother made her first flight over the New Polar Lands to map Rubutanland," I told her. "I thought she was amazing. And are you really the granddaughter of Pierre Neville?"

"Yup." She smiled, which made her even prettier.

"I don't understand," Zander said. "What could have happened for them to take his membership away?"

"I remember people saying that it had something to do with the BNDL Code for Explorers," Sukey told us. "I wish I'd paid more attention."

"Nackley and his son seem to hate him for some reason," I said.

Sukey shrugged. "I can try to find out something for you."

Zander was silent for a moment and then he said, more to himself than to the rest of us, "There's got to be a way to figure out whether he went to Arizona."

"Arizona?" Sukey asked. "What does Arizona have to do with anything?" Her eyes widened as she watched the lump on the front of Zander's sweater move slowly up toward his face. Zander pushed it back down.

"I can't tell you why," he said. "But we're trying to find out if our dad ever went to Arizona. We were hoping the Expedition Log would tell us, but—"

Sukey started to say something, then stopped. She stood up, walked over to the door, and closed it.

"What?" Zander asked her.

She spoke in a low voice, almost a whisper. "Well, it's just that... he was a cartographer, wasn't he?"

"He was the best American cartographer of the New Modern Age," I said indignantly.

Sukey walked around the room, her head down, mumbling to herself. Suddenly she said, "Come with me. I'm going to show you something."

"What is it?" Zander asked.

"Just follow me." She stood up, opened the door again, and led the way back through the Hall of Explorers to the reception area. "Wait here."

Sukey disappeared into one of the small rooms off the main area.

"What's going on?" I whispered to Zander.

"I have no idea," he said. "But she seems to know something."

A couple of minutes later, she was back.

"It's clear. Come on." She led us into a small office, and then, looking around to make sure no one was watching, opened what looked like a closet door. She let us through, followed us in, and shut it carefully behind us.

It wasn't a closet. We were at the top of a long wooden staircase, carpeted in pale blue, the banister and walls painted blue to match. Following Sukey's lead, we went down the stairs and along a dark hallway lined with ornate frosted-glass doors, each one labeled with a number written on in silver ink. There were no windows, so I figured that we had descended underneath the street. At the end of the passage, I could see more hallways heading off in different directions.

"Sukey," Zander said, sounding, for the first time since we'd left home, a little nervous. "What is it? Where are we going?"

She stopped. "Shh. We're not supposed to be down here. It's off-limits even to members."

"But where's 'here'?" He had stopped walking, too, and I knew he wouldn't go any farther until we had an answer.

"The Map Room, you idiot," Sukey said, pulling him along the hallway. "I'm taking you to the Map Room."

Fourteen

"It's kind of a secret," Sukey whispered as she led us along the hallway. "I don't understand why. Expedition Society members make maps of the places they visit. Certain ones get hung up in the Hall of Explorers and then others get stored in the Map Room. They do research down there, too. Nobody's supposed to know about it, but I discovered it when I was looking around down here once. Let's see, it was 209, I think." She stopped in front of a door marked 209 and tried the handle. It was locked, but she reached up, took a key from the top of the molding over the door, and used it to open the door.

"Just 'looking around down here once'?" I asked her.

She shrugged, smiling mischievously, and led us into a dark room. "Now," she whispered, "I think the light switch is here somewhere." Moments later, the lights came on and we found ourselves in a big room filled with tables and frosted-glass filing cabinets. The most remarkable thing about the room was that all four walls were covered with framed maps of different shapes and sizes, with many more stacked on tables or piled into boxes on the floor.

"Zander!" I said, staring up at the maps. "Look!" They were all here, all the exotic places in the world that we had heard about and read about: Peru and Grygia and the Grand Canyon and Micronesia and the Solomon Islands, and many I'd never heard of, with strange names that conjured up images of sun-washed beaches and snow-covered steppes and thick, dangerous jungles. It reminded me of the way the wall in the library at home had looked before BNDL had taken all of Dad's maps away.

"We'd better hurry," Sukey said, "in case someone saw us coming down here. What are we looking for, anyway?"

I thought for a moment. What *were* we looking for? Dad's maps had gone with the agents, and we didn't even know if he'd ever been to Drowned Man's Canyon.

"I guess anything that says 'Arizona,' or has Dad's name on it. You can look for 'Azure Canyon' or 'Drowned Man's Canyon,' too," I told them. We split up, each of us scanning one of the four walls we'd been assigned to, then looking through the piles. It took everything I had not to get lost in the incredible maps. Many of them were signed by well-known Explorers and there were more than a couple of Dad's I'd never seen before, though they turned out to be of other locations.

"Why are these maps down here?" Zander asked as we looked. "Shouldn't they be up where people can see them?"

"I don't know," Sukey said. "Maybe it's for security. I can't ask my mother, because I don't want her to know I came down here. We're underground and these rooms go on for miles and miles. I think it's some kind of secret headquarters."

I looked around at the tables. On one of them there was a box filled with framed maps and magnifying glasses and file folders scattered around. "It looks like someone's been cataloging these," I said. I flipped through the frames. "These are Dad's maps!" I cried out. "These are the ones that they took out of our house! They've been studying them."

Zander came over to look.

I kept flipping through the maps. "I don't understand why they wanted these so badly. I mean, Dad published all of his maps, right?" Zander and M.K. shrugged, so I looked over at Sukey. "When your mother explores a new place, she makes maps for BNDL, doesn't she?"

"Those are the rules," Sukey said. She recited, "'*The cartography of all Explorers of the Realm is the property of BNDL. The reservation of any cartography or knowledge for personal gain is punishable by the suspension of exploring privileges.*'"

I thought for a minute. "So they must have taken the maps because they thought there was something he hadn't revealed to them, right?"

"One of these?" Zander asked.

"No, we know about all these places." I looked around the room.

"Hold on, remember the treasure map he made for M.K.'s birthday?"

"The what?" Sukey was looking confused, but Zander and M.K. jumped to it, slipping the maps out of their frames and testing the corners. I did the same.

"You could separate it only at one corner," I reminded them. "So try all four."

"I don't know what you're talking about," Sukey said, cutting me off, "but we better hurry up. We don't have a lot of time."

"He once made a map that peeled away from… I don't have time to explain. We've got to find it." I tried a map of the Canadian Rockies, but there wasn't anything on top of it.

"We've *got to* not get caught," Sukey said. "Come on. Put those back." I picked up a map of Istanbul and started to take it out of its frame, but she grabbed it. We stared at each other for a minute, her eyes flashing a darker shade of amber. "I never should have brought you down here."

"You don't understand," I said finally. "We have to find the map. I can't tell you exactly why, but we just have to…"

"I've got it!" M.K. called. "Right here!" Sukey let go of the map I was holding and we rushed over. M.K. was carefully peeling the corner away from a map of a mountain range somewhere in Munopia, and as we all watched, another map was revealed underneath. It had been adhered to the very thin paper of the Munopia map so that you never would have known Dad's secret if you didn't know to look for it. It looked vaguely familiar to me. "*Drown*," the title read, then ended.

"This is it!" I called out. "It's Drowned Man's Canyon. Just like Mr. Mountmorris said. It's the other half of the map! Careful, M.K., Zander, make sure there aren't any others hidden like this."

"Mr. Mountmorris? And what do you mean the other half—?" Sukey started, then stopped, cocking her head toward the door. We heard voices coming along the hallway, too far away to make out what they were saying. "We've got to go."

"Any others, Zander?" I folded the map of Drowned Man's Canyon and tucked it into the front of my sweater with its other half.

"I've got one more to check." He had replaced the other maps in their frames and was testing the corner of the final one. "Nope. That's it." He put it back in the pile. "They can look at these ones all they want."

"Come on," Sukey was saying. "Hurry." We ducked out of the Map Room and she locked the door and replaced the key. We started back toward the staircase, but the voices were coming from that direction, so we turned around and went the other way. "Keep going," Sukey whispered, "to the end of the hallway. There's a door there that leads to another staircase." She, Zander, and M.K. were ahead of me, and we ran as quickly as we could along the hallway. Sukey opened the door, and she and Zander were inside when I heard a man's voice, vaguely familiar, say, "The light's on. I think someone's been down here." I didn't think there was time for both of us to get through the door without being seen, so I pushed M.K. through and shut it behind her. Then I ducked through an open doorway that led to a dark, basement-like boiler room. I ran along the wall, crouched behind a water tank, and tried to keep my breathing as quiet as I could.

"It must be the West children." Another man, his voice also familiar.

"How should I know? What are they doing here anyway?" said a third voice.

"I should think that would be obvious." Suddenly, I recognized Mr. Mountmorris—his formal way of speaking and the high, squeaky quality of his voice. "They came to see if they could find the other half of the map they showed me." My heart felt like it was going to beat right out of my chest. *Mr. Mountmorris!*

"Well, is it here?" The first voice was bordering on angry.

"No, we looked through everything we took from Alexander's house," said the second voice. "The Drowned Man's Canyon map wasn't there. Damn! We should have had them arrested as soon as my boy Lazlo told me who they were. At least we'd have half of the map." *Leo Nackley.* But who was the third man? I knew I'd heard that voice before.

"I saw it, Leo," said Mountmorris. "On its own, it doesn't tell us anything. We need the other half."

I was terrified, my leg muscles screaming from crouching perfectly still, but I couldn't help smiling. We'd outwitted them.

They moved down the hallway, their voices growing fainter. Now I could hear only a few snippets of their conversation.

"…went out to the house," one of them said. "…contacting agents… no… word yet. Soon."

"…associate of Alex's," Mr. Mountmorris's voice said. "…the Mapmakers' Guild, perhaps… the…" His voice disappeared, and I couldn't hear anything more.

The Mapmakers' Guild? It rang some sort of bell, deep down in my brain. Maybe it was something I'd overheard a long time ago, but I couldn't remember if Dad had ever mentioned anything about it.

I counted to one hundred and when I was sure they were gone, I snuck out. I checked the hallway to be sure, then found the staircase where the others had gone. They were waiting at the top for me.

"Where were you?" Zander asked angrily.

"I panicked," I told them. "I hid in some sort of boiler room and could hear them talking. I think they're going to the house to figure out what happened to the agents."

"We've got to go," M.K. said, "before they get there."

"Why?" Sukey turned to look at her. "What's at your house?"

"Well, I kind of knocked out some BNDL agents at our house," M.K. explained, shrugging. "I had to, though. Seriously." She blinked innocently.

Sukey's eyes narrowed. "'*Kind of knocked out some BNDL agents*'? I wish you'd told me that. You three are full of mysteries, aren't you?" We burst through the door and hurried through the lobby toward the front door, ignoring the looks we were getting from the Explorers standing around talking. We stopped running and Pucci scrambled up Zander's chest, popping up through the collar and settling himself on his shoulder. The parrot bobbed his silver head to Sukey in greeting.

"What are you, some kind of pirate nanny?" she asked with a smile. But the smile disappeared as she took a good look at Pucci. "Is that a modified Fazian black knight parrot?" Her eyes were very wide.

"Kind of." Zander pushed Pucci's feet back under his collar.

"Where did you get him?"

"We adopted him. Or he adopted us." Zander smiled and she rolled her eyes.

"I don't even want to know. Run," she said. "I'll hold them off."

"Thank you for everything," I said to her. Her cheeks were flushed and her curly hair looked even curlier. People always say that things look copper, but her hair really was the color of pennies, dark and red and alive against the vivid blue of her jumpsuit.

"Don't be ridiculous," she said. "Now go!"

It was only once we were back out on the street, navigating the crowds of people and running toward the train station, that I realized why the third voice in the downstairs hallway was familiar to me.

It belonged to Francis Foley.

Fifteen

The New Modern Age steam trains were remarkable inventions: huge, shining silver machines that could carry hundreds of people from place to place in record time. When we were small, Dad had often brought us to the railyards outside the city so we could watch them sailing in, one after another. He had told us how the trains could no longer be run by computers, as they once had, so they'd been engineered to respond to the expert handling of experienced drivers. "A great steam driver can convince you you're sitting still, even if the world is flashing by outside your window," he'd tell us as we waved to the men and women seated in the steering cabins of the big trains.

The train to Philadelphia was a gleaming new Fronsne 2000, and we leaped on just as it started to move—so smoothly that we barely knew it had started—out of the station and west out of the city.

"Did anyone follow us?" Zander whispered as we settled ourselves in a second-class compartment. The only other inhabitant was a white-haired Archy reading a newspaper and chewing dramleaf. He looked up as we came through the door and his eyes widened in alarm when he saw Pucci, who had found himself a comfy perch on top of the luggage rack. He squawked *"All aboard"* once before dozing off to the almost imperceptible motion of the train.

"I don't know," I whispered back. "But that was Mr. Mountmorris and Francis Foley with Leo Nackley in the basement. I recognized their voices. We never should have shown Mountmorris the map." I felt sick. "We never should have gone to the Expedition Society."

"We wouldn't have the other half if we hadn't gone to the Expedition Society," Zander pointed out, a little too loudly. The man in our train compartment seemed very interested, and I nodded toward him so that Zander and M.K. wouldn't say anything else.

Zander waited until the man was looking down at his paper again, then made a clicking noise that called Pucci to his shoulder. He whispered something to the parrot, who rose into the air, flapping his wings and cawing at the man in the corner, his metal legs out in front of him, ready to attack.

"Sorry," Zander said. "He hates newspapers. Weird."

The man, pale now, dropped his paper on the floor and stood up carefully. "Yes, yes, I think I'll just find a different compartment." Taking his leather briefcase with him, he slunk out the door.

"Good bird," Zander said as soon as the man was gone. We were alone now. "Okay, Kit. Take it out. Let's see what we've got."

I pulled the curtain across the window in the compartment door and took the two halves out. They matched up perfectly.

"*Map*," Pucci announced. "*Whole map*." We all looked up at him for a second, then back down at the map.

The complete map now showed Azure Canyon and the entirety of Drowned Man's Canyon, as well as mesas and hills and other formations created by ancient floods and washes. I studied it carefully. Drowned Man's Canyon was a squiggly worm of a canyon that widened in the center and then narrowed, branches jutting off the end like fingers on a hand.

As far as I could tell, there were no *X*'s for *X marks the spot*.

"Tickets, please," bellowed a train conductor, coming into our compartment. I jumped up and spread our former seatmate's abandoned newspaper out on top of the maps.

"Sorry," Zander said. "We didn't have time to get them at the station." He smiled up at the conductor, a Neo with a large silver ring through one side of his nose and a couple of flashing lights in his ears. His name badge said Harry Craps. I tried not to look at Zander, knowing he would make me laugh if he saw it, too. "Can we buy them from you?"

The conductor sighed as though we'd just asked him to push the train up a mountain, and he got three tickets out of his pocket. "How far are you going?" he asked.

"Flagstaff, Arizona." Zander gave him another smile, as if people asked for tickets to Flagstaff every day. "Three tickets to Flagstaff."

Harry Craps looked surprised but jotted something down on the tickets and said, "All right. That'll be two hundred thirty-seven Allied Dollars." He eyed us suspiciously, three children alone in the train compartment with a parrot perched on the luggage rack.

I stared up at him. Two hundred thirty-seven AD! No wonder it was only rich government workers who traveled by train anymore.

"Come on, Kit, give him the money," Zander said with a confident smile.

My hands shaking, I reached into my backpack and took out the money we'd collected from the house before we'd left. It was all that remained of the cash Dad had given us before he'd gone to Fazia, and we'd been trying to save it, trading copper for food and using a dollar here or there only when we had to. I counted out the fare and Zander and I exchanged a glance. We were down to about four AD. I felt my stomach drop.

Harry Craps took the money, handed over the tickets, and left us alone.

"I hope you know what you're doing," I told Zander. "Now we don't have any money to get home."

"We'll figure it out," he said. But he looked scared. "Take out the map again."

"I don't see anything about the treasure here," I told them.

"But the important thing is that he left us the map." Zander was excited, pacing around the train compartment and looking out the window. "Dad wants us to go to Arizona. He left us a map of the place where he wants us to go. He thought it would be in the house when we found it, of course, but Foley took it and we found it anyway. Maybe there's some kind of hidden message."

I couldn't help thinking that he was getting ahead of himself. "Yeah, maybe the message says, 'Don't go to Arizona,'" M.K. suggested sarcastically.

"*Do not go to the place on this map.*" I laughed.

Zander stopped pacing and sat down, giving us a nasty look. "There must be more to it. Let's all think."

I tried to keep my voice down. "Zander, what are we doing? We're on a train. We have no food. They've probably found Wolff and DeRosa by now and there are a whole bunch more creepy government agents looking for us, agents who would probably kill us for Dad's map if they thought they could get away with it."

He looked scared for a minute, and I realized that even though Zander always seemed to know what he was doing, he hadn't really thought this through.

I started thinking about what I'd just said. If the agents were willing to do anything to get the map, there must be something in it. *Dad must have found something.* And the man with the clockwork hand had risked everything to get the book to me. I felt a tingling all down my back. Whatever this was, it was big.

"Look," Zander said finally, "for some reason, Dad gave us this map. Dad wouldn't have joked about something like this. There must be some really important reason why he did what he did. That gold is… well, you know how much gold is worth now that there isn't any more to find. Maybe he wanted us to find it so we can fix up the house, go to the Academy. Maybe he wants us to go to Fazia and try to find him."

"What?" This was the second time he'd talked about this, and I stared at him. "You think he's alive?"

"Maybe. You said yourself that nothing they told us about his disappearance makes sense." He looked so much like Dad, his blue eyes wide and pleading, that it freaked me out a little and I had to look away.

M.K. and I didn't say anything. I was excited now, but the idea of actually making it to Arizona seemed… impossible.

"I've been thinking about something," I told them after a minute. "Why did Mr. Mountmorris tell us about the treasure? Telling us about it only made us less likely to give him the map, right?"

Zander looked up. "You think it was a trap?"

"Think about it. Why else would he have told us? If they can't find the map, the next best thing is to let us find it and follow us. Maybe that's why they sent the agents."

Zander and M.K. were silent and I kept talking, thinking out loud now. "We've always wondered why they didn't put us in an orphanage after they told us about Dad. Maybe this is why. Maybe they *wanted* the man with the clockwork hand to find me and they knew he couldn't if I was locked up. They've been watching us the whole time so they can get their hands on Dad's map and the gold. We all know how valuable gold is now. It's the only money that's worth anything. They need it for trading."

"We just have to make sure they don't catch up to us, then," Zander said after a long moment. It was very quiet in the train compartment. Although we could barely feel the motion of the train, we could see the suburbs flying by outside our window. Along the train tracks there were little lean-tos where people had made their homes. Dad was always telling us how lucky we were, that his status as an Explorer of the Realm had meant that we could stay in our house, could get food and clothes and things. So many people were much worse off since the shipments from the New Lands had dwindled, he had always said. I watched a boy about my age scavenging by the side of the tracks as we flashed by, and I knew Dad had been right.

Above the racing train, the sky was bright blue and full of long, wispy bits of cloud. In the distance I could see a couple of dirigibles chugging along, emitting clouds of black smoke behind them.

The train slowed as it stopped at various stations, and a voice came over the loudspeaker saying that we'd be arriving in Philadelphia soon.

"We need to talk to someone," I said finally. "We need to talk to someone who knew Dad well, who can tell us if he ever talked about Drowned Man's Canyon."

Fifteen minutes later the train slowed as it approached Thirtieth Street Station in Philadelphia.

I had been staring out the window, watching the crowds of people waiting for the train, when I noticed a couple of blue-uniformed security agents running onto the platform. They seemed upset about something, looking around wildly and then leaning in to talk to each other. As I watched, Harry Craps stepped down from the train and said something to them, pointing back toward the car where we were sitting.

"Well, we should think about who Dad might have told about Arizona or the treasure, if he found it or knew where it was. So who would he have—?" Zander was saying.

"Zander?" I reached out and pulled his arm to get his attention. "Zander, I think they're here for us." I tucked the map back into my sweater.

"What?"

"Damn!" M.K. exclaimed. "Look out the window!"

"They must have called the police," Zander said. "We've got to get off this train."

"But where are we going to go?" M.K. asked us. "We spent all our money on the train tickets. How are we going to get to Arizona?" She was already standing, ready to move.

"Welcome to Philadelphia," came a voice over the loudspeaker.

"Come on. We're going all the way to the back of the train," Zander said. "Get ready to run."

"Run where?" M.K. asked. "Where are we going to go?"

"I wish we knew someone here," I said, realizing as I spoke that, in fact, we did.

"Hold on," Zander said, his eyes brightening. And I knew he'd had the same thought I'd had. "Actually, we do know someone here." We poked our heads out of the compartment and, seeing no one, headed toward the back of the train. People were coming out of the compartments as the train slowed, and we had to push past them.

"Hey!" someone called after us. On the other side of the clot of passengers, I could see a couple of uniformed policemen trying to make their way through.

"Excuse us, excuse us," I murmured as we rushed along the corridor, but we were still getting some pretty nasty looks.

"Who do we know?" M.K. whispered, bringing up the rear.

"Think, M.K., think," Zander turned around to say. "Philadelphia?"

"Oh," she said, as it dawned on her. "You mean…" We'd reached the last car and we opened a door at the very back of the train, where the caboose would have been if they had cabooses anymore.

This was it. We jumped from the back of the train onto the tracks and clambered up the end of the platform, Pucci flying ahead to show us the way. The policemen were still on the other side of the platform, and we ducked down, keeping low to the ground as we ran toward the stairs that would take us up and out of the station. The three of us said it at exactly the same moment, "Raleigh McAdam!"

Raleigh and Dad were ten years old when Harrison Arnoz discovered the Grygian Alps. They didn't know each other yet, of course; Raleigh grew up in Philadelphia and Dad in New York. But I think that they must have had pretty much the same reaction to the news that Arnoz had scaled a mountain pass that had been declared impassable and discovered a difference between the old government-issued maps of the region generated by the Muller Machines and what he was seeing as he camped in and hiked through the thick forest, looking for bear tracks.

Dad said that the world had suddenly opened up before him, new possibilities stretching and turning and expanding like the lines on the new maps. After the Muller Machines were outlawed, no one had had much hope for a while. The discovery of the New Lands was like an electric charge. Dad would be an Explorer; he would travel the world, just the way he'd dreamed when he'd played with the wooden puzzle his father had made.

Four years later, when he joined the first class at the brand-new Academy for the Exploratory Sciences, Dad became friends with Raleigh McAdam. Dad was always telling us stories about Raleigh, about the things they'd done together at the Academy, about their classes on navigation and mapmaking and wilderness survival and the biology of the Fazian violet anaconda or the new Grygian bear.

Raleigh had visited us a couple of times, armed with fake excuses about collecting supplies from Dad in case the agents asked questions about his trip. I remembered those trips vividly because Dad had seemed younger when he was with Raleigh. They stayed up late playing harmonica and drinking Rubutan whiskey and talking about the old days at the Academy. It had really been something to be an Explorer of the Realm in those days, when there was still so much to discover and explore.

We had visited Raleigh once, too. Dad had come up with some excuse to tell the agents, and we'd taken the train to Philadelphia, found our way to Raleigh's house, and spent an afternoon with him. "Raleigh is the most trustworthy person I've ever known," Dad had told us on the way home. "Don't ever forget that."

A year or so before Dad disappeared, Raleigh had had some kind of accident. Dad didn't tell us much about it, except to say that Raleigh had lost the use of his legs. Dad went to visit him once and when he came home he had seemed depressed. I'd wondered if Raleigh might get in touch with us when he heard about Dad, but he never had.

"Do you think he'll even recognize us?" M.K. asked.

"Probably not," I said. "We were just little kids the last time we saw him."

We were standing in front of the door of Raleigh's big, ramshackle row house, exhausted by our sprint from the train station. It looked the way I remembered it, just more dilapidated, the shutters missing or hanging at odd angles, and bright green graffiti to one side of the door. Years ago, Raleigh had cemented little gargoyles to the windowsills, but most of them had broken off. The few that remained looked lonely and angry on their perches.

"Well," Zander said, putting out an arm for Pucci, "we can't stand out here on the steps all day. Someone'll see us." He pulled his fist back and knocked, hard, on the door. We didn't hear anything for a long time, and then there was a jangling and clicking on the other side of the door and it swung open.

It was Raleigh, looking twenty years older.

He stared up at us from an old wheelchair, his straggly brown-

and-gray-streaked beard grown almost to his chest, his hair an unruly mess on top of his head. There was a tin of dramleaf in his lap, and I could smell the spicy scent of it in the doorway.

He stared up at Zander. "As I live and breathe. Alex? Is that really you? Have you come back?"

Sixteen

"I thought you were a ghost," Raleigh said for what must have been the twentieth time since we'd knocked on the door. "My god, you look so much like him. You look exactly the way he looked when I met him." He stared at Zander for a long moment, then looked away. "What are you kids doing here, anyway?" He looked up at Pucci, who was inspecting the clutter of knickknacks on his mantel. There were four huge candelabras, one on each wall, tall wax candles burning away in them, and the faded red wallpaper was scarred by old ports and wires that had once connected to the Muller Machines.

"We're kind of in trouble, Raleigh," I told him. "BNDL's looking for us and there's this map and we thought maybe you could tell us if Dad ever went to Arizona, to a place called Drowned Man's Canyon."

Raleigh was sitting straight up in his chair, staring at us. "BNDL? Drowned Man's Canyon?" he asked. "Tell me everything."

I did, leaving out the part about the man with the clockwork hand. The Explorer had risked a lot to get the map to us, and I think we had all started feeling protective of him.

When I was finished, Raleigh looked up. "I'll say you're in a lot of trouble. These people are very dangerous." He ran a hand through his crazy hair, not meeting our eyes, and tucked a new wad of dramleaf behind his lower lip. I could see the relaxation wash over his face as it took effect. "You shouldn't be fooling around with these things."

"But what *are* 'these things'?" I asked him. "We can't figure it out. Obviously they think that Dad made a secret map and that he knew where the treasure is. But there isn't anything on the map. Did he know about the treasure of Drowned Man's Canyon, Raleigh? Did he go there?"

Raleigh didn't say anything. He just wheeled himself over to the fireplace and poked at the fire halfheartedly. He had regular firewood—Raleigh had inherited a lot of money when his parents died and he must have been able to buy firewood on the black market—but it wasn't a very good fire and the room was quite cold.

When he turned around, his eyes settled on Zander. "I still can't believe how much you look like him," he said again. Zander smiled, embarrassed. I just felt irritated, the way I always did when people commented on Zander and Dad's similarity. But then Raleigh looked at me and said, "And damned if you don't look exactly like Veronique. 'Nika,' I always called her. God how I miss her. Him, too." Raleigh's eyes filled with tears and we looked away while he got ahold of himself.

"In answer to your question," he went on after a long moment, "yes, your father went to Arizona, looking for the treasure. In fact..." He started to wheel himself over to a big bureau on the other side of the room and then stopped and said, "Kit, do me a favor and open the second drawer from the top. There should be a stack of photographs there." I opened the drawer and started hunting under the piles of envelopes and mail for the photos. "This chair isn't working well," Raleigh said. "I don't know what's wrong with it."

"Don't you have a set of IronLegs?" M.K.asked him. Zander and I glanced at each other. I'd wondered why Raleigh was using the old-fashioned chair, too, but neither of us had had the nerve to ask.

"Ah, they're over there, against the wall." He pointed to the mechanical brass braces leaning up against the far wall. "They don't work, either." He smiled sheepishly. "Nothing works around here. Your father had a knack for mechanics. I don't. I should get them to a shop, but I just..." Raleigh looked embarrassed. "I don't know. I can't seem to get around to it. It's not like I have anywhere to go. Maybe I should become a Neo and use one of their crazy devices." We'd heard about strange new leg braces made by Neo engineers that allowed the user to stand and walk without any clanking or awkwardness.

"I'll take a look," M.K. said. "I'm good at things like that." She went over and started inspecting the braces as I found the stack of photos and brought them to Raleigh.

"Here we go," Raleigh said. He flipped through them and laid a couple down on the table. "We shouldn't have kept these pictures,

of course. But your dad had some film from somewhere and he knew how to develop it. That's why I keep them hidden. Anyway, there we are: the treasure hunters."

The picture showed three young men laughing into the camera, squinting against the bright sun that washed everything with a bleached, sandy light. I recognized Dad right away, even without his beard. He was the tallest of the three, his blond hair almost white from the sun, his eyes crinkling with happiness, but only a small smile on his lips. I would have known Raleigh, too; even then he'd had a roundness that was the opposite of Dad's tall slimness. Raleigh's brown hair was cut short and he was grinning from ear to ear, looking as though he'd just told a dirty joke. The other boy in the picture had light hair like Dad, a pointy chin, and thin, rangy build. He was making a funny face and holding a walking stick. "That's our school friend John Beauregard," Raleigh said. "What a group we were. We'd heard about the golden treasure of Drowned Man's Canyon and we were convinced we were going to find it. We'd practically started spending the money. Your father and I were going to use it to finance a trip to the New North Polar Sea. Hah! We didn't find it, of course, but we sure had a good time trying."

Raleigh pointed to another picture of Dad, leaning against a solid rock face. "There he is, the intrepid explorer. It was the summer after our second year at the Academy. We hitched rides, jumped trains, whatever we had to do. It was easier to get around then. The government didn't care so much about what people did. Took us three weeks to get out there."

"But obviously you didn't find the treasure," Zander asked after he'd gone through all the photos.

"No, but your dad had some ideas," Raleigh said. "It was the legend of Dan Foley that first got us interested in Drowned Man's Canyon, but there were all kinds of other stories about that part of Arizona, crazy stories…" He trailed off.

"What stories?" M.K. asked, looking up from the leg braces, which she'd disassembled on the carpet.

"Oh, weird things. Some people think that there are aliens in the canyon, or that a race of giant ant people lives in tunnels inside the rocks. We met an Indian guide who told us that the ghost of Dan Foley haunts the canyon, that there are other ghosts that appear in the night and take you away. I have to admit, some of those stories scared the bejeezus out of me. But your father was very interested in them. He said it showed there was something there." Raleigh waited for a minute before saying, "He believed there was a secret, undiscovered canyon somewhere near Drowned Man's, a canyon that contained Dan Foley's treasure. And he believed the stories supported the idea that it was there. Not that they were true, but that the stories had been created to keep people out of the canyon. He went back to Drowned Man's Canyon, you know, just before he met your mother. Nika."

There was a long, thick silence. "Do you remember her at all?" he asked us finally.

"A little," Zander and I said at the same time. M.K. didn't say anything; she'd been only a few months old when our mother had died.

"He was so in love with her. She was so in love with him, too.

126

She was smart, Nika, one of the smartest people I've ever met. She understood all about the Muller Machines, how they worked, how they had malfunctioned. Your dad was so proud of her."

"He never talked about her," I said angrily. "It was like she never existed at all. I didn't even know that, about the Muller Machines. He never told us that."

"It broke his heart," Raleigh said simply. "I think it hurt too much even to say her name." He took a deep breath. "Anyway. He went out there again. Alone."

I wanted to ask him more about our mother, but instead I took the two pieces of the map out and laid them on the table.

"There aren't any other canyons here," Zander said. "But maybe he made this map before he'd found it."

"If he *had* found the treasure," Raleigh said, "we would have heard about it. Your father was scrupulous about bringing his findings to museums."

I looked at the picture of the three boys again. They were standing in front of a desert landscape, red-brown rocks and a waterfall behind them. A dark shadow fell across the right-hand side of the picture. "Wait a second, Raleigh," I said. "Who took this picture of the three of you? There's a shadow there."

Raleigh looked surprised. "Oh, didn't I tell you? There were four of us. Your father and John and I and…"

A dark look passed across his face as though he was remembering something especially unpleasant. "Leo Nackley."

Seventeen

We were all silent for a moment. "Leo Nackley?" Zander asked. "Leo Nackley was with you, too? In Arizona?"

"Of course. Didn't you know that? When you said you heard him in the basement of the Explorer's Society, talking about your father's map, I thought you knew that he was after the treasure, too. Yes, Leo was there when your father, John, and I went to Drowned Man's Canyon the first time. He was a good friend of ours from the Academy... back then, anyway."

"Do you think he knows where it is?" I asked. M.K. had stopped working on the leg braces. She had them standing up and was testing the joints.

"No, if he'd found it you can bet we would have heard about it. Leo is one of those Explorers who does it for the glory. The money and the resources, too, but always the glory." The dark look passed over Raleigh's face again.

I thought for a minute. "Why would Dad want us to have that map, Raleigh? Do you think he wanted us to find the treasure? Did he say anything to you about leaving it to us?"

Raleigh tried to stand up, as though he'd forgotten for a minute that he couldn't. Beneath his beard, his face was red and his eyes were angry.

"God forgive me. You have to understand. After my accident, I... well, I've kind of kept to myself. I let self-pity get the better of me. Alex visited me a couple of years ago. I think he had something to tell me. He kept circling around it, waiting for me to be in the mood to listen. But I couldn't stand seeing him. He was so. . . vigorous. So full of life. He just reminded me of all the expeditions I'd never go on. I picked a fight, basically drove him away. If I could go back and..."

I don't know what made me do it, but I glanced at Zander and said, "Raleigh, I found the map because Dad left us a code in Mr. Mountmorris's book. A man brought me the book when I was out in the market. He was being chased by agents and I think he got away, but..."

Raleigh struggled in his seat again. "Who was he? Who was the man?"

"We don't know," I said. "Just a man, an Explorer, I think, no one I'd seen before. He had a clockwork hand. Do *you* know who he is?"

There was a long, long silence before Raleigh said, "No, I don't know who he is, but I think I know what he is." He settled back into his chair, looking defeated.

"*What* he is?" I repeated. "What do you mean?"

Raleigh didn't say anything, and it was M.K. who broke the silence. "I've got these done for you," she told him. "Here, let's try them on."

Once M.K. helped Raleigh buckle them on, Raleigh stood up and the IronLegs started moving, walking him around the room as he engaged the clockwork gears at the top.

He grinned, though the look of pain was still there beneath his smile. "I should have known one of Alex's kids would turn out to be a mechanic." He sat down again and looked at me.

"If I'm not mistaken," he said, his eyes very serious, "that man is a member of the Mapmakers' Guild."

Eighteen

I jumped out of my chair. "They were talking about that in the basement. They said something about the Mapmakers' Guild. What is it, Raleigh?"

"The Mapmakers' Guild," Raleigh told us, as we all looked at the dying fire, "is a secret organization outlawed by the government, ever since the Muller Machines were hacked."

"Are you a member?" M.K. asked in a hushed voice.

"Me? No way." Raleigh laughed, tucking a new wad of dramleaf into his lip. "The Guild—from what I've figured out—was the elite of the elite. Cartographers, I think. It goes way, way back, to the time when they built the first Muller Machines. The Guild put all the information into the Muller Machines that made the maps. People didn't know much about them, but they worked for the government and they did some exploring. They were about the only ones who were allowed to travel.

"But then, the Muller Machines were hacked. And the new government came in and outlawed them. This was President Barbado, the guy before Hildreth. When Harrison Arnoz discovered Grygia, they went on a witch hunt, trying to figure out how everyone had been duped. The government figured that the Mapmakers' Guild must have known and that they were helping the government to keep the New Lands for the rich, rather than bringing the resources back for the good of the country and our allies. Barbado and his goons tracked down a bunch of them and put them in jail.

"Everyone figured they were gone, but I've heard rumors that they aren't at all, that they still operate in secret. When I was still around the Expedition Society, I remember hearing about people getting interrogated by BNDL agents. They reported that the agents asked them about this Map Guild or Mapmakers' Guild. They seemed to have inside knowledge."

"And you think the man who gave Kit the book is a member of the Guild?" Zander asked him.

Raleigh looked at me. "Guys with clockwork hands give you mysterious packages every day, do they, Kit?"

I sat there for a minute, staring at the fire, trying to put it together. "So the guy was part of some sort of secret fraternity? But what does Dad have to do with all of this?"

"I don't know." Raleigh's face clouded over. "Your dad was a great Explorer. He…"

"Do you think he was part of this Mapmakers' Guild?" I asked.

Raleigh just stared at the fire.

"He was weird before he left for Fazia," I said suddenly. "There was something going on. When he said goodbye to us, it was like there was something he wasn't telling us." Zander and M.K. nodded.

"You think that's why he was kicked out of the Expedition Society, don't you?" I asked Raleigh. "Because he was in this organization?"

He took a deep breath. "Maybe. But I was hoping it was about him standing up to land grabbers like Leo Nackley."

"Land grabbers?"

"After the New Lands were found," Raleigh told us, "there were some explorers who thought that BNDL and ANDLC—you know about ANDLC, right?" We nodded. "Well, they thought that the government had the right to take anything it wanted, to move people off their land, relocate animal populations." He pointed to Pucci. "To modify animals to use against their own people, take natural resources, anything they wanted. Leo Nackley was one of them. Your father and I thought differently. The government decided it for us, of course, and your father and I... well, I suppose you could say that we went along so we would be allowed to keep exploring. I'm not proud of it, but there it is." He hesitated for a minute and I had the feeling that he'd been about to tell us something, then stopped himself. "There were things that happened that...," he started. "There are things that it would be dangerous for you to know."

"We're already in danger, Raleigh," Zander said. "And I don't know who the guy is, but he risked his life to get us the map. We owe it to him and to Dad to try to find the treasure."

Raleigh looked up at Zander. "To try to find the... You don't mean that you're going to Arizona?"

One look at our faces told him all he needed to know.

"Of course you're going to Arizona. You're Alex's kids, aren't you?" He stood up awkwardly and paced around a bit on the IronLegs, still getting a feel for them. The candles were burning down, their light flickering against the walls.

"If I thought I could stop you, I would," Raleigh said. "But if you three are half as stubborn as your dad was, there isn't any point. There is... one other thing."

He lit a candle and slowly led the way up the stairs to the second floor of the house, opening a large closet in the upstairs hallway. He reached behind the jumble of coats and explorer's jackets hanging there and pulled out a large cardboard box, holding the candle over it so we could see. *For Zander, Kit, and M.K.,* Dad had written on white tape on the top of the box.

"He left these when he came to visit," Raleigh said. "He must have hidden them up here when I wasn't looking. I found them only a couple of months ago. Obviously, he wanted you to have them. And I think you're going to need them." He took the top off the box and brought out three identical Explorer's vests. We slipped them on over our sweaters and adjusted them so that they fit perfectly. They were just like Dad's, made of different hides and synthetic fabrics, lined with namwee fur and sporting multiple gadgets and utilities embedded on the outsides of the vests. There were more in the many inside and outside pockets.

We didn't have time to inspect them properly, but I could see that my vest had a compass embedded in the front, along with other devices. I found a large map pouch on the back inside lining and zipped the maps of Drowned Man's Canyon inside.

"Reminds me of him," Raleigh said, studying us in our vests for a minute. He went back into the box and took out three pairs of Explorer's leggings made of black cowhide so supple it was like someone had been wearing them for years. The leggings were complete with cargo pockets all along the legs. "You'll be well outfitted, at least," Raleigh said wistfully. "All right, gang. It's time for bed."

We'd been asleep only a couple of hours when Raleigh woke us, striding into the room on the IronLegs, saying, "Get up, kids. Now. It's important." He'd put us in a bedroom on the second floor, and as he waved a lit candle around the room, I could see that it was cluttered with remnants from his travels, statues and figurines and paintings. At first, I thought I was still asleep, dreaming that I was surrounded by tiny people made of jade and stone.

I sat up in bed, nudging Zander, who was sleeping next to me. M.K. was on a mattress on the floor, and Pucci hopped over and started pulling at her hair. M.K. could sleep through almost anything.

"What?" She sat up suddenly and looked around the room.

"Some men just came to the door," Raleigh said, walking on the clanking leg braces over to the window and pulling aside the curtains to look outside. "It's two o'clock in the morning and some men just came to the door." He peeked out the window again and paced around the room. "There were a whole bunch of them, agents and police on IronSteeds."

Zander was already out of bed and getting into his clothes and I followed suit. M.K. ducked into the bathroom and came out dressed in her leggings, shirt, and vest, lacing up her boots.

"They were lying," Raleigh said. "They told me they were concerned about your safety. They said that they'd learned I was a friend of your father's and they wondered if I'd heard from you. I told them no, of course, but I'm not sure they believed me. Now there are a bunch of people out there." Zander went to look out the window. "No! Zander! They'll see you."

"We have to get going," Zander said.

"You can't go out the front," Raleigh said. "Look."

I stepped to the window and peeked around the edge of the curtain and gasped. Raleigh was right. The street in front of the house was filled with people and IronSteeds.

I looked at the group. "That Neo guy in the red jumpsuit… Mr. Mountmorris's secretary. Jec something. He's out there. He isn't just Mr. Mountmorris's secretary, he must also be a BNDL operative."

"They're everywhere," Raleigh said with a scowl. "I know Explorers who swear BNDL has tapped their phones and tailed them when they're on expeditions."

"We've got to go," Zander said. "Now."

Raleigh looked nervous. "Are you sure this is a good idea?"

"What else can we do?" Zander asked him.

"You could stay with me. I could hide you. I have money. I—"

"They'd find us," Zander said. "We're committed to Arizona at this point. If we can find the treasure before Nackley does, then we can bargain with them."

Raleigh watched as we got ready.

"All right," he said. "You can go out the back. The train lines run parallel to the street about half a mile that way." He pointed toward the back of the house. "There's no station, but the trains make a stop there to switch tracks. I think you should be able to get into one of the empty cargo cars. Be careful, though, the rail riders can be a nasty bunch. Oh, and I almost forgot. I made these for your parrot. I don't even want to know how you guys ended up with one of them, but if you don't cover up his feet, you're going to attract some pretty unwelcome attention." He handed a set of leather booties to Zander and helped tie them over Pucci's feet and legs. He still didn't look like a normal parrot, but at least the metal talons weren't so noticeable. Pucci hopped over and nuzzled Raleigh's neck in thanks.

We all trooped downstairs and Raleigh gave us each an awkward hug that smelled overwhelmingly of dramleaf and sour wine. "I should have food to give you or something. Hell, I shouldn't be letting you go at all. Do you want some cookies?" He tucked a few stale cookies into a rolled-up newspaper and handed it over. "Hey, how about some money?" He took a pile of hundred-dollar bills out of a jar on the kitchen counter and handed a few bills to each of us. We exchanged wide-eyed glances and stuffed the money into our vests.

"I'm not much of a grown-up," he said.

"You're the only grown-up we've got," M.K. said, kissing him on the cheek.

"Then you're in more trouble than I thought." He grinned.

We thanked him again and slipped out the back door, already running into the last of the night.

Nineteen

L ulled by the motion of the train and curled up on piles of hay, we slept through the darkness in an empty cargo car on the Philadelphia—Los Angeles line.

It wasn't until daylight angled through the half-open door that we really looked at the leggings and Explorer's vests. We examined them as we sped across the country.

"Look," M.K. said, "there's a tool set on mine." She showed us a little flap on the front of her vest that concealed a complete miniature tool set. "And Dad put a bunch of utilities in these pockets. This one has a picture of a sleeping person on it. Wonder what that does." She laid three more brass boxes out on the floor of the car and poked and prodded them. "I can't figure out what they do, though."

There were a lot of buttons and flaps on M.K.'s vest, and she pressed them one after the other, trying them out. "Hey, what's this?"

"Ow!" Zander grabbed his right shoulder and we all looked up to see a small arrow embedded in the wall of the cargo car. "You shot me!"

"It just nicked you," M.K. said, inspecting a tiny wound on his upper arm. "Don't be such a baby."

I checked my own vest. Aside from the shining brass compass embedded in the animal hide on the front, there was also a small pocket on the inside that contained a sextant, just like the little tool Dad had used for navigation. I opened another inside pocket and found a brass spyglass. "Look at this," I told them. "It has ten degrees of magnification, like a really powerful set of binoculars!"

"What do you think this is?" Zander asked us, holding up a small brass utility about the size of a pack of playing cards that he'd found in one of his pockets. He pushed a button on the box and a flame shot out of one end. A little fire started in the hay and he jumped on it to stamp it out. "That might come in handy," he said. He held up another one, this one a bit larger, and when he pressed a button, a large piece of silver fabric, complete with zippers, shot out. "It's a sleeping bag!" Zander said, delighted. "Thin but warm. And I think we each have a light on the vests. He thought of everything." He reached over and pushed a button on the left shoulder of my vest. A light shone out into the train car, illuminating a large area in front of me.

Zander also found a small hunting kit, containing a few arrows and a foldable bow, and we all found utilities in our pockets that we couldn't quite figure out. We put some of them in the pockets on the leggings and left the rest in the vests.

"We'll be all right now," M.K. said, settling back against a pile of boxes at one end of the car. "He knew we'd need the vests."

We were all quiet, thinking about Dad, wondering if this was what he had imagined when he'd hidden the gear in Raleigh's closet. It was one of those moments when I missed him so much that I could feel the pain of it deep in my skin, like a hidden burn that wouldn't ever go away. And somehow, Raleigh's mention of our mother had seared a twin burn next to it. All the years of her absence, the way Dad's eyes would cloud over when we asked him about her, it had all lodged there in my body and I felt something I'd let myself feel only a handful of times since he'd disappeared: pure, hot anger at him for leaving us.

I looked around at the graffiti-covered walls of the cargo car; symbols and pictures that I knew had been left by rail riders who had used the empty cargo cars to move around the country. Soon after the invention of the ultra fast trains, Neo kids who didn't have anywhere to live had started riding the empty cars, defending their turf with the long-handled knives they carried.

The train moved quickly across Pennsylvania and down through Virginia, Tennessee, and Arkansas, and then straight across the wide fields of Oklahoma. Outside the cargo car, the sun rose slowly and we could feel the air get hotter and more humid as we raced west across the country. We took off our sweaters and opened the door of the car a bit, but there wasn't much of a breeze and it wasn't long before we were drenched in sweat. Even Pucci looked miserable, his feathers bedraggled and limp. The cookies Raleigh had given us were gone by the time we crossed the Oklahoma border. I had visions of us starving to death and dying of thirst in the hot train as the train chugged on for hours and hours.

We were speeding through a huge expanse of cornfields when all of a sudden, as the train slowed down around a bend, the door flew open and a Neo boy with spiky blue hair came crashing into the car.

He hit the floor hard and when he looked up and saw Pucci, he grinned and said, "Hey, where am I, the zoo car?"

"*Funny*," Pucci squawked. "*Very funny!*"

He sat up and we all stared. He wasn't too much older than we were. He was a thin, wiry boy who looked five inches taller than he really was because of the blue spike of hair that stood up like the blade of a circular saw. He had a pile of chains around his neck and little flashing lights embedded in his ears and neck. When he grinned at us, we could see that the insides of his lips were pierced with the lights, too.

"Whew. Hot in here. You got anything to drink?" Something about the way he said it put me on my guard.

"No," I said. "Wish we did."

"Ah. You're thirsty, too? I've come down from the North myself. Didn't know it would be so hot." He studied us for a moment, his brown eyes wary. "You don't look like the usual rail riders," he said. "Not at all. You're Archys, aren't you? Where you ridin' from?"

"Canada," Zander said.

"That right? Huh." He watched Zander for much too long, as though he was trying to see the lie on his face.

"Yeah," Zander said, but not very convincingly.

The guy nodded at M.K. "She looks a little young to be ridin' rails."

"*Looks* can be deceiving," said M.K, putting a hand on the sheathed knife on her belt. The guy looked surprised for a minute and then he smiled and said, "So they can, so they can."

The train slowed and then stopped, and we were all quiet as we listened to the sleek sound of the doors whooshing open and the voices of passengers getting on and off. A few minutes later we were moving again. The rail rider was sitting with his back against the wall of the car, still watching us. The little lights in his ears and lips flashed in time, as though they were sending out some sort of message.

He laughed quietly. "So you don't have a thing to drink, do you? That's what you're telling me?" He stood up. He was very tall, six-feet or more. "What about money, then? You got any money, four-eyes?" Self-consciously, I pushed my glasses up on my nose. "Riders share with each other. That's the tradition."

There was a long silence as we all looked at him, and then M.K. jumped up, the little knife out of its sheath and up in the air where the guy could see it. He sat back down again, laughed nervously, and held his hands up where we could see them.

"Hey, hey, sorry about that. Gotta try, you know, gotta try. But you three are all right. You're all right. Yeah, yeah…"

M.K. stood there for another couple minutes, just to be sure he got the message, and then smiled sweetly at him, put her knife away, and sat down again.

He was quiet for a few minutes and then said, "Look, like I said, you three are all right. So I'm gonna tell you something. I'd get off this train if I were you. Word on the rails is that the next station up ahead is crawling with cops looking for three kids traveling with a black parrot. Modified, I heard. If I'm not mistaken, that's you. Something about assaulting federal agents. I'm pretty impressed, I've got to tell you. Wouldn't have thought you had it in you."

I was already on my feet. "How much farther to the station? What are we going to do?"

Blue Hair put a hand out. "Easy now. You can make it. We'll slow down up here on the final approach. The grass is pretty high there on the side of the tracks. I think you can jump out as we slow down and hide pretty well next to the rails. Crouch down until the train is gone and then you might want to lay low awhile. That's my advice, anyway."

"Thanks," Zander said, standing, too, and holding on to the side of the rocking train.

"Hey," Blue Hair said, "good luck and don't forget this." He pressed Raleigh's newspaper into M.K.'s hand. "You're probably going to want some reading material. Now go." He slid the door open for us. Outside the car, we could see the cornfields flashing by.

And we could feel the train slow as it leaned into the curve.

We jumped.

Twenty

I'm not going to lie—it hurt to hit the ground.

M.K. yelped.

"Ow!" I rolled over and lay there on my back for a second, then reached up to make sure my glasses weren't broken.

Zander didn't say anything, but when I looked over at him, he looked like he wanted to say "Ow!" too.

"Everyone okay?" he asked, once he'd gotten his breath back. "You two made it?" It wasn't any problem staying on the ground until the train was out of sight around the bend, and once it was gone, we stood up and walked out of the field toward another large open one that had just been mowed. M.K. had her right arm cradled against her body, her shoulders hunched up. Pucci squawked and made a wide circle in the air as though he was trying to tell us something, but when we searched the sky and the horizon, we couldn't see a thing but clear, blue sky for miles and miles. No dirigibles, no nothing. The only object on the horizon was a big commercial airship, far away to the south of us, heading east. A huge, rolling irrigator sat at the edge of the field, and we took off our vests and sat down under it to rest. It would shield us from anyone flying overhead, but if the police came by ground, we were out of luck.

My left hip throbbed where it had slammed into the ground and my back ached from the long journey on the floor of the cargo car. We leaned back against the irrigator, Zander and I breathing hard. M.K. was still holding her arm.

"You okay?" I asked her.

"Yeah." She rubbed at her biceps, and winced. "I think I hit a piece of metal when I landed. Can you see what happened?"

I pushed up the sleeve of her shirt, finding a long gash, oozing blood. "This looks bad," I told her. "I need a cloth or something so I can clean it. Zander, do you have anything in your vest?"

"I think there was a little…" He went through the pockets, coming out with a small chamois cloth. I used it to soak up the blood and then pressed it against the wound, hoping it would stop bleeding.

"Look in ours, too," I told him. "We should put something on it." He searched through our vests and in mine and found a small first-aid kit. He tossed me a small tube. "'*Roweben juper berry cream*'," I read. There was some very small writing on the tube and I scanned it until I read, "'*antibiotic properties*'."

"This is the stuff, M.K." I spread some on the wound, but I didn't like the way the sides opened up. It was deep. It might need stitches. Zander had found a bandage in the first-aid kit and he came over and spread it carefully over the cut.

M.K. tried to grin. "Good as new," she said. "Thanks, guys."

But there was something about her voice that made me nervous. M.K. didn't cry when she got hurt, never had. She wasn't crying now, but she looked a little pale and her grin stayed on her mouth, never reaching her eyes. I felt panic creep through my veins. If that cut didn't heal, we couldn't just walk into a hospital and ask them to stitch it up.

"What are we going to do now?" I asked Zander. "We can't hop another train out west. They'll be looking for us. In fact, when they discover we're not on the train, they'll probably come searching for us. We're not exactly good at blending into the scenery, you know."

"I know," Zander said. "It's a problem."

"A problem! Dying of thirst and hunger in a field in the middle of I-don't-even-know-where is a little bit more than a problem, Zander." My glasses were dusty. I polished them on my shirt and then replaced them on my face. Everything was brighter: the green fields, the blue sky. "And what if M.K. needs a doctor?"

"I'm fine," she said in a stubborn voice. "I won't need a doctor."

"Dad wants us to find the treasure," Zander said in the annoyingly calm way he has when he's arguing. "Do you wish you'd never opened the book? Do you wish you'd put the map back in the drawer?"

I hesitated. "No, of course not. But we don't even know what Dad meant for us to do with it. It's crazy. It's a wild goose chase."

"Dad would never have sent us on a wild goose chase." Zander folded his hands over his stomach and leaned back against the big metal contraption.

Zander and I sat on opposite sides of the irrigator, not talking. M.K. picked up the newspaper and looked through it while Zander and I sat, mad at each other and getting hotter in the bright sun.

We'd been sitting there for a good five minutes before M.K. said, "Zander, Kit, look at this."

She held up the newspaper that had held the cookies, folded so that we could read the story on the back.

EXPLORER AND SON TO EMBARK ON SOUTHWESTERN TREASURE HUNT

By Dolly Frost
Exploration Correspondent

Famed explorer Leo Nackley and his son, Lazlo Nackley, a student at the Academy for the Exploratory Sciences, leave today on a hunt for Dan Foley's famed golden treasure in a remote canyon in the American Southwest. The senior Nackley told our reporter that new information has come to light that will help his son pinpoint the location of the treasure, which has long been rumored but never found despite considerable effort and outlay of funds. Nackley said that the

treasure is priceless, in terms of both
monetary and cultural/historical value.
We await news from our intrepid treasure
hunters.

"New information? Hah!" I said. "Mr. Mountmorris told him about the map!"

"You're right." Zander shrugged. "But he doesn't have it. We do."

"For what it's worth," I grumbled.

"We've got to beat them out there," Zander said. "Maybe we could hitchhike."

"Hitchhike? Are you crazy? Who's going to pick up three children and a bad-tempered parrot with the ability to rip a man's face off?"

Pucci murmured indignantly.

"Something's bound to turn up."

I didn't even bother answering. It was so hot out in the field, the sun beating down on our heads. The dust from the dry ground was making it hard to breathe.

"I just think," Zander said, to fill the silence, "that it's going to be all right. I don't think Dad would have sent us out to Arizona if he didn't think we could find the treasure."

"Dad didn't send us to Arizona," I reminded him. "He didn't send us anywhere."

"He wouldn't have left the map for us if he didn't think we were going to go after the treasure. I know that."

"You don't know anything," I said. I stood up and glared at him. "Maybe the man with the clockwork hand works for BNDL. Maybe *that's* the trap. I don't know what we were thinking. You convinced us to come all the way out here, with no plan, with no food. M.K. attacked those agents. We broke into the Map Room. They could put us in jail!" I pushed my glasses back up my nose. I was sweating and they kept slipping down.

Zander hardly reacted. He just bent down and plucked a straggly piece of grass from the dust. "Dad wanted us to—"

I cut him off. "Did it ever occur to you that maybe *Dad* didn't have the best sense of direction? *Dad* got lost, remember? That's why he's dead! He left us! Maybe his judgment wasn't so great, Zander. Did you ever think of that?"

By the time I finished, I was almost shouting. Zander just stared back at me with a stunned look. He was about to say something when Pucci flew up into the air, very excited, and squawked, "*Plane! Plane!*" We looked up to find a small plane approaching.

"It must be security agents," I said, scrambling to get up. "That rail rider must have told them about us. Quick! We've got to hide." We put our vests on and started running. But as I started moving, I realized how improbable it was that they'd send a plane for us rather than a dirigible. Hardly anyone used planes anymore because they used too much gasoline. I stopped for a minute and listened, but I couldn't hear anything.

"It's unmarked," M.K. shouted. "And it's not a plane. It's a Router Glider 432. The same kind Delilah Neville flies."

The three of us stopped and looked up as the glider sailed closer and closer. It was a graceful, birdlike machine, painted a creamy white that made it look like a huge airborne swan. The glider's wings were much bigger than the wings of an airplane, broad and flat and shaped to make the most of the thermal air currents that Neo machines depended on. Most of the gliders used by Neo explorers were combination machines, with an engine to get them off the ground and huge flat wings to help them stay up once they were airborne.

"Do you smell anything?" I asked, sniffing the air. "Doesn't it smell like popcorn?"

"That's not popcorn," M.K. said. "That's a late-adapted biofuel engine burning pure-grade corn oil!"

"Do you think…?" Zander started as the glider circled lower and the lone figure in the cockpit waved to us. We heard an engine kick on and then the aircraft made a long approach, setting down neatly in the unplanted field. We all stared as the door opened and the tall, copper-haired pilot stepped out and strode over to us wearing her bright blue flight suit, her brass and blue-leather goggles pushed up onto her turquoise leather flight cap.

"What's the story with the matching vests and pants?" Sukey Neville asked, grinning at us, her eyes an intense amber-brown. "You three starting a singing group or something?"

Twenty-one

Y ou should have seen the Expedition Society once they figured out what you'd done to those agents," Sukey was telling us. She was eating an apple, talking with her mouth full. "It was crazy. Leo Nackley and Francis Foley were all up in arms, saying that the children of Alexander West had assaulted federal agents and broken into the Expedition Society. Even Mr. Mountmorris was there. And he almost never comes to the Society. Luckily, they didn't realize I'd been in the Map Room with you, but I got into trouble for signing you in as guests. I just said it was a misunderstanding and I didn't know who you were, but I'm not sure they believed me. You know who Mr. Mountmorris is, don't you?"

"We do now. He's an advisor to ANDLC, right?"

"Yeah, he's an 'advisor' to ANDLC, an 'advisor' to BNDL. The truth is, he runs the whole thing. He was working for President

Barbado when Harrison Arnoz discovered Grygia, and he made sure the Bureau got rid of any Grygians who were in the way. That's what Delilah says, anyway."

"I wish I'd known that before we showed him the map," I grumbled.

"*The map*," Pucci squawked. "*Show her the map!*"

"That bird is really weird," Sukey said. She looked up at me. "Are you going to tell me what's going on here or not?"

"Uh…" Zander and I glanced at each other, not sure about trusting this girl again. It was true that she'd saved our hides twice in the last couple of days, but still…

It was M.K. who decided it for us. "Come on, let's tell her," she said. "If it wasn't for her, we wouldn't even have the second half of the map."

M.K. was right. We explained the whole thing, starting from the beginning, when the man with the clockwork hand had given me the book. The only thing we left out was the stuff about the Mapmakers' Guild. From what Raleigh had said, it would be dangerous to reveal that Dad might have been a member.

"We think the treasure's in this canyon and that our father wanted us to find it, but we don't have any idea *where* in the canyon it is," I told Sukey. "And now Leo Nackley is heading west, and he and Lazlo are going to get there before we do, and if they catch us, they'll probably put us in jail."

Sukey just nodded. "Well, we can't let them beat us there, can we?"

"How did you find us, anyway?" I asked her.

"I heard something about how you'd gotten off the train in Philadelphia, but then I overheard Foley and Mountmorris talking about how they thought you'd be trying to get to Arizona. I figured you didn't have a lot of options. When I checked the schedules, I saw there was a cargo line heading out and, well… It's what I would have done in your place. Delilah's on an expedition so I took the glider and I just flew low and followed the tracks and pretty soon, there you were." She cocked her head and looked at me for a minute, then pitched her apple core over the wing of the glider. "I snooped around a little bit yesterday and I found out some information for you. About your father and why he got kicked out of the Society." She stopped talking for a second and listened. "Did you hear something?"

We all listened. "No," I said. "I don't think so."

"Okay, I'll tell you what I learned, but I'm not sure you're going to like it."

"It's okay," Zander told her. "We want to know."

Sukey's eyes met mine. In the bright sunlight, they were a liquid light brown. "Well, after everything calmed down, I found a good friend of my mother's—Billi Pan, she's an Explorer who defected from the Chinese Protectorate after the plagues—and asked her if she'd ever met your father. She said she'd known him well and that even if he was an Archy"—she grinned at us—"he was a wonderful man and a good Explorer. That's what she said. She said he'd stood up to the land grabbers and that people like her, who agreed with him, thought he was a real hero for it. I asked some other Explorers why he'd been kicked out of the Expedition Society, and they said that it had never been explained completely, but that BNDL told them that he'd engaged in some kind of forbidden activity…" She hesitated.

"We want to know," Zander said. "Go ahead."

"Billi thought it was Leo Nackley who accused him, and that he'd accused your dad of fraud and belonging to an outlawed organization. She wasn't sure what it was, though."

Zander and M.K. and I exchanged glances. I had a pretty good idea.

"But if he was kicked out of the Expedition Society, how did he get to take the trip to Fazia?" Zander asked. "He needed boats, supplies, a crew."

"I don't know. Billi said everyone had wondered about that, but they were all too afraid of Foley and his agents to ask too many questions. They didn't say anything after he'd disappeared."

We sat there in silence for a couple of minutes, just taking it in. I couldn't stop thinking about his face as he'd gotten into the SteamTaxi to leave for Fazia. Had he known he wasn't coming back? Or had he just been scared? I remembered the way his eyes had darted around the yard. Had agents followed him on the expedition?

"He didn't say anything to you about all of this?" She seemed incredulous.

"No," I told her. "As far as we knew, he was going down there on BNDL's dime, same as always."

"That Foley guy didn't say a word about it when he came to tell us Dad had died," M.K. said. "That seems pretty weird to me."

"Well, Delilah says that you can't trust Francis Foley as far as you can—" Sukey sat up, listening, looking out across the expanse of cornfield. "I could swear I heard something."

"Pucci, what is it?" Zander asked, and Pucci rose into the air and made a wide circle.

"*SteamCycles,*" he called down as he circled back. "*SteamCycles!*"

"Someone's coming!" Zander stood up, searching the horizon, one hand shielding his eyes from the sun.

"Did that bird just say 'SteamCycles'?" Sukey asked.

M.K. gestured to Zander to bend down and boost her up on his shoulders. "I don't see anything," she said once she was up. "Do you think it's BNDL?"

"I don't know," I said. "But if it is, we'd better get out of here."

"Wait," Sukey said. "Hold on. Did that bird really say 'SteamCycles'?"

And then we heard the engines, just the faint sound of them in the distance.

"Looks like he did," I said.

We were all up and moving in a couple of seconds.

"Where are we going to go?" Zander was asking us. "There's nowhere to run. We're like sitting ducks out here. Sukey?"

But Sukey was ignoring him. "I might have to dump some supplemental fuel," she was saying to herself, doing some kind of arithmetic on her fingers. "Twenty times forty and..." She sprinted over to the glider, where she started fooling around with some knobs and dials on the outside of the fuselage. Then she took a thin wrench out of her pocket and tightened something on one of the rear wheels. "Come on, you three. I think we can do it."

"Do what?" Zander asked.

"Take off," Sukey said, her curly hair springing up all around the edges of her helmet as she pulled it on, her eyes huge behind the goggles. "What do you think, Pirate Boy?"

Twenty-two

It took us four tries to get off the ground. Sukey kept revving the glider's supplemental engine, but we could all feel that there was something wrong. It just didn't seem to have any power.

"Let me take a look," M.K. said, jumping out and getting a wrench out of the tool kit on her vest.

"Does she know what she's doing?" Sukey asked us.

"Dad always said she was a better mechanic than he was," I said.

"You've got a loose connecting wire to the bio supp," M.K. called out. "I'm just fixing it now." We could all hear the SteamCycles, the engines' *put, put, putting* getting louder.

"Hurry, M.K.," Zander called.

A couple minutes later, she was jumping back into the cargo hold behind the cockpit. "Try that."

Sukey revved the engine and we could hear the difference, but as the glider raced along the open ground, I could feel how heavy and unwieldy we still were.

"We're too heavy," I told Sukey.

"No, we should just be able to do it." She circled around and tried again, but I could feel that gravity was not on our side. As we all watched, a line of black SteamCycles came into view on the horizon.

"You're going to hit them!" I called out.

"Only if we don't get lift," Sukey said in a determined tone.

"Try again," M.K. called out.

Sukey revved the engine and we sped along the ground, heading right for the SteamCycles. The riders wore the uniforms of local policemen and they looked absolutely terrified.

"Come on, come on," Sukey muttered under her breath. I could feel the little glider straining and working and then suddenly, just when I thought we would hit them for sure, the glider's nose rose into the air, and we were heading up, up, up into the bright blue sky.

The glider climbed for a couple of minutes and then we leveled out, slicing neatly through the air. Sukey settled us just below the cloud cover, and we all looked out the window at the patchwork of fields below.

"We did it," Sukey said, patting the controls. "I wasn't sure she was going to do it. Should be just a couple of hours to Arizona."

I looked around the tiny cabin. We were crammed in there like pickles in a jar. "It's safe, right? Flying with this many of us?"

"I guess we'll find out," Sukey said, giving me a wide grin over her shoulder. "I've never done it before."

Pucci cackled. *"Never done it before."* I gulped and tried to focus on the view outside the window.

"That bird is really weird," Sukey said. Pucci cackled again.

"That's a late-adapted engine, right?" M.K. asked her. "How does it run?"

"Runs great," Sukey told her. "She can burn any kind of vegetable oil. The engine gets us up in the air and the glider and the thermals do the rest."

"How long have you been flying?" Zander asked her.

"Since I could walk, practically. I was born in a dirigible. This was before my mother started flying gliders. Delilah was making a run up to Greenland and I was early, so... Anyway, what were we saying about your dad and Leo Nackley?"

I looked out the window. We'd left the SteamCycles far behind.

"We found out that Leo Nackley and Dad were friends when they were younger," Zander said. The glider was beautifully quiet. He told Sukey what we'd learned about their Arizona trip and about the Nackleys' expedition.

"I know all about that," she said. "They started talking about it after they realized you were gone. Nackley does whatever Foley and his agents tell him to do. Delilah can't stand him."

"What are we going to do when we get there?" M.K. asked.

Zander and I looked at each other. "I guess we've got to get down into the canyon and follow the map," I said after a minute.

"I figured you'd have a better plan than that," Sukey said. "Foley and Mountmorris are after you and Leo Nackley has decided he's going to find the treasure before you do. You did assault those agents. What are you going to do when you see them?"

"The whole point," Zander said, "is not to see them."

Sukey just raised her eyebrows.

I was so tired I could barely think anymore. I leaned against the wall of the glider and I must have dozed off because when I looked up next, we had dropped down even farther and the reddish-brown ground was spread out below us, close enough for us to see fields and houses and barns, cars moving like tiny insects along the string-like roads and highways.

The low, flat plains of the Midwest gave way to the high, ridged mountains of the Rockies and then the beige and green high desert of Colorado and northern Arizona. Huge, gray-white clouds had rolled in from the West, and they sat there below us like a wall of fog, just where we needed to go.

For the first time, I noticed that the walls of the glider were decorated with a collection of little dolls, woven out of plant fiber and decorated with beads. "What are those?" I asked her.

"Oh, those are Delilah's Rubutan idols," Sukey told us. "There's one up there for every flight she's made to Rubutanland. They're supposed to be guardians. They watch out for her when she's flying."

I looked up at the little beaded faces and hoped they were watching out for us, too.

"We're almost there," Sukey called back to us. "Brace yourselves. I don't like the look of the weather up ahead and it may be a little bumpy as we drop down for the landing."

We all braced ourselves against the sides of the glider as it started to pitch and roll and Sukey switched over to the engine. As she struggled to keep the plane even, Sukey went pale, her eyes squinted in concentration behind her goggles, and her hands gripped the throttle. I remembered Dad saying that after the Mass Failures, aeronautical engineers had had to completely reinvent the controls on new dirigibles and gliders since aircraft had become so dependent on computers. The dirigibles and gliders were made to be flown by expert pilots, and as I watched Sukey flying the pitching glider, I knew we were in the hands of an expert.

At least I hoped we were.

"Hang on!" she shouted. "I've got to get us out of these clouds." There was a loud rumble of thunder and a few seconds later we saw lightning flash across the nose of the glider. And then we dropped. It was a terrifying feeling. We were in free fall, plummeting through the sky toward the earth as rain suddenly pelted the windshield. Finally, after what seemed like a year, we leveled out.

"Sorry," Sukey called back. "I had to get us out of that. It should be better now. Everyone okay?"

We sailed below the gray clouds rolling across the western edge of the mountains, and suddenly I could see a huge gouge in the reddish surface of the ground.

"There it is," Sukey called, pointing out the window to the left side of the glider. "The Grand Canyon."

We looked down and it took me a moment to take in the sheer depth of the thing. The canyon was a giant scar in the solid, rocky earth, winding out of view over the landscape, the Colorado River a tiny, silvery thread in the distant bottom. The afternoon sun filtered through the clouds, and it hit the red and pink and orange rock of the canyon so that it looked like it was lit up from within.

I don't think I understood until that moment the thrill that Dad must have gotten exploring new places. I had always wondered how it was possible that there were hidden, undiscovered places on the Earth. But up here, looking down at the hugeness, the vastness of it all, it finally made sense to me. We were so small and the Earth and all of its mountains and canyons and rivers and oceans... they were so *enormous.* Of course we didn't know all there was to know about the Earth. How could we?

"Look," Sukey said as the plane dropped, "that's Azure Canyon right there. I see a little village where we can probably leave the glider. Then we'll have to get some IronSteeds for the ride into the canyon. I'm a little worried about the weather."

She made an adjustment on the dash.

"We?" Zander asked.

"That's what I said."

"You're coming with us?" He looked happy all of a sudden. "Really?"

She looked sideways at him and grinned. "Of course I am. You have no idea what you're doing. And you don't think I'm going to miss out on my first treasure hunt, do you? You better share the gold with me if we find it."

"But you don't have any equipment," I said.

"Of course I do." She gestured toward a stuffed backpack in the corner of the plane. "I'm always packed and ready to go. Learned that from Delilah."

She must have seen the worried look we exchanged because she said, "Don't worry. I know what I'm getting into. And I won't slow you down. I'm a student at the Academy. I've taken more outdoor survival classes than you have. Besides, I know these guys."

And with that, she brought the glider down in a little sandy lot, a few trees dotting the ground here and there. We ran along the ground for a few minutes, the racing red rock landscape slowing through the windows.

Pucci squawked.

We'd arrived.

Twenty-three

It wasn't raining as we got out of the glider, but the clouds overhead were gray and threatening and the air was humid, a swift breeze coming from the East. We looked around and found ourselves in a vacant lot behind the straggly little village. Sukey threaded a chain and padlock through brackets on either side of the cockpit door, closed the lock, and we started walking. It felt good to be on solid ground again, and despite the fact that we were, by any read of our situation, in pretty serious trouble, I felt oddly cheerful. We had made it to Arizona. I hadn't ever traveled very far from home and here I was, in the great outdoors, ready to embark on a treasure hunt.

And Sukey was coming with us.

My mood changed when we got to the town. Someone had been having fun when they'd called it "Azure City." It wasn't anything more than a dozen or so trailers parked in little yards decorated with cacti and old washing machines and toilets and rusting cars. Azure Canyon had been discovered at the very beginning of the New Modern Age of Exploration, when Dad was in his teens, and for ten years or so it had been a fairly popular place for Explorers to visit because of its famous blue waterfalls. The canyon had been carved out of highly reflective limestone and travertine rock, and the water that collected beneath its many waterfalls appeared to be a brilliant Caribbean Ocean blue.

Pretty soon, though, it had become clear that there weren't any resources that could be taken out of the canyon, and the Explorers had moved on to more exotic locations in the New Lands. Now the little village looked run-down and desperately poor. I couldn't help but remember Dad ranting about how Native Americans had been treated during the New Modern Age. "You would think we would have learned our lesson already," he would bellow whenever the subject of the new discoveries out west came up, "but here we are, doing it in our own country, taking everything out of the land for ourselves and leaving a mess behind for those it belongs to!"

We walked past a couple of little market stalls advertising Food for Campers and Hikers, and a withered old man wearing a feathered headdress, standing on the street with a hose, who filled up our water bottles for fifty cents a pop. There was a stall with a sign that read Exotic Foods from the Territories, but when I went to look, the old woman in the stall just had a couple of dried-out Juboodan grubfruits. A group of young guys on rusty IronLegs were sitting in front of a broken-down building, holding a sign reading Veterans. Hungry. Please Help. They stared at us as we passed by.

At the end of the short road was a huge, handmade billboard: Bongo's IronSteed Rental. The Best Way To See The Canyun. IronSteeds Nevur Neid Food or Water. Underneath was a picture of Azure Canyon's famous blue waterfalls and a childlike drawing of a mechanical horse. A parking lot next to the sign was filled with the big machines that had always reminded me of medieval horses in armor ready for jousting.

In front of the sign sat a young guy in an old lawn chair. He was a Neo, but a strange kind of Neo, with bleached-out blond hair that hung halfway down his back. He had sunglasses on and was staring up at the sky as though he was expecting to see something appear there. "Are you Bongo?" Sukey asked him. I glanced around nervously. I had gotten really paranoid about the BNDL agents, but I didn't see any here.

Slowly, he raised his sunglasses. "Yeah, that's right. You looking for IronSteeds?"

"Yup," Zander said. "Four, please. How much?"

Bongo looked up at us, blinking as though Zander was speaking a different language. After a minute, he pointed to Pucci. "But, dude, what's he going to do?"

"Uh, he'll fly," Zander said. "He's a bird."

"You don't want a horse for him, then?"

"No, I don't think so." Sukey and I looked at each other, trying not to laugh. The hot desert sun must have gotten to this guy's brain.

"I like his little boots." Bongo stared at Pucci for a minute. "Well, anyway, I can't. Sorry, dude."

"Can't what?"

"Can't rent you any IronSteeds. I don't have any."

"There are about twenty of them out there," Zander said. "I can see them."

"No. Those are all reserved. Big group of people. Some kind of archaeological expedition."

"Who reserved them? Was his name Leo Nackley?" Zander asked.

"No... local guy. Tex somebody. Said he had a big group coming out from the East Coast."

It had to be the Nackleys. Zander and I exchanged a worried look.

"Couldn't you spare a couple?" Sukey asked. "Surely the party you've got coming in doesn't need all of those."

"Dude," the guy said, "they do. They already paid and everything. They have a lot of stuff to carry."

We stood there, not sure what to do, when, out of the corner of my eye, I saw movement in a field behind the little restaurant. There were seven real-live horses grazing in the late-afternoon sun.

"Hey," I said to Bongo. "What about those horses?"

"What?" He looked where I was pointing. "Those? But they... they need food and water."

"Well, we can give them food and there's water in the canyon. I mean, people rode horses into the canyon before IronSteeds were invented, right?"

"Sorry, dude. They're not mine."

"Well, who do they belong to?" I asked him. I was getting annoyed. We didn't have much time. We needed to get down into the canyon before anyone figured out we were here.

"I don't know. They just kind of hang out there."

I rolled my eyes at Sukey.

"Did the big party say when they'd be getting here?" she asked Bongo.

"There's gonna be a big party?" He looked really excited. "Dude, I love parties."

"No, the… the party that you said reserved all the IronSteeds. When are they getting here?"

"Oh, yeah, today, dude. Later today."

"Okay," Zander said. "We better get going, then. We don't have a lot of time."

"You sure you want to go down there?" Bongo asked. "I think it's gonna rain soon. You don't want to be in a canyon when it rains."

"We'll be all right," Zander said. "We've got to get going." But he looked nervous, and when I looked up at the sky I could see that the clouds were moving in, dark and menacing.

"Can you do us a favor?" I asked him. "When that group gets down here, don't tell them you saw us, okay?"

"You in trouble or something?"

"No, not exactly. Just don't tell them about us."

"You got it. Tell them about who?" He winked and handed over a grubby square of paper. "Here, take one of these maps."

We were just about to leave when I thought of something. "Bongo, you've heard about the legend of Drowned Man's Canyon, right?"

He looked a little less dumb and a little more scared. "Yeah. I heard it," he said. "About the gold and everything. They say there's a ghost of that dead miner down there. He comes out of the rocks and takes you away if you go near his treasure. You couldn't pay me to go down that way. Stay in Azure Canyon. It's real pretty. That's where the tourists like to go."

"We'll keep that in mind," I said. "By the way, you should really fix your sign. There are some typos."

"Yeah, dude. I know. The horse has three legs and in real life horses have four."

"No... that's not... forget it," I said. "Thanks anyway." We started walking away. I turned back to wave at him, but he was staring up at the horse on the sign as though he'd forgotten what it was.

"What are we going to do now?" Zander asked. "If we walk down, it'll take forever. There's no way we'll beat them."

"Go see if you can find some food and then meet me over by that barn," Sukey said. "I just want to see something." She took off at a run for a falling-down little barn near the horse paddock. Zander and M.K. and I looked at each other. I shrugged and we did as she'd asked.

There wasn't much food to be had, but we bought a couple of cans of beans and some beef jerky from an old Indian lady and went back to wait by the barn. The air was hot and close and I was itching to get moving. If we had to walk into the canyon, we'd better get going. "What's she doing?" I complained. "They're going to be here any minute."

"Want me to check?" Zander asked.

"No, I'll check," I told him. I started for the barn, but Sukey was already coming out. "No need to fight, boys," she said. "I think we're in luck."

She was leading four horses, all saddled and bridled. They were skinny, but they looked excited to be out of the paddock, dancing around and sniffing the air. "Good thing Delilah dragged me on all those pony treks on the Grygian steppes," she said.

I stared at her. "Did you just steal them?"

"Kind of." She grinned. "Now we're all criminals. That keeps it nice and even. Let's get going."

Twenty-four

We descended as quickly as we could into Azure Canyon, the horses picking their way along the path, which zig-zagged down the steep canyon walls. The gray clouds overhead were gathering faster, but it was so hot that it seemed hard to believe it could ever rain.

My horse was a gentle palomino and she responded to my hands on the reins better than any machine ever could. After a while I relaxed into the Western saddle, letting her carry me along. I checked Dad's map and the one that Bongo had given us every once in a while so I would know when to look out for Drowned Man's Canyon. It was beautiful down there; the red limestone walls of the canyon were marbled with brown and gold and darker red and there were bright green cottonwood trees along the way. Every once in a while, a clear stream formed little waterfalls before it disappeared into the ground. The water tasted delicious, cold, and sweet. All along the walls were caves and crevices in the rock and it all made the canyon seem otherwordly, like some kind of desert paradise. I remembered reading about the ancient peoples of these canyons, who had built their houses high in caves in the cliffs in order to defend themselves from attackers.

"Yahoo!" I called out. "We're free! There aren't any pictures of President Hildreth to salute down here!"

"Yeehaw!" Zander called back.

"Yodeleheeho!" Sukey answered.

Pucci squawked, then mimicked Sukey's yodel.

M.K. laughed and yelled, "Whoo whoo! It's beautiful down here!" We gave the horses free rein and galloped along the path into the canyon.

Before long, we'd reached the canyon floor and we set off toward the West, into the thin sun. I took the compass out of my vest pocket to get our bearings, and once I'd established that we were heading west, just as the map indicated, I noticed a tiny counter in one corner of the compass. As the horses walked along, the numbers slowly went up. After I'd consulted the map, I realized it was tracking our mileage.

"Dad put a sort of odometer on it," I told them. "It's counting out the mileage as we go, like a pedometer for horses. I can compare this to the scale on the map and I'll be able to figure out exactly where we are."

"As long as we're heading for Drowned Man's Canyon, that's all I care about," Zander said.

"What do you think about those?" I asked Zander as we rode, pointing to the gray mass in the distance. The ugly bank of clouds we'd run into in the glider seemed to be settled to the North. "Anything we should worry about?"

"Maybe," he said. "They're pretty far away. And they don't seem to be doing anything." Pucci was flying up ahead of us, making big lazy circles in the sky, as though he was enjoying stretching his wings.

We rode as fast as we could, conscious of the Nackleys and Foley and his agents somewhere behind us. I didn't know how they'd get out here, airship, maybe, or train, but I knew they'd be here soon.

I gave my horse a gentle kick in the side and trotted a little bit ahead of everyone, then fell back into step next to Sukey and her tall red mare. "So where do you live, anyway?" I asked her.

"That's right," said Zander, catching up to us and falling in on the other side of Sukey in a way that annoyed me a little. "We don't know anything about you."

"Oh, it's not very exciting," Sukey said. "Delilah and I live in the city and during the school year I go to the Academy."

"How do you like it?"

Her whole face lit up. "It's so great. This was only my first year, but the classes are amazing. This past year, I took the Science of Flight, Celestial Navigation, Introduction to Outdoor Survival, and Carnivorous Amphibians of the Southern Hemisphere. Next year I get to take Flight Strategy in Remote Jungle Regions and I forget what else. I can't wait."

"I heard you have to take Cartography and Compass Mapping," I said.

"Is it true you learn how to fix engines and construct gliders?" M.K. asked.

The three of us listened in envy as Sukey went on about her teachers and fellow students. We had gone to the local elementary school for a while, but Dad hadn't thought we were learning anything but government propaganda, so he'd been teaching us at home for the last couple of years.

"Lazlo Nackley goes to the Academy, too," Sukey said. "He thinks he's so much better than everyone. On the Final Exam Expedition last fall, he put tacks in a friend of mine's hiking boots so he wouldn't make the top of the peak we were aiming for. And once in our geography seminar, he and I got into an argument about the Grygian War. He said that the U.S. and the Allied Nations deserved the land because we had found it and the Grygians were too stupid to hang onto it. He said the Treason Camps were the Grygians' own fault because they didn't give in when we tried to take their land. I called him a dirty land grabber and he said he was proud of the name!"

"I think I remember Dad telling us about the Final Exam Expedition," Zander said. "That's where you have to plan a whole expedition all by yourself, right?"

"That's right. And then the teachers pick the ten best plans and the kids whose plans don't get picked get assigned to the other expeditions, and we go on them during the spring semester. How you perform on the expedition makes up 50 percent of your grade for the year."

We rode on, stopping for a quick look at the famous blue waterfalls. They were pretty amazing; a bright turquoise color that didn't seem like it could be natural. But the sun was going down and we knew we didn't have much time. We had the lights on our vests and we decided that we'd keep going into the night, to stay ahead of BNDL and the Nackleys.

I'd been tracking the mileage, and Dad's map showed the entrance to Drowned Man's Canyon at eight miles along the floor of Azure Canyon, but when we'd been traveling for only five miles, we saw a narrow opening in the rock and a canyon that seemed to jut off in the right direction.

"That's strange." I checked the map again. "Dad's map says it shouldn't be for another three miles."

Zander kicked his horse and trotted over to the entrance. "But this looks like it, right?"

I fumbled with the map that Bongo had given me. "Yeah, I guess. This map has it at five miles."

"So Dad's must be wrong," Zander said.

"But Dad was never wrong. You guys wait here. I have to make sure that it isn't up ahead."

"But that'll be six miles," Zander protested. "We can't waste that much time. This must be it, right? What else could it be?"

"We have to find out," I told them, "just in case it's the wrong one. Then we'd really be in trouble."

"All right," Zander said, looking exasperated. "I'll go. I'm a faster rider."

"I'll go," I said. But he'd already given his horse the heel of his boot and pulled up next to me, taking my spyglass out of my hands. He was off in a cloud of red dust before I could even put the map away.

"Let him," M.K. said. "He is fast."

"Three miles!" I called after him. "Check in three more miles!"

The three of us waited silently, watching as the sun sank and the walls of the canyon turned the colors of the sunset: red and pink and rippling orange. Zander was back twenty minutes later, racing along the floor of the canyon.

"I was right," he said, giving me an 'I told you so' look that made me want to punch him. "Nothing up there. The canyon just gets narrower and keeps going. This must be it."

"Fine." I pulled my horse around and made my way into Drowned Man's Canyon.

The opening was pretty narrow—just wide enough for the four of us to pass on horseback side by side—and water wouldn't have drained out of it very quickly. I could see how Dan Foley had gotten into trouble. Once it started to rain, it would have been like being stuck in a giant bathtub.

As the horses trudged along the canyon floor, we saw that we'd entered a completely different landscape. For one thing, it was narrower, the walls steeper and made of a darker limestone, pocked with sinister-looking caves and crevices. Maybe it was the darkening skies and the fact that it was getting late in the day, but suddenly I thought about Bongo and his story about the ghost.

"Do you feel like we're being watched?" M.K. asked.

I nodded, looking nervously over my shoulder. Pucci had come to sit on Zander's saddle, as though something was making him nervous, too.

Twenty minutes later, the clouds were darkening, moving fast across the sky. When I felt a couple of drops on my face, I called out to the others, "What should we do?"

"Keep going," Zander said.

It was raining harder and in a few minutes the rain started to fill up the canyon. The horses went more carefully, plodding along in the swirling water.

We kept pressing on along the canyon floor. Pucci had flown ahead a bit and now he circled back, calling out a warning. Sukey found a rain poncho in her pack. But the three of us were getting soaked. "Hey!" M.K. called out suddenly, and we turned around to find her sitting there, completely sheltered by an umbrella that seemed to have sprung out of her back. "Try your vests!" she shouted over the rain. She gestured toward the back waist of the vest and Zander and I both felt around on our own. I pushed the button that appeared under my fingers and, sure enough, I heard a *whoosh* and, two seconds later, was shielded from the rain by a large umbrella. Another two seconds and Zander was sheltered, too.

Sukey looked surprised, and a little jealous. I motioned for her to ride next to me, but she waved her hand to say she didn't care if she got wet.

The horses were soaked now and they started moving nervously in the water, turning their heads and snorting in protest. Pucci, still on Zander's saddle, was wet and bedraggled, his shoulders hunched against the rain.

"We've got to get up higher," Zander called back to us. "It's going to be a flash flood in a minute." He pointed toward a steeply climbing bridle path that wound up the sides of the canyon. "Kit and Sukey, you go first." The walls were almost completely vertical. I kicked my horse hard in the side and Sukey did the same to hers and we led them up the steep slope ahead of Zander and M.K. I was leaning so far back in my saddle that I was afraid I was going to fall, and every time I looked over the edge, I saw the swirling water and the steep slide down to the bottom.

It kept raining as we climbed, and down below us, in the canyon, the stream of water had turned to a river. If we had stayed down in the riverbed, the water would now be up to our chests. It was just as I'd thought: there was nowhere for the water to go and it was rising fast.

I peered through the torrential rain beyond my umbrella. A couple yards ahead, I could see a shelflike cave in the rock. It looked to be seven or eight feet high and I waved wildly at the others, pointing them toward it. Sukey and I pulled in and dismounted and Zander and M.K. did the same. Once we'd figured out how to return the umbrellas to our vests, we squeezed under the overhang and looked out at the veil of water cascading outside our shelter. The horses seemed unfazed now that we'd found higher ground, putting their heads down as the water ran off their backs and waiting for it to end.

Pucci found his way inside and he sat on the ground, squawking at us as if to ask what we were doing in such a terrible place.

"What is this?" M.K. asked, looking around. "Hey, it goes back farther. Look, it's really big!" She felt along the back of the cave and disappeared into the darkness at the back.

"M.K.?" I called out after a couple of minutes. We didn't hear anything and I was starting to worry when she popped her head out. "It's huge," she said. "And look at this." She pointed toward the back, where I noticed, for the first time, the sound of falling water. When I ducked my head, I could see that there was a wide hole carved through the rock. There was a hole underneath that seemed to be draining water away from the cave. When I pointed my vest light at it, I could see chisel marks on the inside.

"It's a chimney!" I told them. "Someone lived here and made that hole in the rock for a chimney."

"What do you mean someone lived here?" Sukey asked, looking nervous all of a sudden. Outside, the rain was pelting the rock and we heard a clap of thunder.

"Long ago, maybe," I told her. "There were lots of cliff dwellings in this part of the Southwest. I remember reading something about the geology. The rock is soft and the caves and tunnels formed easily."

We sat at the mouth of the cave and looked out at the downpour. "When are we going to be able to get going again?" M.K. asked.

"I don't know," I said. "It's bad out there. We're going to have to spend the night here and get going in the morning."

"If the Nackleys are on IronSteeds, the rain won't slow them down." Sukey looked worried.

"Well, we might as well make a fire and have something to eat." Zander stood up and started looking for dry firewood that had been blown into the cave.

Pretty soon there was a nice pile of firewood and some pine branches to use as kindling, and Zander was hunting around in our vests for matches.

"I would think there would be some," he said.

"I've got some," Sukey said, but when she got them out of her pack, she found that they were soaked. I tried to strike one against the box, and then on the wall of the cave, but the match just hissed a bit and didn't light.

"All right," Zander said, picking two sticks—one large and flat and one thin and small—out of the pile of firewood. "We're going to have to do this the hard way." He took out his pocketknife and started whittling away at the smaller one, and in a couple of minutes he had a long, needle-shaped stick. With his knife, he made the other stick into a flat plane, then carved a little hole in it and inserted the smaller stick's point into the hole.

"There's an old saying: Know how to make a fire with two sticks?" he asked us as he started to twirl the needle-shaped stick between his hands.

"How?" Sukey asked.

"It's easy as long as one of them is a match," Zander answered and we all laughed.

He kept twirling the stick quickly between his palms, but nothing happened. M.K. went over and started rummaging around in our vests, taking out all of Dad's brass utility boxes.

"Hang on," Zander said. "I've almost got it." He kept twirling when suddenly there was a *whoosh* and the little pile of wood erupted in flames. Pucci squawked and retreated to the mouth of the cave, and when we looked up, we saw M.K. standing there holding Zander's flamethrower utility.

"Wish Dad had given this to me," she said. Twenty minutes later, a large fire was crackling in the cave. Pucci kept his distance. Zander had noticed he was afraid of fire, and we thought maybe it was from dropping bombs or whatever awful things they'd made him do in the territories.

We buried two cans of beans in the coals to heat them, making a meal of them and some beef jerky we'd found at the little market in Azure City. It wasn't much, but we were so hungry we ate every last bean.

We all sat around the fire drying our clothes, watching the smoke curl upwards through the chimney, looking up at the stars outside the cave. Pucci dozed on a stick away from the fire, making little murmuring coos in his sleep. The sky was an inky blue-black, the stars brighter than I'd ever seen them. The air even smelled different out here, wet and piney from the rainstorm, now filled with the sweet, woody scent of our fire.

"*Clear the square*," Pucci murmured in his sleep. "*Big fire.*"

Sukey raised her eyebrows. "Did he just say 'Clear the square'?"

"Yup," M.K. said. "He says that a lot in his sleep."

"You know that's weird, right?"

"Zander thinks he has flashbacks," I told her. "About things he had to do when he was working in the territories. Dropping bombs and stuff."

"Okay... Where did you get him, anyway?" she asked.

"There was a stray cat that used to hang around our house, to catch mice," M.K. told her, "and one day, Zander looked out the window and saw it playing with something. When he went out, he found Pucci, almost dead. Zander saved him. A couple of weeks later, when he was strong again, he picked up a rock with his legs and dropped it on the cat's head. That cat never came back."

"Have you been by yourselves since your dad died?" Sukey asked us. She hesitated. "You never said anything about your mother. Delilah's friends said they never met her."

Zander and M.K. were silent so I said, "She died when M.K. was a baby."

"I'm sorry." Sukey poked at the fire with a stick. We all stared at the tiny orange-hot sparks that popped and shimmered between the burning logs.

Something about the darkness, the silence, made me say, "Dad never talked about her. He refused to. So we stopped asking. But when we were at Raleigh's, he told us she was called 'Nika' and that she was really smart, that she knew all about the Muller Machines and how they worked. Dad never told us that. Not once."

Sukey hesitated again. "How did she die?"

"SteamCar accident," Zander said.

"What about her family?"

"We never met her parents, if that's what you mean." I stared at the fire. "They died before Zander was born."

"When Dad disappeared, we kept expecting them to make us go to an orphanage or something, but they never did," M.K. said. She reached up to rub her arm and I realized I'd forgotten about her cut.

"They had agents watching us, though," I told Sukey. "I'd see them every once in a while. They must have known about the map. They took all of the maps in the house and when they didn't find it there, they must have figured that the guy with the clockwork hand would try to get it to us. We think that's why they didn't send us to an orphanage. They wanted to use us as bait." I'd been thinking about it some more. "And they must have had someone watching me by the markets. They didn't see me talking to the man with the clockwork hand, but he was spotted."

"So this map is pretty important," Sukey said, "if they'd go to all that trouble."

"I guess it must be."

"M.K.," Zander said, "how does your arm feel?" She'd been rubbing it the whole time I'd been talking. "Let me see it."

She leaned down toward the fire and pulled her sleeve up so we could see the gash. I felt a little wave of fear wash over me. It looked swollen and angry red, the edges of the cut pulling away.

"That's nasty," Sukey said. She refused the juper berry cream I took out of my vest, getting a real first-aid kit out of her backpack

and dressing M.K.'s wound. "Here, this should take care of the infection, M.K. But you have to tell us if it starts hurting again." M.K., already looking happier, agreed, and Sukey put the juper berry cream and the first-aid kit back in her pack.

I got out the map and laid it out carefully by the fire so I could study the route and check it once again for any sign of where the old mine might be. We would be hiking farther into the canyon tomorrow and we still had no idea where to look. With the Nackleys behind us, we didn't have much time.

As I studied Dad's map, I was bothered again by the fact that the entrance to Drowned Man's Canyon hadn't been where it was supposed to be. According to Dad's scale, it should have been eight miles along the floor of Azure Canyon. But we had entered it at five miles. What had happened to those additional three miles? Time and rivers could make canyons wider and longer, but nothing could have altered where the canyon *started*.

"What are you doing?" M.K. asked, coming to sit beside me.

"I don't know. There's something funny about this map." I showed her how I'd compared it with the tourist map that Bongo had given us and my own calculations as we'd ridden through the canyon, and found that Dad's map was wrong.

"But he was never wrong," I muttered, as much to myself as to M.K. I fooled around with the two halves of the map, making sure I'd matched them up precisely. They fit perfectly when I placed the two halves together so that they didn't overlap at all, but I started experimenting, overlapping the edges and trying to match up the contour lines representing the depth of Drowned Man's Canyon on one side with the lines on the other side.

Dad's map represented Drowned Man's Canyon as a series of closely spaced squiggling contour lines, each one representing points connected at the same elevation.

Contour lines were only invented in the sixteen hundreds, when a French mapmaker came up with them as a way of representing the actual features of a landscape, the mountains and valleys and lakes and rivers. Until then, maps had been able to represent places in only one dimension. You could draw a blue circle for a lake, but you couldn't see how deep the lake was or how steeply the edges of it dropped off toward the middle. You could draw mountains and hills, but on paper Mount Everest would appear to be the same height as a little foothill. But once topographical maps—that is, maps that represented the rising and falling of the landscape—came along, you could read a map on paper or on a Muller Machine and get a feel for the landscape, for whether it was flat or hilly or wet or dry. It was funny, sitting in the cave high in the walls of Drowned Man's Canyon, looking at a map representing those walls.

I shifted the sides of the map.

"Wait a second," I said. Zander and Sukey looked up from their conversation.

"What?" M.K. watched as I fiddled with the edges of the two halves, overlapping them and then making a few calculations. Instead of matching up at the edges, the right side of the map—the side we'd found in Dad's desk—was now laid over the other half—the half we'd found in the Map Room—covering about three inches of the left side. The contour lines still matched, but the strange lines that I had assumed were mesas and hills to the north of Drowned Man's had now come together.

"The map wasn't wrong," I said. "I was."

"What do you mean? And what's that?" M.K. pointed to the squiggly contour lines. Zander and Sukey had come over and were looking at the map over my shoulder.

"We haven't been thinking about why there are two maps or, I mean, two halves," I told them, so excited by my discovery that I was talking too fast. "Dad wanted us to find the map, right? He wanted us to find both halves of it. But why split it in half? Look." I placed the maps next to each other. "Here's Dad's map of Drowned Man's Canyon and here's the one Bongo gave us."

I went on. "Remember when I said that we reached the turnoff to Drowned Man's Canyon too soon? Well, we did, according to Dad's map, anyway. Because Dad's map is wrong."

"But you said Dad was never wrong," M.K. said suspiciously.

"Well, he wasn't. Or at least, he was wrong on purpose. Because the two halves of the map aren't meant to be matched up perfectly. It's meant to go like this."

I pointed to the two halves, now overlapping by three inches rather than matching up exactly. I waited, for dramatic effect. "It goes like this instead."

Now we were all looking at the same canyons we'd seen before, but Azure Canyon was a bit shorter than it had been and branching off from Drowned Man's Canyon was another canyon. I was too excited to stop and calculate the depth but I assumed it was about the same as Azure and Drowned Man's.

"When you do it like this," I told them, so excited now I could barely contain myself, "there's another canyon there. See?" I pointed to the spot where it broke off. "There *is* a secret canyon. He found it and included it in his map. He split the map in two so that we could put it together only if we actually came here! He knew that I would map it as we came through the canyon. He knew that I would notice that it wasn't right. It must be where the treasure is. And we're the only ones with this map. We're the only ones who know there's a secret canyon and the only ones who know how to get there."

Twenty-five

I didn't sleep well that night. The rock floor of the cave was hard and M.K. was a terrible snorer. Once our fire died down, the temperature dropped and I was cold even in the reflective sleeping bag Dad had tucked into my vest, folded into a bag the size of a pack of cards. I must have drifted off to sleep a few times because I had terrible dreams, about giant rattlesnakes and ghosts and monsters and, finally, one in which Dad was rowing away from me in a boat and I was trying to throw a rope to him, but the rope kept falling in the water and disappearing beneath the dark surface.

When I woke up from that one, the sky was just getting light and I decided to get up and explore a little bit. I figured I could go ahead on foot and find the entrance to the secret canyon so that we'd be ready to go once the others were up.

I put some wood on the fire before leaving. Pucci was perched on a rock near the mouth of the cave, making his funny little clucking noises. I gave him a little scratch on the top of his head and he chortled before falling back to sleep.

I tucked Dad's map back into the hidden pocket of my vest and started out, scrambling down to the almost-dry canyon floor. Suddenly the sun cleared the rock walls and the canyon was full of pink morning light. It was still cold, the air smelling of our campfire, and I felt incredibly awake and alive as I hiked along. I imagined the look on Sukey's face when I came back to the cave. "Thought I'd just see what's up ahead," I'd tell them. "Oh, I found the secret canyon, by the way."

According to Dad's map, the entrance was another three miles along the floor of Drowned Man's Canyon from our cave. I set off, walking briskly through the morning.

It took me almost an hour on foot and I found myself wishing I'd brought my horse. As I went, I measured the distance with my spyglass's pedometer, and as I approached the place where it was supposed to be, I heard the crash of falling water and felt a mist in the air. I came around a bend in the canyon, and right where the entrance to the secret canyon was supposed to be, there was a giant waterfall.

There was a little stand of cottonwood trees and, above, a vertical cascade of water to the canyon floor. It was easily as high as the waterfalls in Azure Canyon, but where those had been magical, this waterfall was a little spooky, the water falling from the top into the pool below, which was black as night. I knew it probably wasn't that deep, but when I peered over the edge, it looked as though it reached down into the center of the earth. According to Dad's map, the secret canyon was right here, but when I looked up, all I could see was solid rock and the river spilling over the edge of the canyon wall, where it had worn away the earth for thousands of years.

I walked around the side of the waterfall, looking for breaks in the rock, but the limestone was completely solid, without any of the caves and crevices we'd seen at the other end.

The only part of it I couldn't see was the area behind the waterfall itself. But in order to examine the back of the pool, I'd have to get into the water. I bent over and cupped my hands, filling them with water and gulping it down. It was freezing cold.

I was trying to figure out what to do when I caught movement out of the corner of my eye and ducked behind one of the cottonwood trees. Slowly, I got the spyglass out of my vest and lifted it to my eye. I turned the eyepiece, zooming in. Across the canyon, riding back in the direction from which I'd come, was a lone figure on horseback.

He looked like an old-time miner or cowboy, in cowboy boots and a wide hat and beard. I increased the magnification and saw that he wasn't as old as I'd thought at first. His face was set in a grim scowl, his eyes searching the canyon as he rode. The spyglass gave me a perfect view and I played around with it, turning it this way and that to see if I could get better magnification. I hadn't noticed a small button on the side, but I must have pressed it by mistake because there was a little buzz from the spyglass and all of a sudden I could hear the sound of a horse's hooves. It took me a minute to realize that the sound was coming from the mysterious rider's horse and that Dad must have invented some sort of sound-amplification system for the spyglass.

I tried to figure out what to do. I had to go and tell the others. This man, whoever he was, might be with the Nackleys or he might be a BNDL agent. We would need to come back with ropes and look for the entrance to the secret canyon before anyone saw us. I watched him through my spyglass, not sure how to get back to the cave without him seeing me. And then, as I watched him through the glass, he disappeared into the wall of the canyon.

One minute he was right there, riding along in the morning sun. And the next he was gone. I put down the spyglass and searched the canyon with my naked eye, but he wasn't there.

He couldn't have just disappeared, of course, I told myself. He must have ridden out of my view and around a bend. Or it may have been the low light in the canyon. Perhaps he'd just blended into the wall. Or there was a cave there like the one we'd camped in.

Or maybe I hadn't seen him at all.

Either way, I wanted to get back to the others as soon as possible. The Nackleys might already be on their way and our only hope was to get to the secret canyon before they did.

I jogged all the way back, much more quickly this time, and I had almost reached the cave when I heard, off in the distance, a sort of low metallic rumbling. It was so faint that I wasn't sure for a minute I'd heard it at all, but as I ran it got louder and louder, resolving itself into a distinctive clanking: IronSteeds.

I felt my stomach sink. They were already here.

High above us, I heard Pucci's warning call, "*Careful, careful, careful,*" and looked up to see Zander, Sukey, and M.K. in front of me.

Approaching along the floor of the canyon, clanking loudly, was a small army of IronSteeds, twenty of them, the machines we'd seen at Bongo's. In the morning light, their metal armor gleamed.

I thought about running, but we were no match for those robot horses and all the people they had with them besides, so I just stood there, terrified, aware of Pucci still circling high above us in the air. At least they couldn't get him.

The IronSteeds clanked and then stopped.

"Hello there," Leo Nackley said as he dismounted. He had a pistol holstered at his belt and he took it out, holding it loosely in his right hand, reminding us it was there. "Mr. Foley will be glad to hear that we've found you. There are a lot of people looking for you."

There was a flash of red behind him and Mr. Mountmorris's secretary, Jec Banton, got down from his IronSteed. His Mohawk looked even sharper than it had yesterday and he was wearing red leather boots with little lights embedded along the laces. "That was fast," he said, raising an eyebrow at us.

Leo Nackley must have noticed Sukey because he smiled at her and said, "Does your mother know where you are? I should have known you'd join up with these young criminals."

"They're my friends," Sukey told him, her hands clenched in fists at her side. "What are you going to do about it, you dirty land grabber?"

Twenty-six

Leo Nackley stared for a minute, the pistol twitching a little in his hand, and then he waved and the people behind him dismounted together and sprang into action, unloading bags and boxes from the backs of the giant machines.

Lazlo Nackley was wearing his shiny Explorer's gear, the jacket gleaming black over his snowy white shirt. On his head was a broad-brimmed black hat with wicked-looking knife points on the brim. It had gotten hot now that the sun was up and there were little drops of oily sweat running down his cheeks. "How did you get hooked up with these kids, Sukey? Did you know they almost killed two BNDL agents? Not that you'd care."

He walked toward us, his black boots stamping out a rhythm on the floor of the canyon. He looked from me to Zander and then back at me again. "Well, where is it? Where's the treasure map?"

"I don't know what you mean," I said, stepping back. I looked over at M.K., who was glaring at Lazlo, her chin jutting out and her fists curled at her sides like Sukey's. Pucci had disappeared into the sky.

"Yes, you do." Lazlo leaned forward and lifted one side of my vest and then the other, looking for inside pockets. I could feel the map, hidden away in its secret compartment, burning against the small of my back.

"That's enough, Lazlo," Leo Nackley said coldly, brushing some imaginary dust off his own black jacket. Lazlo's face fell. He took a few seconds to look us over with his cold blue eyes. "You're in a lot of trouble."

The men and women unloaded shovels and picks, steam-hydraulic digging machines, and other contraptions I'd never seen before. We watched as they unpacked and began unrolling what looked like a series of elaborate Gryluminum tents.

"I don't know why," Zander said in a calm voice. "We're just down here to enjoy some camping and hiking in the canyon. Same as you."

"Not exactly," Jec Banton said. "This expedition is sponsored by BNDL. The location of the possible treasure has been kept a secret from the general public, and BNDL agents are deputized to do whatever they need to do to keep it that way. Besides which, there's a directive for your detention. You assaulted government agents."

"And I would do it again," M.K. said, stamping her foot.

The workers rolled out Gryluminum tents, and as I watched, they pulled on the tops and the tents popped up, creating a little compound of waterproof shelters in only a couple of minutes. I'd heard about these tents from Dad, who always liked to build his own shelter when he was in the field.

"What treasure?" Zander asked. I recognized the tone of his voice as the one he used when he was trying to keep me from finding out about something he was up to.

Leo Nackley smiled, a slow smile that rippled across his lips, just barely shifting his mustache. "Is that how you're going to play this?"

Zander didn't say anything.

The men and women who had ridden in on the IronSteeds were milling around and Leo Nackley turned and nodded at a tall, bearded guy mounted on the only real live horse of the bunch. "Tex," he said, "take these children to a tent as soon as one's ready."

"Yes, sir." The guy looked like an old cowboy in his leather boots and wide-brimmed hat. It was hard to see his face beneath his bushy gray beard, but his eyes stared out from his sunburned face, hard and mean.

He was the lone rider I'd seen in the canyon. I hadn't imagined him, after all. He was as real as Zander. It had been the morning light shining in my eyes that had made it seem like he'd vanished.

"What are you doing?" Sukey demanded, as they started pushing us toward a tent. Tex had ahold of my arm and I could feel the strength of his fingers on my elbow. He smelled of sweat and woodsmoke. "Where are you taking us?"

In answer, they pushed us roughly through the flap that served as the tent's door. A couple of agents followed with chairs, and before we knew it, they had seated us with our backs to each other, our hands and feet tied to the chairs, and the chairs tied together so that we couldn't turn them around. My wrists throbbed.

"Don't try to get away," Jec Banton said as they left the tent. "You'll just cut yourself."

We all sat there for a minute in silence. "This is insane," Sukey said finally, struggling against the ropes. "What do they think they're doing?"

"I don't know," Zander whispered. "But we've got to get out of here. Did you see all that equipment out there? They're going to get to the treasure ahead of us." He was sitting next to me, and out of the corner of my right eye, I could see him trying to turn his head to look at me. "Please tell me you don't have the map with you."

I was silent.

"Great. It's all over. Why did you bring it?"

"I was looking for the secret canyon," I hissed back at him. "Why did *you* come after me? If you hadn't, you all could be rescuing me right now."

"Stop it, you two," Sukey said. "We've got to figure something out. M.K., can you get to your knife?"

"No," M.K. said. "Not tied up like this. But I'm trying to rub the rope against the back of this chair. There's a little piece of metal and I think I can do it." We listened for a moment to the sound of her struggling.

"They're keeping us prisoners!" Sukey said. I could hear voices outside the tent.

"Shh," I told her. "They're coming back."

But she didn't lower her voice. "When my mother hears about this, she's going to be furious."

"Your mother," Leo Nackley said, coming into the tent, Lazlo, Jec Banton, and Tex trailing behind him, "depends on BNDL for permission to fly to all of the exotic places she likes to fly to. I don't think she'll make too much of a fuss. And don't be so dramatic. Until Mr. Foley gets here, we're just going to ask you a few questions and keep you from trampling all over the site of what may be a very important find for the United States and the Allied Nations."

He stood right in front of Zander. "All right. Where's the map? If you hand it over in aid of the expedition, I think you may have an easier time once Mr. Foley gets here."

Zander hesitated. Then he said, "I don't know what you're talking about."

Leo Nackley pointed his pistol at us. "Damn it! Where's the map? Who has it?"

None of us said anything, but I must have flushed because Lazlo Nackley called out, "He looks guilty, Papa. The skinny one with the glasses. He knows something."

Banton came over and put a finger under my chin, forcing me to look up at him. His skin was very cold. "Kit? That's your name, isn't it? Where's the map, Kit? Where's the map you showed to Mr. Mountmorris?"

As long as we were talking, they couldn't look for the map, so I decided I had to keep them talking.

"Oh, there wasn't anything on that map," I said, much too fast, my words tumbling over each other nervously. "Nothing more than what you'd find on a tourist map or something. We thought if we came out here, maybe we could just find it, you know. But, wow, it turns out it's a really big canyon and there's nothing out here but rocks and more rocks, so we were just about to go home when you—"

"Where is the map?" Leo Nackley interrupted. "We know that *criminal* friend of your father's gave it to you at the market. This is the last time I'm going to ask." Tex stood behind him, looking menacing.

I couldn't think of anything to do but just keep talking. "Nobody gave me anything," I said. I met his cold, pale blue eyes and actually felt a chill go through my body. "We know you were friends with Dad and we know that you came here a long time ago looking for the treasure. But we don't know anything more than that."

Something flashed across Leo Nackley's face and then he scowled. "There's no secret about that. We were good friends once."

"What happened?" I asked him, desperate now. "Why did you get him kicked out of the Expedition Society?"

Nackley looked genuinely surprised. "Me? He got himself kicked out. I had nothing to do with it."

"But why was he kicked out?"

"I'll tell you why." Francis Foley came into the tent, looking dusty and mad. "Your father had been lying to us. Last year, he was sent on an expedition to Munopia, to look for a new source of water for the cattle farms. We know that he found one, but he said he didn't.

207

He turned in incorrect maps to hide his discovery. That's a violation of the BNDL statutes."

Jec Banton raised his eyebrows. "He didn't tell you any of this?"

"No," I said. "None of it."

"Well," Foley said, "he was probably embarrassed. He got caught taking money from a local group of criminals to keep the knowledge of the water source secret. He had lots of unsavory… associations. The truth is that he cared more about money than he did about being an Explorer."

"That's not true," M.K. said.

"It is," Foley said. "Now, where is that map? I know you have it. And if you won't give it up, we'll have to find it ourselves." He nodded to the Nackleys and Tex. "Let's search him."

I was desperate. "You can't do that," I protested. "I'm a U.S. citizen."

They stepped forward and Banton said, "Under the provisions of the Act Creating the Bureau of Newly Discovered Lands, section 9, paragraph 2, civilians possessing knowledge of the location of undiscovered lands or natural or cultural resources are hereby required to share said information with the government under penalty of imprisonment."

"But I don't know where the treasure is," I protested. "How can I tell you if I don't know where it is?"

"He really doesn't know," Sukey said. "And the BNDL provisions apply only to people actively inhibiting the exploration of—"

"Enough of this. Stand up," Leo Nackley interrupted her. I felt my heart sink as he and Tex untied me from the chair and pulled me to standing. I could still feel the bite of the ropes on my wrists. They untied my hands and Tex tore my vest off and handed it to Banton, who started going through the pockets. I felt my heart sink as utility boxes clattered out onto the floor.

I had run out of options, so I started shouting and flailing around. "This is against the law!" I yelled at them. "You can't treat me this way. That's unlawful search and seizure." Leo Nackley pushed me back into the chair and Tex tied my hands and feet again.

"Here it is," Banton said, with a little gleam of excitement on his face. He was holding up the plastic bag in which I'd put the two halves. "Hidden pocket. The whole map's here. They must have found the other half." He replaced all of my utilities in the vest and tucked it under his arm. My heart sank. Everything was there, everything but the spyglass, which I'd shoved into my pants pocket after listening to Tex near the waterfall.

"Thank you," Francis Foley said.

Leo Nackley turned to me. "You *are* a little liar, then. Your father was a failure. He had the whole map and he couldn't even find the treasure." He held the two halves of the map up to the light, and then he and Tex turned to go. "Alex must be turning in his grave. Lazlo, stay here and make sure they don't go anywhere while we look at the map. We'll see what he was up to."

He looked up at Foley and put his hand to his forehead. "Hail President Hildreth!"

Twenty-seven

They left with the map and my vest, leaving us alone in the tent with Lazlo.

"Your father's a coward and a criminal, Lazlo Nackley," Sukey spat at him. "He's going to hear from my mother's lawyers when we get out of here."

Lazlo studied her for a minute and then he pulled a chair up in front of me and straddled it so he was facing me, his eyes only six or seven inches from my glasses. I could see every detail of his face: the freckles that spread out over his nose and a big, red, angry-looking pimple just under his chin.

"Did you really think they wouldn't find the map?" he asked after a minute. "Did you really think you could hide it in your vest?"

I didn't say anything and my silence seemed to make him mad.

"We're going to find the treasure," he said. "We're going to find it and the reporters are going to call it 'the Lazlo Nackley Treasure.' I'll be famous. They'll name the new Mountaineering Club clubhouse after me. Neville here knows what that is since she goes to the Academy."

We ignored him. I tested the strength of the rope that was holding my hands and feet to see if it was looser now. I could hear Zander and Sukey and M.K. trying to pull out of their constraints, too.

Lazlo watched us. "What, you think you're going to escape and go find the treasure yourself? BNDL would never allow that. They think this treasure is one of the most important ones in the New Lands. Do you know how much it's worth?"

"You think they'll let you have any of the money, Lazlo?" Sukey asked him. "Think again."

"They want my father and me to find it and we're going to. And they don't care what happens to you."

"We're just kids," I told him. "What are they going to do to us?"

He laughed. "They don't care how old you are. All they care about is making sure the treasure doesn't fall into the wrong hands. You don't know what they can do."

"So they're going to keep us locked up until you and your father find the treasure?"

"Pretty much."

"Well, we don't know anything," Zander told him. "That's the truth. They found the map, so they can let us go."

"They won't do that," Lazlo said. "You don't know these—" Suddenly, there was a *whoosh* and the beating of wings and a black form sailed in the open door.

"Pucci!" said M.K. He had gotten the leather booties off and his metal talons gleamed. He gave a low squawk. I heard something hit the ground and then the parrot went for Lazlo's face, beating his wings, threatening him with the metal talons.

"Aaaaaaaaaa!" Lazlo hollered. "Get it off me!" He was waving his arms around wildly, which was just making Pucci beat his wings harder.

"Be quiet, Lazlo," Zander said in a low voice. "Or I'll let him use his feet on you. You know what they did to the faces of protesters in Fazia, don't you?"

Terrified, Lazlo stopped yelling.

"He brought my pistol," Sukey whispered. "But I can't get my hands free. Unless Wonderbird here has opposable thumbs, we're still tied up."

"Actually," M.K. said, standing up and shaking her hands free of the rope, the edges frayed where she'd been rubbing it against the chair, "*you're* still tied up. But not for long."

Twenty-eight

MK. picked up the pistol and trained it on Lazlo with one hand while she untied Zander with the other. Zander untied me and we called Pucci off, stuffing a length of rope in Lazlo's mouth so he couldn't call for help. Then we tied his hands and ankles.

"Let's get out of here before Foley and his goons show up," Zander said.

"But what about the map?"

Zander swore. "You're right. But where did they take it?"

"It must be in one of the other tents." I looked down at Lazlo, who was still watching Pucci with a scared expression. I lowered my voice again. "We can't leave Dad's map behind. We're going to have to listen to them talking and figure out where it is."

"Too dangerous," Zander said. "We'd have to be right up next to the tents. We'll be caught."

"Not with this." I took my spyglass out of my pocket and showed them the listening feature I'd discovered. "I think I can figure out where he is without getting too close. Then someone can go get it. We'll have to get them out of the tent somehow, though. Let's go."

M.K. pinched Lazlo's nose as we left the tent. We made our way along the outside of the group of tents and found a place to stand where we could see most of them but were shielded from view. I lifted the spyglass and pointed at each tent, listening for Leo Nackley's voice. It was daylight now, but from the small number of IronSteeds left in the camp, it seemed that most of Nackley's party had gone out scouting in the canyon. Somewhere, someone was frying bacon and eggs, and the smell that wafted over the camp made me so hungry I was ready to go in search of breakfast instead of the treasure. When I aimed the spyglass at a tent at the far end of the camp, I could hear the bacon sizzling in the pan.

"Now that's just torture," Sukey muttered.

From one tent we heard the sound of Tex's voice giving instructions for digging and from another came the sound of music, coming over some sort of scratchy, old-fashioned radio. Just when I'd given up on finding them in the warren of tents, we heard Foley's voice saying, "...isn't clear. But it must be there. Damn it! This map doesn't show anything. Maybe it's a decoy. Maybe there's another one somewhere."

Sukey and I grinned at each other. They hadn't figured out the secret to the map.

"Damn him!" Leo Nackley said. "He knew where it was. He must have! But when did he make the map?"

Foley's voice came through the spyglass's tiny speaker. "Our intelligence sources reported that Alexander West must have completed the map not long after his second trip to the canyon. It's possible that he discovered something. We would have known if he'd brought the treasure out of the canyon, however. And he certainly didn't."

Zander and I glanced at each other. "Intelligence sources"? Dad had been right that the government was watching him.

"Do you think the children know anything?" Foley asked.

"I don't know. There's something about the middle boy. Mr. Mountmorris said he seems to be something of an expert on cartography. It's possible he's figured it out. We'll have to interrogate them all to be sure, of course. We can use extreme measures."

I gulped. I didn't like the sound of "extreme measures," whatever it meant.

The voices were coming from a smaller canvas tent on the far side of the camp and we watched it as we listened. There was some more back-and-forth about the map and then we heard a woman's voice say, "Mr. Foley, he's here."

"Oh good, thank you."

Through the spyglass, I saw them leaving the tent—and leaving the map and vest unguarded.

"I'll go. I'm smallest," M.K. whispered. She darted away, stalking around the outside of the camp like a cat, keeping out of sight.

"Where do you think they're going?" Sukey whispered. "Can you see?"

The four of us peeked around the tent again. I didn't need the spyglass to see the giant silver airship with its BNDL logo on the side, Mr. Mountmorris's face pressed against the glass at the front of the gondola as it slowly descended into the canyon.

Twenty-nine

The airship was called the *Grygia* and I remembered reading about it when it was built. It had cost millions and millions of Allied Dollars and BNDL had held a huge celebration, saying that it would allow Explorers to go into even more remote areas of the New Lands to look for resources. There had been protests, but ANDLC had handed out food rations to the protesters and they hadn't lasted very long. I'd always been curious about the *Grygia*. According to BNDL, it was the biggest airship in the world.

The giant, egg-shaped gas envelope was painted a glittering silver color that made it look like a huge cloud. The BNDL logo was painted in black on the side of the silver gondola, and below it, in fancy script, was the airship's name. The gondola, where the passengers rode in luxury, was huge, and I remembered what I'd read about it being able to carry forty or more passengers for extended trips around the world.

The airship settled down into the canyon and the door to the gondola opened. Agents Wolff and DeRosa got out first, followed by Mr. Mountmorris. Agent Wolff was wearing her military uniform and her hair had been styled in an elaborate arrangement of silver knots and whirls on top of her head. Mr. Mountmorris was wearing a bright green suit made of some kind of shiny material that didn't look like it breathed very well. He looked hot and miserable. Through my spyglass, I could see the huge red welt where Agent DeRosa's head had hit the wooden floor in the dining room.

The three of us shrank back against the tent, out of sight, just as M.K. came up behind us. "Got it," she said, handing me my vest, which was reassuringly heavy. "Everything's there. The maps, too. They left them right on the table." Her eyes widened when she saw the airship and who had been riding in it. "Let's get out of here."

I heard the door of the gondola open again through my spyglass. "Well?" Mr. Mountmorris called to Nackley. "Where are the children?"

"Oh, they're tied up," Nackley said. "We'll have to decide what to do about…"

I didn't need to hear any more. "Let's go," I whispered.

The four of us started running. We didn't look back.

"We don't have long," Zander called back once we were out of sight of the camp. "They'll be after us on the IronSteeds as soon as they realize we're gone. We've got to go straight to this secret canyon."

"Um… about the secret canyon," I started to say.

"What about my pack?" Sukey yelled. "It's back in the cave."

Zander waved her away. "There isn't time. Don't worry, we have everything we need in our Explorer's vests."

We ran as fast as we could and were at the waterfall in forty-five minutes, completely out of breath and drenched in sweat. I couldn't believe they hadn't noticed we were gone and come after us, and I knew we didn't have much time.

"*Waterfall!*" Pucci squawked, alighting on my shoulder. We stood there for a moment looking up at the veil of black water.

"This is where it shows the canyon on the map." I was winded and I struggled to form the words. "If it's there, it's at the back of the waterfall. It's the only place I couldn't see."

"There's something scary about that waterfall," Sukey said.

"You're sure it's not over the top or something?" Zander asked. But we could all see that there was no secret canyon next to or on top of the huge waterfall.

"Hey," M.K. said, "do you remember how Dad used to say that if you couldn't find a way over or around, you had to go through?"

"That was how he discovered the Baltese Pass," I said. "The way through was disguised by some kind of creeping moss."

"Baltese creeping reindeer moss," Zander said. "It covered the entrance to the pass, but when he hacked it away with a machete…"

We all looked at each other.

"Good thing the vests are waterproof," Zander said. "You all stay right here." He dipped a foot in, shivered when he felt how cold it was, and then jumped in. Pucci followed. We watched them take off through the pool and disappear behind the veil of black water.

"Is he afraid of anything?" Sukey asked, admiration in her voice.

I was irritated. I'd figured out the secret to the map, but if Zander found the hidden canyon, he would get all the credit, since he'd been brave enough to leap into a waterfall.

"Where is he?" I searched the water for Zander's blond head. "He should be more careful. If he gets into trouble, we'll have to go save him."

We waited a few minutes before Sukey called his name, trying not to be too loud. When there was no answer, M.K. and I started in, too.

There was something eerie about the silence that followed, and finally, after another five minutes, I said, "We've got to go after him. They'll be here in a minute."

We waded in, calling Zander's name. The vests were waterproof and protected everything inside from the water, but our clothes were soaked within seconds and they became as heavy as if we were trying to swim in suits of armor.

The current was strong; we had to fight to stay on our feet, and as I tried to walk toward the back of the pool, behind the violent splash of water from the falls, I could feel the water swirling around me, trying to pull me under. If Zander had gone below the surface in order to see if there was an underwater entrance to the canyon, he could easily have been pulled into the center of the pool. I ducked my head under, holding my glasses with one hand and opening my eyes against the blackness of the water. I couldn't see a thing.

"Where is he?" I called to Sukey and M.K. "I can't see anything under there." I was starting to panic now, imagining Zander drowned.

Pucci was circling over the water. Suddenly he disappeared, too, a dark silhouette above us one minute and gone the next.

"Do you think he's in trouble?" M.K. called.

"I don't know." I kept scanning the water. "I can't find him. He isn't here."

"He's a good swimmer," M.K. said hopefully. "He once swam two miles from a capsized canoe."

I dipped my head under again. It was so cold that my eyes ached and so dark that I couldn't see anything.

And then we heard a faint voice—Zander's—calling over the clamor of the waterfall.

"That's him!" I paddled frantically, trying to follow the direction of the voice, but the waterfall swallowed any other sound and we still couldn't see him.

"Zander," we called. "Where are you?"

"Over here!" His voice was coming from behind the waterfall.

We waded through the water, feeling the spray of the waterfall on our faces. We waded around behind the veil of water, where the rock rose steeply out of the pool, covered with a pale green moss.

"Up here," called Zander's voice, and we had to tilt our heads all the way back to see him, up above us, perched in a small cave in the rock behind the waterfall. Pucci was sitting on his shoulder, and when he saw us, he squawked loudly.

"I found it!" Zander yelled down to us as we stared up at him in disbelief. "There's a tunnel back here. Just where it shows on the map. It must lead into the secret canyon!"

Thirty

"It took me a minute to see it," Zander said once we'd all scrambled up into the damp little cave. "At first I thought the back wall was solid. See? It's so dark that you can't see what's in that corner." We looked where he was gesturing and saw that he was right. One corner of the cave was nothing but blackness, far enough back that not even the tiny bit of sunlight filtering through the waterfall reached its depths. Pucci, who seemed nervous, hopped along the floor of the cave, looking for light.

"But when I crawled back there, I couldn't find the wall, so I started feeling around and... look." All of a sudden, Zander was gone.

I pushed the button on my vest that turned on the solar light. M.K. did the same. The lights illuminated a huge tunnel ahead of us, stretching away deep into the rock and rising high above our heads.

Zander was standing there, grinning at us, his arms spread out to show us the tunnel.

"Could this be it, Kit?" Sukey asked. "I thought it was going to be a canyon."

"I did, too," I said. I started to take the map out to look at it, but before I could, we heard, through the rushing of the water, a cacophony of clanking and shouting and we all ducked back into the little cave, peeking out into the blinding sunshine to see a phalanx of IronSteeds approaching the falls. The big metal horses stopped and Leo Nackley, after a bit of waving and gesturing, used a pair of binoculars to survey the falls. We quickly ducked back into the darkness.

"They're here. What are we going to do?" Sukey asked. For the first time since I'd met her, she actually seemed scared and I realized that all of Lazlo's talk about BNDL must have gotten to her.

I wanted to make her feel better, so I said, "Remember that they didn't see the map that we saw. As far as they know, there's absolutely nothing special about the waterfall. They're just looking for us."

"You're right. So what do we do?" She sounded relieved.

"We get as far away from them as we can and we find the secret canyon," Zander said. "Come on."

Zander, M.K., and I switched our lights on again, and the four of us, Pucci riding on Zander's shoulder, stepped into the tunnel. It was completely dark—the lights illuminated only small splashes of rock in front of our feet—and we walked for ten minutes or so before

Sukey said, "I don't see any canyon. This just looks like some kind of cavern."

I got the map out of the inside pocket of my vest and looked at it again. "I assumed it was a canyon," I said, embarrassed, "and Raleigh said Dad was looking for one. . . But I guess it could be an underground tunnel, or a series of underground caverns. There are a lot of those in this area. Geologically, it's a fascinating—"

"You guess?" Sukey cut me off. "I thought you were good at reading maps."

"He *is* good at reading maps," M.K. said.

"Well, see these contour lines here?" I pointed my light at the map and showed her the thin lines marking the depth of the tunnel. "The map doesn't show whether or not there's a ceiling. In a sense, this *is* a canyon, an underground one that formed in the center of the rock."

Sukey looked skeptical. "The legend doesn't say anything about the treasure being in a tunnel, does it?" she asked.

"Come on," Zander said. "It's on Dad's map. Whatever it is, let's see where it goes."

We started walking, Sukey in the middle since she didn't have a light, Pucci hopping along anxiously, inspecting the walls.

"Did someone make this?" M.K. asked from somewhere behind me. Her voice echoed strangely in the tunnel, bouncing off the walls and along the passageway.

"I don't think so. I'd have to feel the walls, but they look smooth. It must have been formed naturally, probably by acidic water that dissolved the limestone or by an underground river."

I stopped and touched the stone wall, snatching my hand back when I felt something wet move under my fingers.

Sukey must have felt it, too, because she gasped. "There's something there," she said. "Something on the wall. I just felt it move." Standing still now, we became aware of strange noises coming from the walls of the tunnel, faint sucking, whispering sounds that echoed back and forth across the passage.

Zander swung around and shone his light on the curved wall. At first it just looked like some kind of luminescent stone, the surface a glowing green color. But when I looked closer, I saw that the entire surface of the stone was moving. "They're slugs," he whispered. "But..." We all crowded around to look, and sure enough, I could see that the wall was covered with giant green slugs moving slowly across the rock and making the weird sounds we'd heard. Zander took a knife out of his pack and knocked one off the wall and onto the ground. It was the size of a small banana, its moist green skin almost translucent. When Zander pointed his vest light at the slug, it twitched, shrinking as though the light bothered it.

"Yuck," Sukey said.

But Zander wasn't disgusted at all. "This is incredible! I think we've discovered a new species. I've heard of giant slugs in the Amazon and Fazia and Australia, but I didn't know they could be found in the American Southwest. I think they must be photosensitive. They must live all their life cycle in this cavern. This is amazing! I need to take a specimen." He rooted through his vest and found a small bag, but there was no way the giant slug was going to fit

in it. He stared at it for a moment without saying anything, then put the bag away.

"What do they eat?" I asked.

"That's an excellent question." He knocked another off onto the floor and inspected the wall where it had been. "Moss," he finally announced triumphantly. "There's some kind of luminescent moss growing there."

"Does he always get this excited about slugs?" Sukey asked.

"He wants to be an explorer-naturalist," I told her. "He wants to discover a new species."

"I just did," Zander said. "The Zander West slug."

Pucci went over and pecked halfheartedly at the slimy length of it.

"Too big for you, Pucci, huh?" M.K. patted his head. "Zander, what kind of animal could eat these slugs?"

"I don't know." In the light from my vest, Zander suddenly looked nervous. "Let's keep going."

Thirty-one

Now that we knew what was making the sucking sounds, it was even creepier walking through the tunnel, and I kept looking over my shoulder as we went, catching sight of the pale greenness of the slugs in the light from M.K.'s vest.

"Sukey, did you ever take any classes on isolated species?" Zander asked her.

"No," Sukey said, "but maybe someday I'll be studying the Zander West slug."

I stopped walking so I could check the map again. "The tunnel takes a turn up there," I told them. "Maybe there's something up there."

But it was just darkness ahead.

Maybe that was what gave me the nerve to say it. "Do you think he was telling the truth? All that stuff about Dad taking money?"

"No way," Zander said. "Dad never would have done that."

I wasn't so sure. "He did seem to be worried all the time back then. Don't you remember?"

"Zander's right," M.K. said. "Dad never would have done anything like that. They're making it up."

Sukey was silent. Finally she said, "Sometimes people do things that seem, well… wrong. On the surface. But there's a reason for it. There's a… well, a tradeoff. Maybe he thought there was a good reason for it."

"But he was an Explorer," Zander said, as though that was the end of it. "I think they were lying about him to get us to tell them something."

I wasn't so sure. I just kept thinking about the way Dad had looked before he'd left for Fazia. Something had been bothering him and for the first time I let myself consider the possibility that he'd been doing something illegal.

We walked along for another thirty minutes or so. The tunnel changed as we went, expanding up and billowing out so that we were now in a large system of caverns. My eyes had adjusted to the darkness a bit so that I could see better with the help of the lights. There were only a few of the giant slugs here and there on the walls and the air had a new dampness.

"What's that noise?" M.K. asked.

We all stopped walking and listened and, sure enough, we heard the sound of rushing water. Pucci cocked his head, listening.

"What is it?" Zander asked Pucci, who hunched his shoulders

in a little shrug. "Hmm. There must be a waterfall or something up ahead."

"Underground?" Sukey asked. "How can there be a waterfall underground?"

"There are underground rivers," I said. "In fact, when spelunkers die, it's sometimes because underground rivers flood. In an instant they can... But I'm sure that's not what this is."

But as we came around the turn in the tunnel, I could see that I'd been wrong.

The rushing sound became louder and louder and suddenly we had the feeling that we were right on top of it. We stopped, and when we pointed our lights down at the ground, we saw a wide expanse of swirling, moving blackness.

It *was* a river, an underground river, and when we looked across the breadth of it, we could see that the caverns we'd been following continued on the other side, winding along beside it into the underground darkness. I checked Dad's map, hoping it might show us a different route, but it confirmed what I saw in front of me.

"That's where we need to go," I told the others, pointing across the water.

There were only two choices: we could somehow get across the raging underground river, or we could turn around and go back the way we'd come.

Thirty-two

"The River Styx," I whispered.

"What?" They all turned to look at me.

"It looks how I always imagined the River Styx would look."

"Isn't that the river that takes you to hell?" Sukey asked.

"Yeah."

"That is not a helpful comparison, Kit," Zander told me. "Who's going in with me?"

"I'll try it." M.K. stepped into the river.

"I hope there aren't any piranhas or crabs in there or anything," I said nervously. In the dim glow of my vest light, M.K. turned around and gave me a mean look.

"I'm just saying." I shrugged. "It's dark. We can't really see anything."

"Shut up, Kit." Zander stepped into the water, too. "Come on, M.K., how deep is it?"

"I can't—" One second she was standing there and the next she had disappeared beneath the surface of the water. Pucci called out, *"M.K.! M.K.!"* and Zander reached down and came up with her, then lost his own footing. Sukey and I had to reach down into the cold water and haul them back up onto the rock by the side of the river.

They sat there shivering in the dark. "It was slippery and the current's really strong," Zander said. "And it's pretty deep. There's no way we could all get across." He shivered. "Wow, that water was cold. You okay, M.K.?"

She tried to nod, but her teeth were chattering so hard she just sort of vibrated. Sukey took off her flight jacket and put it around M.K.'s shoulders.

"Are you okay?" I asked her. "Do you want my vest?"

"I'll be fine," she said, but I could tell she was trying not to shiver. I took off my vest and put it over her shoulders.

"What are we going to do?" We all sat there for a moment, staring across the river. The light on my vest flickered and Sukey handed it back to me. A minute later, it died.

"The solar batteries," I said. "They've run out."

"Quick," M.K. told Zander, "shut yours off. We'll use mine and save yours, whatever's left of it."

He did as she said. Now that we had only the light from her vest, the cavern was darker than ever. We sat there for a long time, not sure what to do.

"I'm hungry," M.K. said finally.

"We all are." My stomach gave an involuntary growl and I looked halfheartedly through the pockets of my vest on M.K.'s shoulders, hoping for a candy bar, but finding nothing. The food we'd bought at the top of the canyon was still in Sukey's pack in the cave. Dad had provided us with all the utilities we might ever need, and now we had all the water we could ever drink, but at that moment, I would have killed for a chocolate bar.

"We need to get warmed up and we need to eat something," I said. "Otherwise we're not going to be able to go any further, much less get back to Drowned Man's Canyon. And we're not going to be able to do those things down here."

"You think we should just give up?" Zander turned to look at me. "Go back and turn ourselves in to Foley? Give the Nackleys the map so they can find the treasure?"

"No, but I don't know how we're going to... There's no way across that river. And there's no food or firewood in these caverns."

"But why would your father send you all the way into this cavern if there was no way across?" Sukey asked. "That doesn't make sense."

There were lots of explanations. Maybe it hadn't been much of a river when Dad was here making the map. Maybe he hadn't intended for us to come here at all. But I didn't want Sukey to think I was scared so I said, "You're right. There must be a way across the river, a tunnel under, or stairs in the wall, something like that. Everyone, look carefully."

We did our best, but we couldn't really split up and look with only one light, so the four of us just kind of stumbled around on the side of the river and finally gave up. We sat down on the cold rock.

"I better switch off my light," M.K. said. "Save it."

I didn't like the darkness at all.

"I don't feel right," Sukey said. "I'm so tired all of a sudden."

"I know what you mean." The little bit of exertion had exhausted me, too. "It must be because we're so hungry. Keep drinking water. We won't run out of that."

In the last six months, ever since Dad had disappeared and we'd lost our Explorer rations, I'd been really hungry. A few times, we'd gone a couple of days without meat or milk, but there'd always been something, a box of stale crackers, a couple of apples from one of our trees, a piece of cheese traded for copper at the markets. This was different. There was absolutely nothing to eat down here.

"We ate yesterday," M.K. said, as though she was trying to convince herself.

"We had a few bites of beans and beef jerky yesterday." Sukey sighed. "It feels like it was a year ago. We should have gone back to get my backpack."

"If we'd gone back to get your backpack," Zander told her, "we wouldn't even be having this conversation."

Sukey was silent for a moment and then she said, "You're right. We'd be sitting in some BNDL prison somewhere."

"That's a little melodramatic, don't you think?" I asked her.

"I don't think so. Lazlo wasn't lying. BNDL is ruthless. I once heard my mother talking to a friend of hers about someone they knew. He went on an expedition to China, looking for a mountain pass or something. And he disappeared. Just never came back. Some of his friends, including Delilah, flew out there to see if they could find him. They found some people who said he had been seen talking to a man and a woman wearing black Explorer's uniforms with red patches on their jackets."

"BNDL," I said. "What happened then?"

"I don't know. They stopped talking about it."

"But... they couldn't have... killed him. Could they?" I don't know why the thought was so shocking to me.

"You'd be surprised. I heard..." She hesitated. "Forget it. It's just gossip."

"What's just gossip?" Something in her voice made me think she'd been about to tell us something important.

"Nothing. Nothing definite. I shouldn't have said anything."

I think we were all too tired and hungry to press her. "We have to think," Zander said after a minute. "There must be something to eat down here."

"There's nothing down here but those slugs," I said.

"They *are* protein," Zander said after a minute.

"What?" Sukey's face was shocked in the low light. "You wouldn't...?"

"Hold on." Zander switched his light back on and we saw him searching the walls of the tunnel. A minute later and he was back, holding one of the slimy slugs. He put it on the ground and we all watched as it writhed on the cold stone. Its flesh was plump and green. I felt my stomach turn.

"No," I said. "No way. I'm not eating raw slug."

"We have to have protein," Zander said. "And it won't be raw. We'll figure out a way to cook it. I'm sure there are lots of cultures where they eat slugs."

"Zander," Sukey said in an exasperated tone, "in case you hadn't noticed, there's no wood down here."

"Hang on." M.K. was rummaging in Zander's vest and she came up with the flame thrower she'd used to start the fire. She pressed the button on the top and a flame shot out of the box. She directed it at the slug and it writhed for a few seconds and then was still. A hideous odor of burning flesh filled our noses.

"Aghhhh!" I pinched my nose, trying to keep the awful smell out, but nothing helped. M.K. closed the flamethrower and we all stared at the smoking slug.

"No," Sukey said. "Just, no."

"Yeah," Zander said. "You're right." He kicked the slug into the river, where it hissed as it hit the cold water and was sucked below the surface.

We all stood there, dejected, staring into the darkness.

M.K. spoke up. "Is this it? We can't go any farther."

Sukey went over and kicked the wall of the cavern. "Ow," she said.

M.K. gave Sukey her jacket back and started rummaging around in her vest, taking out a couple of utilities.

"I was just thinking," she said. "Dad made it across the river somehow and Dad left the vests for us."

She fiddled with one of the utilities and some fabric shot out of one end. "I don't know what that is. Maybe it's another tent." She shoved the fabric back in, replaced it, and fiddled with another gadget box, pushing a button on top. "I wonder what——"

Suddenly there was a loud *whoosh* and we couldn't see M.K. at all as a huge expanse of gray plastic ejected from the utility and inflated almost instantaneously.

In a little under a minute, M.K. was standing next to a large boat.

"Wow," she said. "I thought it might be a rope or something."

Thirty-three

We piled into the boat. It was a good vessel, made of an ultra-light rubber coated with something that made it quite durable. There were even some oars that had inflated when the boat did, and Sukey and I each took one while Zander and M.K. huddled in the bottom, trying to get warm after their dip in the river. I laid my vest out on the side of the boat so that Pucci's feet wouldn't puncture the rubber.

We wanted to save whatever was left of Zander's light, so we switched it off and started down the dark river. It was strange, knowing we were moving but unable to see the sides of the cavern passing by as we went.

The river wound on through the rock and we floated along on the swift current, winding our way through the darkness. The caverns were filled with a mossy green scent that reminded me of frogs and fish.

The river was moving so quickly that Sukey and I didn't even need to paddle.

"What do you think the Nackleys are doing right now?" I asked them.

"I bet they're still digging," M.K. said. "Did you see how many shovels they had?"

"They're pretty determined," Zander said. "And now that it's been in the paper and everything, they probably feel like they have to find it. Leo Nackley would be humiliated if they went home empty-handed."

"I wonder why BNDL's so interested, anyway?" Sukey asked after a minute.

"What do you mean? It's a treasure in gold, who wouldn't be interested?" M.K. snorted. "Gold's about the only thing that matters anymore."

"But maybe there's something else that BNDL wants to find," Sukey said. "Something other than the treasure."

"Like what?" I hadn't thought about that.

"Well, I was thinking. Why did they establish BNDL in the first place?"

"For the resources," I said, catching on. "It was after they discovered Gryluminum in Grygia and they realized that there might be all kinds of other resources, metals they could mine, coal, diamonds, agricultural land. All kinds of things."

"Right. So what if there's something here that they're looking for?"

"Like what?" Zander asked. "You couldn't farm very well down here. It's too hot. And you'd need wa—" He grinned. "Oh."

"Exactly," Sukey said. "I was thinking about what they said about your dad and Munopia. The water. A new source of water in this part of the Southwest. That's a big deal. There have been all these droughts lately, right? The legend goes that Dan Foley saw the golden treasure in an old mine, right? Well, you need water for a gold mine. Maybe they think that Dan Foley's treasure will lead them to a river—this river. And then, of course, there's the gold. I'm sure ANDLC would love to take the gold."

We were all quiet for a while, just thinking as the boat took us to wherever it was that we were going. After half an hour or so, the current slowed and we seemed to be in a new part of the cavern.

Next to me, Sukey was alert, her eyes focused on the water, and I sensed that she was tensing up even before I became aware of the feeling that someone was watching us. Pucci seemed to sense it, too. He hopped around at the front of the boat, calling into the darkness as though he was hoping someone would answer him, and then flew up to Zander's shoulder, where he cawed and complained.

"Pucci's nervous," Zander said, and as we looked ahead of us into the darkness, we could see that it was now lit up by what seemed like hundreds of tiny lights.

Or eyes.

There was a new smell in this part of the cavern, something musty that reminded me of a nest of rodents.

"What is that?" M.K. asked. "What's out there?"

We stared up at the pairs of lights shining in the darkness, and as if in answer, one set of eyes seemed to detach from the others and we felt something swoosh through the air over our heads.

"We were wondering what might eat those giant slugs," Zander said. "I think we may have figured it out."

"Quick, turn on your light," I told him. "We've got to see what it is." Zander switched it on, looked up, and in the weak light from his vest, we saw them.

High in the walls of the cavern, on every possible surface, were hundreds of huge nests made of sticks and rocks. And sitting in the nests were giant birds.

They looked a bit like buzzards or vultures, with long necks and bald heads, but they were easily twice the size of any buzzard I'd ever seen. Their beaks looked sharp and their feathers, green and black, gleamed in the darkness. As we stared at them, they realized that we were there. As a group, they stirred, flexing their wings and stretching out of the nests. One launched itself into the air and sailed toward us, making a strange gurgling sound down in its throat.

"What do we do?" Sukey asked. I could barely see her face in the low light, but she sounded really scared.

Zander was now sitting up in the boat and looking around him at the birds. "They must be some kind of vulture," he said. "But their beaks and heads are more like raptors'. I've never seen anything quite like them. Let me see your spyglass."

"Zander," I said. "I don't care if they're a brand-new species no one's ever seen before. They're coming after us."

"We've got to row," Sukey said. "I think we can get away from them. Come on, Kit. Look up ahead." I did and saw what she meant. The ceiling of the cavern got gradually lower ahead of us. If we could squeeze beneath it, we might be able to escape the birds.

As though the birds had noticed our distress, others started detaching themselves from the wall and flying slowly toward us.

"Row harder, you two," Zander called out.

"We're trying," Sukey said. "Here, Zander, you take over. I have an idea." He did as she said.

She crawled to the back of the boat and suddenly a loud shot reverberated through the cavern. "Take that, you freaks!" she yelled.

"What are you doing?" Zander stopped paddling as he looked over his shoulder at her. "Did you just shoot at them?"

"I might be able to scare them off."

"Are you crazy? The bullet's liable to ricochet off the rock and kill one of us."

"Oh, sorry. I guess you're—help!" I turned around to find one of the birds landing on Sukey's back. Its wicked beak struck at her hair and head and I swung at it with my oar. Pucci attacked, his metal talons out in front of him and the bird flew off with a strange clucking sound.

"Come on," I said. "Everyone help us. We've got to get out of here." Zander and I rowed with everything we had and Sukey and M.K. bent over and used their hands to paddle in the water. As I rowed, I felt wings brush my face and I reached up again to swipe at the horrible birds.

Suddenly there was a loud *whoosh* and I watched as one of the birds transformed into a fireball and plunged into the water, sputtering and flapping its wings until the flames were out.

"M.K.!" I yelled. When I turned around she was holding the flamethrower utility and grinning. "You're going to set us all on fire!" We were almost to the place where the ceiling of the caverns dropped.

"I don't think it's high enough," I said, trying to figure out how much clearance there was in the dim light. "We're going to hit the rock."

"We've got to try," Zander said. "All right, everyone, when I get to three, duck."

I felt one of the birds grabbing at my back with its talons, trying to pull me up into the air. It almost succeeded. Pucci squawked and knocked the bird away. I felt something wet splatter against my face.

"Damn it. Get away from me!" M.K. shouted and I knew that one of them was attacking her, too. "Damn! I dropped the flamethrower into the water. I have to—"

"No time to look for it," I called. "We're almost there. One."

I waved my arms in the air. The birds were all around me and I felt one get ahold of my hair and try to lift me off the seat.

"Two," Zander called.

I swung at the bird and felt it detach for a second before trying to get a better grip.

And then we were looking directly at the wall of rock.

"Three!"

We ducked.

Thirty-four

I felt rock scrape against my back and heard Sukey scream, but in a couple of seconds we had cleared the rock and were floating along quietly in a new part of the system of caverns. The river was bordered on both sides by sandy little beaches and a rocky floor that stretched out toward the high rock walls, which were made of the same beige limestone we'd seen in Drowned Man's Canyon.

"Did the birds follow us?" I asked the others. When I turned to look, I could see that we were alone in the cavern. My heart was pounding and I wasn't taking in the details very well.

"I lost the flamethrower," M.K. complained. "What are we going to… Wait. You guys! It's *light*."

It wasn't light, exactly, but as we looked around we realized that there was late, orangey light coming through the ceiling of the cavern, filtering through holes in the rock into the shapes of little moons and stars and other symbols, so that the sun hit the floor and the water through the openings, decorating every surface with dancing spots of golden light.

There were no birds.

"It's beautiful," Sukey said in a quiet voice. "I didn't know how nice it would be to see the sun again, even like this."

But Zander and I were staring up at the holes in the rock.

"Someone drilled those," Zander said. "Those aren't natural." Pucci flew up to examine them, squawking loudly as if to confirm Zander's opinion.

"Of course they're not." I pointed up at them. "M.K., how would you do something like that?"

"Mechanical drill," she said. "That's a lot of precision. Something pretty good." There was something thin about her voice and when she reached up to rub at her arm, I felt fear wash through me again.

"M.K.?" Sukey asked her. "Does your arm hurt?"

"Just a little." But she looked pale and I knew that it must be bad for her to admit that it hurt at all.

"Let me see." Sukey moved next to her and rolled up her sleeve. I heard her gasp when she pulled the bandage aside. "This is really bad. We need to put some of that antibiotic stuff on it..." She trailed off and her eyes widened in alarm. Her backpack. The first-aid kit was in her backpack, back in the cave.

"Where's that other stuff, the stuff Dad put in our vests?" I put my vest back on and started searching the pockets.

"I put it in my backpack, too," Sukey said quietly.

"I'll be fine," M.K. said. "It's just a little sore, that's all." She pushed her sleeve back up and winced.

"Maybe we can find some kind of medicinal plant when we get to the end," Zander said. The current had slowed and we were just floating along now, the river moving us through this wider part of the caverns.

"Should we wash it?" I asked Sukey.

"Can't hurt," she said.

"The water's moving," Zander said. "At least it's not stagnant." We rowed over to the side of the river and Zander jumped out and pulled the boat ashore as we got out, too.

"Those birds were *creepy*," M.K. said, splashing the cold water on her arm. "What was up with them?"

"They must be some kind of subterranean bird of prey," Zander said. "I think they've evolved to eat those slugs. You okay, M.K.?"

She nodded bravely.

I got the map and my compass out of my vest, trying to figure out where we'd landed. "Where are we?" Sukey asked me, looking over my shoulder at the map. When I looked up, I could see that a little wound on her head was oozing blood. There were drops of blood on her jumpsuit and aviator's jacket, but I was surprised to see the synthetic fabric had held up pretty well to the water and dirt.

"Are you okay? Your head's bleeding."

She brushed my concern away. "Don't worry about me. Worry about M.K. Show me where we are."

I traced our route on the map and did some calculations, then pointed to a spot near the end of the rows of contour lines that described the tunnel and underground river we'd just traveled. Beyond it, the caverns seemed to widen for another six or seven miles and then end. "Here."

"We're near the end," Sukey said. "Do you think that means that we're near the mine and the treasure?"

I didn't say anything, because the truth was that I had no idea. The sun was setting. In an hour it would be almost completely dark again.

"I guess we keep going. Right?" Sukey asked in a small, exhausted voice. But no one answered her. I yawned. I was about as tired as I'd ever been, my muscles aching and my stomach so empty it felt like it was trying to digest itself.

"We're all tired," I said. "I think we should rest."

"But we've got to keep going," Zander said. "According to the map, we're almost there. There may be plants there."

"I'm tired," M.K. said in a thin voice. "And cold. We could get out the sleeping bags. I can share with Sukey."

"Do you think we could build a fire," Sukey asked, "to warm up?" She was looking tired, too.

"There's no wood down here," Zander said. "And we don't have the flamethrower anymore, so we don't have any way of lighting a fire. Come on, guys. We just need to keep going. The river's leading us somewhere. The treasure can't be far away. And we need to find something for M.K.'s arm." He was looking at us as though he couldn't understand why we weren't just following him. It was how he'd always been, stubborn, convinced he knew better than anyone else. I remembered suddenly a hike we'd taken when I was seven and he was eight. Dad had let us go by ourselves if we promised to stick to the trail, but Zander had almost immediately decided that it would be more fun to trailblaze. We'd been lost for a couple of hours but he'd gotten us out of the woods by following deer tracks back to a marshy little field near the trailhead. That was the problem; we usually did what Zander said because he was pretty good at getting out of tight spots. Not this time, though.

"Zander," I said, trying to keep my voice steady, "we have no idea what's up ahead. If we're going to keep going, we've got to have some rest. We can sleep in shifts and the others can keep watch."

"He's right," Sukey told him. "I'm so tired and hungry, I can't keep anything straight in my head." She sat down on the ground, looking forlorn.

It was so rare that Zander didn't get his way that I'd forgotten how angry he could get.

"Come on," he demanded. "We can't stay here. We have to keep going."

"I'm staying here," I said. "We've got the sleeping bags. We have to rest."

"I'm with Kit," Sukey said.

"Me, too." M.K. stared up at Zander, her serious little face fixed in determination. Zander was tough, but M.K., even in pain, was tougher.

He scowled and zipped up his vest. "Fine," he said. "But I'm going ahead to see what's up there."

"Zander," Sukey called after him, "I don't think that's a good idea. What if something...?" But he just ignored her and kept walking until he was out of sight. Poor Pucci looked back and forth between Zander and the three of us, unsure about what to do. Loyalty won out and he followed Zander. From the way Zander kept looking over his shoulder, I could tell that he thought we'd give in and follow him.

We didn't.

"Is he always that stubborn?" Sukey asked once he had disappeared around a turn in the caverns.

"Yes," M.K. and I said at the same time.

"Should we go after him?" Sukey looked worried now.

"He'll come back," I told her. "He just hates it when we don't agree with him."

"All right." But she didn't seem particularly relieved. "I'm not sure I could walk very far, anyway."

The sun must have been sinking fast outside the caverns because one by one the little star and moon shapes disappeared from the rock floor.

"I was just thinking," M.K. said. "Do you remember when Dad used to make pancakes for dinner?"

"Those were the best pancakes." I could almost taste them, warm and floury and filled with blueberries. "I would kill for one of those pancakes right now."

"Is Delilah a good cook?" M.K. asked Sukey dreamily. "What does she make?"

Sukey laughed. "She's an awful cook. But my grandmother… You should taste my grandmother's food. In the summer, when I'm staying with her, we pick blackberries and she makes blackberry crumble, with vanilla ice cream on top. The blackberries get all sticky and on top there's this brown sugar cake with a sort of crust on it. When it's cooking the whole house smells like—"

"Stop," I groaned. "You're torturing me."

She grinned. "Sorry."

"Sukey?" M.K. asked her after a minute. "Do you have a father?"

Sukey picked up a little rock and pitched it into the water. "Of course. Everyone has a father."

"But who is he?" M.K. asked.

"I don't know," Sukey said in a small voice. "Delilah won't tell me."

"But—" M.K. started.

"M.K.," I warned.

"No, it's okay," Sukey said. "I just wish I knew."

The last bit of light died away and we found ourselves in complete darkness again. I switched on my vest light and was glad to see that the faint brightness in the cavern had recharged the battery. M.K. and I got the reflective sleeping bags out of our vests and unfolded them. I gave one to Sukey and wrapped the other one around M.K. and me. We were warm enough, but I was starting to wonder about Zander.

"He has the light on his vest," I said, trying to reassure myself as much as I was trying to reassure them. "And he knows what he's doing, even if he is stubborn."

But the truth was that I was worried, very worried, and every minute that went by that Zander didn't return tightened the knot in my stomach.

We sat there in silence, too tired to talk, and I was just about to say that maybe we should go and look for him when we saw, coming toward us in the darkness, a bobbing light: Zander's light.

He was running and when he reached us he stopped, breathing hard, and said, in a voice full of a fear I wasn't sure I'd ever heard from him, "There's something out there. Something big. A wolf or a cat. It was stalking me through the caverns. I could see its eyes shining in the dark." He took another breath and as we looked at his wide, fearful eyes, Pucci came winging through the darkness and alighted on his shoulder. "Pucci scared it off, but it would have gotten me for sure."

Thirty-five

"**B**ut what was it?" I asked him once he'd calmed down. "Did you actually see it?"

"No. It was too dark. I could just see its eyes. I had the feeling that someone or something was following me but it wasn't until the sun had gone down and it was completely dark that I saw the eyes. They were high up in the rocks on the side of the cavern, and from the way they moved I could tell it was a large animal, not the birds. It was stalking me, keeping its distance, and it ran off only because good old Pucci dive-bombed it about twenty times." He ran a hand through his hair, and on his shoulder Pucci murmured worriedly.

"Is it going to come after us?" M.K. asked.

"Not if I can help it," Sukey told her, taking out her pistol and making sure it was loaded. "Don't you worry, M.K." And she slid over and put an arm around M.K.'s shoulder, resting her hand on my arm. I held my breath for a minute so she wouldn't take it off.

"We've got to get some sleep," I said as I breathed again.

I waited for Zander to tell me I'd been right but instead he said, "We'll sleep in shifts. Kit, you and Sukey first. M.K. and I will keep watch with the pistol. M.K. can nap if she wants. You need to rest, M.K. Then we'll switch."

"I'll stay up with you," M.K. said weakly. "It's only fair."

Sukey and I got into the sleeping bags. The rock was hard underneath our backs, but I was so tired that I fell asleep right away, and it didn't seem like I'd been out very long when Zander was shaking me awake, saying, "Okay, our turn."

Next to me, Sukey stirred, too. "How long did we sleep?"

"Four hours," Zander said. "Something like that."

"Wow. It didn't feel like four hours. How's M.K.'s arm?"

"No better," he said grimly. I rubbed my eyes. They had adjusted to the low light and I felt a bit like a cat, able to see through the darkness. Sukey and I stretched and moved to the outside of the little circle we'd formed, letting Zander and M.K. lie down where we'd been sleeping. Zander gave Sukey back her pistol and gave me M.K.'s knife, telling me to wake him if we heard anything. It wasn't long before we heard deep, even breathing from their direction and knew they were asleep.

"Have your eyes adjusted?" Sukey whispered after a few minutes. Pucci was perched on my shoulder and he had curled himself up against my neck, his feathers tickling me every time he breathed.

It was nice, feeling the warmth of him, the fast, even rhythm of his heartbeat.

"Yeah, isn't it strange? I can almost see down here." With the fading illumination from my vest, I could just make out the outline of her face, her eyes, the contours of her cheekbones. The little lights in her ears had stopped flashing.

"How do these work?" I reached out to touch one. The light felt more flexible than I'd imagined, almost like skin.

"Solar batteries. I guess they've died, huh?"

I nodded.

She scrunched up her nose a little in a way that had started to be familiar to me.

"I don't like the dark. I don't think I'd be a very good mole. What do you think we'll find tomorrow?"

I thought for a moment. "According to the map, we're nearing the end of the first part of the tunnel or the canyon or whatever it is. I don't think my Dad would have sent us on this journey if there wasn't something at the end for us to find, but—"

"But what?" Sukey had moved closer to me so she could hear, and now I could see her face even more plainly.

"Well, a lot of things could have happened. As far as we can tell, he was here, what, twenty years ago, something like that? Maybe someone else found it in the meantime."

"But wouldn't we have heard about it? I mean, who wouldn't jump at the chance to announce they'd discovered a species of giant slug, or giant vultures?"

"Maybe there was a lot of gold there and whoever found it decided to keep it a secret so BNDL couldn't claim the treasure."

"I hadn't thought of that." She was quiet for a long time. Then she said, "Your father." She hesitated. "I'm sorry to bring this up, but... what did they tell you? About his disappearance?"

"Nothing, really. They said they found an oar and some debris from the boats they were using near Bartoa. But I've done a lot of research on this. I've redone all the maps a hundred times. That can't be right. They were way past there. They must have gotten it wrong. Why do you want to know?"

"Oh, it's just... something Delilah said when we heard about him. I'm not sure I should tell you." She looked away and I felt a small knot start in my stomach.

"Tell me."

"Okay, well, it was in the newspapers, you know. And Delilah was really upset when she saw the story. As I told you, she respected your father a lot. And she said, 'Perished in the jungle, my foot! He no more perished in the jungle than I would! I bet BNDL had something to do with this.' I asked her what she meant and she wouldn't say anything more."

"Zander wants to go there, try to find out what happened," I said. "Maybe we will someday. If we ever get out of here."

She was silent for a long moment and then she said, "The man who gave you the package. He didn't have a tattoo, did he?"

I was astonished. "How did you know?"

"Never mind. What did it look like?"

I pointed the light at the ground and drew an approximation of the symbol in the scanty dirt. "Like this," I said. "Like a partial eclipse or something, two circles, one bigger than the other, overlapping. You've seen it before, haven't you?"

She studied it for a moment, leaning close to the ground. "My mother used to have this friend, Harry Mokwobay, Sir Harry Mokwobay, actually. He was Zimbabwean, a brilliant, brilliant Explorer who died on a polar expedition five or six years ago."

"I've heard of him."

"Yeah, well, he would stay with us whenever he was in New York, and one day he was changing his shirt or something and I saw that he had this tattoo on his shoulder. It was that symbol."

"Did you ever ask your mother what it meant?"

"No. She was really broken up when he died. I think maybe she was in love with him. What did your guy look like?"

I described him for her. "It's awfully dangerous, being an Explorer," I said.

"More than it should be, I would say."

"That's just what I was thinking." I was quiet for a moment, deciding. "Sukey," I said finally, in a voice barely louder than a whisper, "Raleigh said that he'd heard rumors about a secret organization, the Mapmakers' Guild. They were supposed to be the ones who fed the wrong information into the Muller Machines. They were outlawed, but Raleigh said that there were rumors that they weren't gone. I think maybe that tattoo was their sign. Have you ever heard anything about it?"

There was a long silence. "Not directly," she said. "But I always wondered about Harry. He was, well… there was something about him that made me think he had a lot of secrets, that's all. And there's a lot of stuff Delilah doesn't tell me."

And then the light flickered once and finally gave out. We were in complete darkness. Sukey reached out and took my hand, something that surprised me more than the slugs and vultures combined. It was soft and her fingers laced with mine, fitting neatly into the spaces between them. The funny thing was that after a minute, it didn't feel weird at all. She moved closer and leaned into me and I put my arm around her and sort of held her against me, the smoky, sweet smell of her hair in my nose. It seemed like a strange, grown-up thing to be doing, holding her like that. I could feel her breathing against me, the gentle rising and falling of her body. Pucci mumbled in his sleep. M.K. snored.

We let the darkness sit around us. We were quiet for a long time, a good kind of quiet, and then the sun started rising outside, the little stars and moons and suns starting to glow pink, then orange, then yellow. Sukey and I watched the day arrive out there, in the real world, and it seemed so far from where we were that I couldn't imagine we'd ever get there.

Thirty-six

We woke Zander and M.K. once the cavern was light again and got going as soon as we'd packed everything back into the vests and had some water to drink. It felt good to have had a little sleep, but we were even hungrier than we'd been the night before and we were now on the lookout for whatever it was that had been following Zander last night. I was still thinking about what Sukey had told me the night before, but I'd decided not to say anything to Zander and M.K.

M.K. seemed a little better after sleeping, though her arm looked worse than ever, and we were quiet as the boat wound its way through the cavern. Now that we could see our surroundings better, we saw that we'd entered a magical section of the network of tunnels and caverns. There were huge stalactites and stalagmites everywhere we looked and the minerals in the water showed up pink and yellow and green in the strange, dappled light. I was lightheaded from hunger and I almost wondered if I was imagining it, but when I looked at the others, they were staring, too.

We were so mesmerized by the formations in the caverns that we didn't notice at first that the current was moving faster and that the light in the tunnel had increased, even though there didn't seem to be any more of the holes drilled in the ceiling.

"Hey," I said all of a sudden, when the scenery had started passing by so quickly I couldn't ignore it anymore, "the current's really picked up." I got the map out of my vest and checked it. "We should be coming around a bend in the river up here and then…"

"And then what?" Zander asked nervously.

"Hmm. That's strange." It was hard examining the map in the bottom of the boat.

"Why's the water moving so quickly?" Zander asked. "Wait. What's strange?"

"Well, I haven't been able to look at the map in really good light since I put it together about the secret canyon, but the contour lines are… This is very strange." I was trying to do the calculations in my head, but the lack of sleep and food was making me slow. "There's some sort of big drop in elevation up here."

"Drop in elevation? What does that mean?" Sukey was sitting up now, holding her pistol.

"It could mean some sort of geologic event that changed the shape of the caverns," I said, still looking at the map, trying to figure it out.

"Pucci, go see what you can see," Zander said, and Pucci rose into the air, his black feathers shimmering, his helmet of silver feathers pewter in the light, and disappeared into the cavern ahead.

As we came around the bend, we were blinded by the bright sunlight coming in the open end of the cavern.

"It's the end," I said. "But here is where it should..." I didn't need to say *drop* because suddenly all we could see was sky, way out in front of us, and all we could hear was rushing water.

"*Waterfall! Waterfall!*" Pucci cried out.

"It's a waterfall!" I shouted.

"You think?" Sukey had to shout to be heard.

"There's no need to be sarcastic!" I shouted back.

Sukey yelled, "What are we going to do?"

"There's nothing we can do," I told them as the boat was swept closer and closer to the edge of the falls. "Hold on tight. Stay in the boat. It's our only hope."

But M.K. was fiddling around with the buttons on the back of her vest.

"M.K., stop that! Just hold on!" I screamed at her as we came closer and closer.

"I'm just going to see what this one does," she yelled over the noise of the water. "It's the only one left." I turned and watched as she poked at the back of her collar, just as I felt us being pulled into the center of the river.

There was a loud *whoosh* and light blue fabric streamed out of the back of her vest, covering us in the boat and momentarily blinding us.

"What are you doing?" I screamed at her. "We can't see. We're going over!"

With a loud snapping sound, the fabric billowed and filled with air.

It was a parachute, a huge parachute, blue as the sky.

"There are two hooks on it!" Zander called out to us as the parachute jerked and M.K. started to lift off her seat in the bottom of the boat. "Hook them onto those rings on the boat!" We did as he said, hooking the long ropes dangling from the parachute onto the D rings on either side of the boat and felt ourselves lift off the surface of the churning water and into the air.

We must have been 150 feet over the ground, out in front of the waterfall now in our strange airship, the inflatable boat hanging beneath the giant blue parachute and the four of us in it staring out with enormous, entirely surprised eyes. It was an incredible feeling, just hanging there in mid-air for a moment before we started to drop, and we sailed gently down, mist in our faces as we looked around at the incredible place where we'd arrived.

We bumped gently to the ground.

Thirty-seven

For a long time, we were absolutely silent.

"Whoa…," whispered M.K.

"You guys." Sukey whistled. "I don't think we're in Drowned Man's Canyon anymore."

We stepped out of the boat. M.K. unhooked the ropes, pushed the button on her vest, and the parachute retracted back into her collar. Then she pushed a button on the bottom of the boat and it retracted back into its utility box.

She replaced it in her vest and we looked around. We were standing at one end of a small canyon, about the width of two football fields, with steep walls that rose straight up toward the blue skies. There was no way of telling how long it was, as both ends curled away from us, out of sight.

Directly across from us were more waterfalls like the one we'd just come over, the little rivers emerging from the canyon walls and

spilling into small pools that glittered like— M.K. was tugging at my sleeve.

"Is it... is it *gold*?" she asked.

"I think so." I just stared. I couldn't help it. I had never seen anything like this golden canyon.

Every surface shone with white and yellow light. The pools below the waterfalls seemed to be filled with liquid gold; the walls sparkled in the sun.

"I think it's a huge gold deposit," I told them after a moment. "An enormous vein of quartz shot through with gold ore. I've read about these but I've never seen anything like... Come on, let's go look at it." I took off for the nearest wall at a run. They followed me, Pucci flying in crazy circles as though he was intoxicated by the sight of all that gold.

When we'd reached the wall, I could see that my initial impression had been right. The canyon had been carved out of one giant quartz deposit, with a huge vein of gold running through it. Every surface was shining white, with lines of bright gold running here and there.

"It's a gigantic gold mine," I told them. "The biggest in the world! This is the most incredible thing I've ever seen." I ran a hand over the wall, tracing the veins of gold and the bright white stone.

"No, it's not," Sukey whispered and when I turned to look at her in surprise, I saw that she and Zander and M.K. were all staring at the other side of the canyon. "That is."

I followed their gaze and nearly fell over.

Farther down, a good four hundred yards past the waterfall, high up in the canyon, tucked under the slightly overhanging walls, was an elaborate series of cliff dwellings, terraces, and the squared-off apartment buildings I'd seen in books about the ancient peoples who had made their homes in these canyons. But instead of having been formed of mud or adobe, they all seemed to have been carved out of the quartz and gold walls of the canyon.

They glittered in the bright sunlight. Beyond them were terraces of green. "They're cliff dwellings," I told the others. "The ancient groups of people who lived here built them up high in the canyon walls like that to protect themselves from invaders. They sometimes had secret staircases carved into the rock, or they built ladders out of plant fiber. This is incredible. This has to be one of the most exciting archaeological finds of the last century. I mean, this is on par with the tomb of Tutankhamen, with the ruins at Mycenae, with the ice temple in Lundland!" I was so excited I had to stop to take a breath.

"Did Dad get here?" Zander asked, looking confused. "Do you think that Dan Foley's treasure is here?"

"I don't know," I said. I stared up at the incredible structures. "But if he did see this, I don't understand why he didn't tell anyone. This would have made his name. It would have made him the most famous Explorer in the world. We've got to get over there and document this. This is incredible. We're going to be famous! Archaeologists will call these the West Cliff Dwellings." I saw Sukey scowl and added, "I mean, the West-Neville Cliff Dwellings. I can write a paper on the geology of the canyon and draw the maps."

"I'll bring back specimens of those animals in the cavern," Zander said. "And they'll name them after me."

"We'll be rich!" M.K. added. "We can do anything we want."

"*Gold,*" Pucci called out suddenly. "*Rich!*"

"I'm glad you're all with me," Zander said. "Otherwise, I'd assume I was imagining this."

"If we were imagining it, I wouldn't still be so hungry," Sukey said. "We need to get something to eat and see if we can clean M.K.'s arm."

"You're right," Zander said. "I think I saw some fish in the pool underneath the waterfall. Why don't you all go look for some firewood and I'll look for plants we can use. Then I'll see if I can spear a couple fish with M.K.'s knife."

"You won't really be able to do that," Sukey said.

"Dad taught him to spearfish," I told her. "He used to catch striped bass from the beach near our house with a sharpened stick."

Sukey looked impressed. "Okay," she said. "Let's split up. We'll find it quicker that way. M.K., are you okay or should someone go with you?"

"Of course I'm okay," M.K. said in an insulted way and walked off, her small legs striding across the canyon floor.

It didn't take long for me to fill my arms with dry cottonwood branches, and when I returned to the waterfall, I saw Sukey had been similarly lucky. She used Zander's stick-twirling trick to start a small fire.

"I can't wait to tell him it took you only two minutes," I told her.

"Are you guys ever not competitive?" she asked me.

Zander came back holding a fistful of fleshy leaves from some sort of cactus and chattering with excitement. "I think this may be some kind of aloe plant. And I saw these incredible finches. Not any species I've ever seen. They must be some variety that lives only in the canyon. I still don't understand, though. If Dad came here, then how come we never heard about any of these species? Why aren't these called West finches or something like that?"

Sukey had been looking around warily and she said, "I was just thinking that. Why haven't we heard about this place?"

"Maybe Dad never made it here," Zander said.

"But then how did he make the map?" I had taken it out and was checking his calculations. They were perfect.

Sukey had her pistol out now. "I just don't like it," she said. "There's something strange going on here. Where's M.K.?"

We all looked around, but M.K. was nowhere to be seen. "M.K.?" we called. "M.K., where are you?"

There was only silence.

"M.K.?"

In one direction were the waterfalls and pools. In the other, the canyon narrowed and wound out of sight.

"I think she went that way," Sukey said. "Looking for wood. Up around that bend over there."

We followed her path along the canyon floor, running as fast as we could and calling M.K.'s name. As we came around the bend in the canyon, we saw more waterfalls and some huge rock formations, all of them quartz shot through with gold. Next to one of them there was something lying on the ground. I felt my heart seize up.

"There's something up there," Zander said. "Look up ahead."

Sukey's voice was shrill and panicked. "I think it's her vest. Is it her vest?"

We rushed over.

It was M.K.'s vest, and it was lying in a small pool of blood.

Thirty-eight

There's something out there," Sukey had her pistol out in front of her now. "Something got her! M.K.! Where is she? We've got to find her!"

We took the vest and rushed ahead, calling M.K.'s name, but we could hear only the waterfalls and the singing of the birds.

"Pucci, go see if you can find her," Zander ordered, and Pucci took off, calling her name as he disappeared up ahead.

We jogged along the canyon floor, searching the glittering walls for any sign of her, but there wasn't anyone there, just the echoing canyon, and the blue sky above its walls.

It seemed to take forever to reach the end of the canyon; about a mile past the waterfall the walls narrowed down so much that there was no way to get through. "She's not here," I called out as I scanned the canyon walls. "We'll have to go back in the other direction and see if we can find her."

"But there's no way we missed her," Sukey said. "There's nowhere she could have gone. I don't understand."

"Well, she's not here." At that moment, I caught movement high up in the canyon walls, but when I tipped my head back to see what it was, there was nothing there. I didn't want to tell them what I was thinking, that whatever creature had stalked Zander in the cavern must have attacked her and dragged her off.

"Did you see something up there?" I asked Zander and Sukey. "I thought I saw something."

"Maybe it's Pucci. Maybe he found her."

But the rocks looked just the way they'd looked before and the sky was empty.

We started hurrying back the way we'd come, toward the waterfall. But as we went, I had the feeling that someone was watching us. I kept searching the canyon walls. A couple of times, I again thought I caught movement among the rocks, but I didn't see anything.

Sukey and I were breathing hard from the running and she had to stop to catch her breath. "I'll go ahead," Zander called back to us and disappeared around a turn in the canyon.

Sukey and I rested for a minute, then started running again. I was so tired, so scared for M.K., that I might not have seen them right away if Sukey hadn't gasped.

"Zander!" she whispered, pointing, and I looked up to see my brother standing stock-still in the middle of the canyon. Ten or so feet in front of him, poised in position to attack, was the hugest mountain lion I had ever seen.

It was much bigger than the cougars I'd seen in zoos or in books, the size of a small horse, with a slick tan coat stretched over its rippling muscles. Its jaws were huge, its mouth lined with shining teeth like pictures I'd seen of prehistoric saber-toothed tigers.

And there was something strange about its eyes. They were bigger than the eyes of most wildcats I'd seen, and they protruded like a fish's.

"Zander," I said in a low voice, "don't move. Just stay still."

"Look for rocks," I whispered to Sukey. "Look for rocks."

"I've got my pistol."

"Not yet. He's in the way."

The cat gave a low growl and sank down low on its haunches, every muscle poised as it got ready to attack. We knew it was for real this time.

Suddenly, Pucci appeared out of nowhere, squawking and swooping, his metal talons out in front of him. He flew at the cat, beating his wings in its face, but the cat just ignored him so Pucci got more aggressive, dropping quickly to take a swipe at the cat's back with his talons. That got the cat's attention. He turned quickly to see what it was that had hurt him and batted Pucci out of the air with his paw. The parrot floundered on the ground for a moment before taking flight and trying again.

I caught movement out of the corner of my eye, and when I turned around, I found that Sukey had drawn her pistol and was pointing it at the cat. "Come on now, Zander, move out of the way," she was murmuring under her breath.

I put a hand up. "Sukey, be—"

The cat moved, just a bit, the beginning of its spring, and I felt Sukey tense next to me, ready to fire. But before she could pull the trigger, there was a sort of *whooshing* sound and then the cat was yelping in pain. From where we stood we could see the long arrow, tipped with black and green feathers, now buried in its leg. It squealed in pain and another arrow flew through the air and pierced the cat's chest. It died instantly, keeling over, its blank, protruding eyes staring up at the sky.

Pucci screeched and flew down to make sure the cat was dead, then landed on Zander's shoulder, nuzzling his cheek.

I looked up quickly in the direction from which the arrow had come and blinked once, then twice, unable to believe I was seeing what I thought I was seeing. Standing there, about twenty yards away, holding a huge bow made of highly polished wood, was a girl. She was dressed very properly, in a long, black Victorian sort of dress with golden buttons in a neat row down the front and a ruffled white blouse underneath. The skirt of the dress was hitched up at the bottom for hiking and she wore tall lace-up riding boots of black animal skin. Her long, glossy black hair—topped by a black hat—lay heavily over her shoulders.

"Hello," she said, breaking into a grin, her broad nose and dark eyes and high cheekbones all seeming to laugh at us. "You must be from the other side."

Thirty-nine

We stared at her. Sukey was still holding her pistol, and the girl, so quickly we almost missed it, reached over her left shoulder and came back with an arrow, stringing it on the bow and aiming it at us.

"Drop the pistol on the ground," she said quietly.

Sukey seemed to be arguing with herself about what to do. Finally, when the girl pulled one hand back, increasing the tension on the bow, Sukey looked down at the dead cougar and threw the pistol down on the ground. The girl moved quickly forward, picked it up, tucked it into her clothes, and had the bow up again before we knew what had happened.

"Thank you," I choked out. "You saved my brother, but our sister was out here and now she's missing. She's hurt and we're worried she got attacked by the cat, too."

The girl studied me for a minute as though she wasn't sure if I was telling the truth.

"She's only ten," Sukey told her.

The girl seemed to think for a moment, then she said, "Everyone stand over there. Don't move. I can shoot you in a second if I need to. You saw what happened to the cat." She spoke perfect English, but with a strange accent, one I couldn't place.

Zander and I glanced at each other and I knew what we were both thinking: there were three of us and only one of her. But there was something about her that made me think we didn't have much chance of escaping. Besides, we had no idea where M.K. was and we weren't going to leave the canyon until we'd found her.

As though she knew exactly what we were thinking, the girl said, "I wouldn't try to escape. I'm the best archer in the canyon other than the *Keedow's* guards, and you don't know how to get out." Then she nodded at Pucci, who was still on Zander's shoulder. "I don't trust that bird."

Zander whispered something and Pucci flew up into the rocks at the side of the canyon.

We did as she'd told us, walking awkwardly past the cat, our hands in the air, while she watched us intently. Strangely, it struck me at that moment that she was probably the most beautiful girl I had ever seen. Her cheekbones were sharp as knives, and her eyes—dark brown, almost black—were slightly turned up at the corners, like a cat's. Why was she beautiful? I couldn't quite figure it out. It wasn't anything specific about her face. It was the way everything fit together.

When I turned to look at Zander, he was staring at her, too. "Thank you," he said. "You saved my life."

"You're welcome. They're really terrible, those cats," she said. "We call them Arktos. They mostly live in the caverns and hunt the gertom birds. But they probably followed you here. You came through the caverns, didn't you?"

"Yes," I said. "But—"

"I saw you come over the waterfall. That's the third one I've killed today," she said. "They must have been hunting you in a pack. They usually don't do that." She smiled and held her bow up again, replacing an arrow on the string and pushing it back so the string was taut. The wicked-looking tip of the arrow was pointed right at my heart. "You shouldn't be here, you know. It's not good. The *Keedow* will be mad."

This was getting weird.

"Where are we?" Zander asked.

She looked at us in surprise. "You don't know? But why did—" She was interrupted by a grinding noise from above us and we all looked up to see the sky over the canyon disappearing as—I couldn't believe it—some sort of stone ceiling closed over us. The huge stone plates seemed to slide right out of the walls of the canyon and I couldn't begin to imagine the engineering that had gone into it.

The three of us stared up at it. I didn't even know how to begin to figure out what was going on. Pucci flew up into the air as though he was trying to figure it out, too, squawking and darting around.

When it had closed, we found ourselves in low light, as though it was late afternoon, the sun now shining through star- and moon-shaped holes in the ceiling that were just like the ones at the far end of the cavern.

"Oh, that's too bad," the girl said. In the strange low light, she looked older, suddenly, her features sharper and her eyes less friendly, more knowing. She smiled again and I found myself smiling back at her, wondering if the coffee-colored skin on her cheek was as soft as it looked.

The corners of her mouth turned down just a bit. "Someone must have seen. Now I'm going to have to kill you."

Forty

"What? No, don't do that. Why would you want to do that?" Zander must have been thinking about the skin on her cheek, too, because he blinked once, looking dazed, as though he'd just woken up. He put his hands out in front of him and started walking toward her. "We don't even know your name."

"Stop. Don't walk any farther," she said. The bow was up, the string taut under her hand. But she said, "My name is Halla."

Zander tried to smile, but it looked more like a strangled grimace. "Please don't kill us. I don't understand. Why would you do that? We just want to find our sister. She's out there somewhere. She was with us and we don't know what happened to her. We're worried one of those cats attacked her."

The girl hesitated, as though she was trying to figure out if he was making it up. "Where did you see her last?"

"She was heading in that direction," he said, pointing, "where the cat was. I'm worried one of them got her and she's hurt and can't call for help." Zander didn't usually show too much emotion on his face, but I could see how worried he was and she must have seen it too.

"I'm sorry about your sister. I just wish they hadn't seen you. They'll be worried you'll tell someone about us. If they hadn't..." Whatever she said was drowned out by a loud grinding as the gears in the ceiling started moving again.

It took only a minute or so for the ceiling to open completely, filling the canyon with glittering, golden light again. "Oh, maybe that was just one of your flying machines. If they'd seen you, they wouldn't have opened it up again."

Finally I realized what she'd said. "'Tell someone about us'?" I asked her. "Who's 'us'?"

She pointed down the canyon toward the cliff city.

We looked at the sparkling buildings, high in the canyon walls, and I couldn't believe we hadn't noticed it when we'd looked up at them before.

They weren't the abandoned dwellings of an ancient people. If I squinted, I could just barely see movement on the terraces and in the windows of the buildings. Past the structures, on the canyon floor, a couple of horses grazed in the hot sun.

"You mean...?" Zander started to ask, but I already knew what she meant.

The city was full of people.

Forty-one

"It's a whole city," I said, gaping. "A hidden city that no one knows about." I looked up at the girl. "But I don't understand. Are we the first people to find it?" Even as I said it, I knew that we couldn't be. An idea started that I struggled to keep up with— an idea about why Dad had left the map for us and why he had made it so difficult for anyone but us to find the canyon.

"Oh no, there have been others," Halla said.

"Did you kill them, too?" Sukey asked.

"Well, not me personally, but yes, some of them got killed. Not all of them, though. It used to be different. There were people who came and stayed with us. That's why we speak your language. But now the *Keedow* believes that no one can be trusted. So everyone gets killed." She shrugged and smiled a small smile. "Anyway, I have to figure out what I'm going to do with you." She kept the bow aimed at us and seemed to think for a couple of minutes, her forehead wrinkled and her eyes narrowed.

Finally she said, "Okay, you have to come with me. I'm going to put you somewhere safe while I figure out what to do about your sister. Walk slowly. We're going back toward the waterfall. Don't try to get away or I'll shoot you. And don't make any noise. We have only ten minutes before the other guards reach this end of the canyon."

Sukey and Zander and I exchanged a glance. Zander shrugged as if to say *I'm out of ideas*, so we started walking along in single file; Sukey, Zander, and I and then Halla. Pucci was making tight circles in the air high above us.

We walked for only five minutes or so, scanning the canyon walls for M.K. as we went. Before long, we had reached a dead-end offshoot of the canyon, a little hollowed-out place in the rock about the size of a large house. We followed Halla to one end of it and then stopped, waiting as she looked around, searching the canyon to make sure no one was watching us. "Don't move," she said in a stern voice before she kneeled down on the ground and used her hands to brush away a pile of dirt and sand and rocks. After a few minutes, she had uncovered what looked like a wooden plank, and after kicking around in the dirt with the toe of her boot, she reached down and pulled on a rope, lifting a wooden trapdoor. We could see stairs disappearing into the ground. "Go quickly!" she said. "They'll be here any minute."

No one moved.

Halla held the bow up a little higher, looking frantically over her shoulder. "Come on. If the guards see you, there's nothing I can do. They'll kill you. Go!"

"What are you going to do to us?" Sukey asked suspiciously. "I don't know if I want to go down there."

"I don't know what I'm going to do with you, but whatever it is, it's better than what they'll do if they see you."

We descended, Halla bringing up the rear and slamming the trapdoor down once we were far enough down the stairs. It was completely dark now that the entrance had been sealed, but Halla fiddled with some kind of mechanism that lit a large torch mounted on the wall. It illuminated the rectangular underground space where we now stood.

"Whoa," Sukey whispered.

"Oh my god." I think I heard my own voice say the words, but I couldn't be sure. I was too mesmerized by the sight in front of me. The light from the torch was bouncing off the glittering walls of the room, and it took me a minute to really take it in.

The space was completely filled with gold.

"Look at this place," Zander said. "It's like Fort Knox."

"It's like a museum," Sukey said.

She was right. There were statues and beautifully carved coins and a few religious idols stacked against the low walls. But mostly there were bars of gold, brick-sized bars of shining gold imprinted with beautiful designs and words in Spanish. I remembered Mr. Mountmorris's voice telling us about the Conquistadores: *In 1567, a group of Spanish Conquistadores—the Spanish soldiers who had come to the new world looking for Aztec gold in what is now Mexico—decided to try to run off with a fortune in gold ingots and bars, unprocessed nuggets, statues, jewelry, an incredible treasure in gold…*

My mind reeled as I tried to calculate how much it must be worth. I couldn't begin to imagine, but I knew that there was enough gold there that we could buy our own house, that we could travel anywhere we wanted, that we could buy our own car, our own dirigible or glider. Forget all that—we could probably buy our own country.

"Dan Foley's mine," I whispered, staring around me. "We've found Dan Foley's mine."

Forty-two

Halla didn't seem at all interested in whose mine it was.

"Sit down over there," she told us. "I'm going to go look for your sister. And I have to go find out if anyone saw you. I'll bring you something to eat, but you have to stay here. I'll be back in half an hour or so."

Zander and I were still staring at all the gold, but Sukey had stepped forward and was standing in front of Halla, her feet apart, her hands at her sides. "How do you know we won't just escape to look for her on our own?"

Halla looked her up and down, as though she found Sukey's Neo clothes very strange. "I just know," she said. "There are more of those cats out there. None of the people from the city leave this area after dusk, unless they're in the *Keedow*'s guard or a trained hunter, like me. And there are guards everywhere. If they find you, they'll probably kill you right away. You're better off letting me look for her. Believe me." She smiled right at me, making my stomach pitch a little, and then she was gone, slamming the trapdoor closed above our heads.

Sukey was the first to move. "Okay, everybody look for shovels, picks, anything like that. If we can surprise her when she comes back, we may be able to get the bow and arrows. Maybe we can take her hostage or something and make her show us the way out of here." She jumped up and started searching around the mine. In one corner, she found a couple of shovels made of highly polished wood.

"These might work," she said. "And you guys still have your Explorer's vests and M.K.'s. Maybe there's another utility in there that we can use to protect ourselves. Come on, let's see what we've got! We've got to get going and find M.K. before that freak girl comes back. If these guards are as dangerous as she says they are, M.K. may not have much time."

I couldn't believe no one had said anything about the mine.

"I know," I said, getting carried away with my excitement. "But do you all realize what this is? It's Dan Foley's mine. We found it! Do you know how much this gold is worth? Do you realize how famous we're going to be when we get back and announce that we've found a hidden city *and* Dan Foley's mine?"

"If we ever get back," Sukey said. "But if we just wait for her to come back and do whatever it is she's going to do to us, our problems are a lot bigger than some mine filled with gold. Not to mention poor M.K."

"'*Some mine*'?" I grumbled. "I don't think you realize how huge this is. Dad was right. He knew the mine was here and he wanted us to find it. We have to find M.K. first, but then we…" Something was still knocking around at the back of my head, an idea about why he'd never told anyone, but the thought of M.K. in trouble and the idea of all the gold was distracting me. "What I can't figure out, though, is why he didn't tell anyone about it. He would have been rich. We would have been rich. Why haven't we ever heard about this canyon? And how did these people get here?"

"I don't know, but you still haven't answered the question of how we're going to get out of here," Sukey said.

"Maybe we can convince her to let us go and find M.K.," I said. "She doesn't seem too worried about us knowing about the gold. Maybe we could hide it in our vests. We'll have to figure out how to get it around the Nackleys. If we report it to someone, a newspaper, maybe, then the Nackleys and BNDL can't take it from us."

"BNDL can do whatever it wants," Sukey said. "And what about M.K.? What makes you so sure she's okay, anyway?"

"You don't know M.K. as well as we do," Zander told her, looking embarrassed. "If anyone could escape from a mutant cougar or armed guards, even wounded, it's M.K. We've got her vest, but she's still got her knife. She's really, really good with that knife."

I was embarrassed, too. Sukey was right. We'd been worried about the treasure and for all we knew M.K. was in serious trouble. "She's right. We've got to find her," I told Zander.

Zander was quiet for a minute and then he nodded. "Maybe we

can ask Halla to help us find her and then show us the way out."

"*Halla?*" Sukey's eyes were wide. "*Halla?* Halla wants to kill us, or don't you remember the part where she told us that? The only thing Halla wants to show us is the end of one of the arrows that killed the cat. She's probably gone to get some of those guards to carry away our bodies."

"I don't think that's true," Zander said. "She seems pretty nice."

"And pretty," Sukey said. "I'm sure that doesn't have anything to do with anything."

"It is quite remarkable," Zander said. "I don't think I've ever seen a girl quite that beautiful before."

"I know," I said. "It's really interesting how—"

"For Christ's sake!" Sukey threw the shovel back down and sat down on the pile of gold bars again. "Are you really just going to wait for her to come back and kill us? Zander, you think you're ever going to make it back to tell everyone about the West birds or the slugs or whatever if we let her shoot arrows through our hearts and seal us up in this mine? Forget being a world-famous naturalist. You'll be a fossil someone will find in the ground a hundred years from now!"

That seemed to do it. Zander thought for a minute. "She's right," he said finally. "We haven't given her any reason to just let us go. But what can we do? Pucci's out there. He can't help us. We at least have to see if she can help us find M.K. The truth is, I don't think we have any choice but to trust her. I just wish we could—"

"What?" Sukey asked.

"I don't know. I wish we weren't being held prisoner, for one thing."

"We don't have any leverage," I said. "That's the problem. She's holding all the cards."

"You think?" Sukey gave me a sarcastic look. But she seemed to be thinking. "There are more of us than there are of her. What if we take her prisoner and demand that she find M.K. for us?"

"How are we going to do that?" I asked.

"Like I said." Sukey stood up and picked up one of the shovels again. "There are three of us. And if she doesn't bring anyone back with her, there's only one of her. Now, she's got a bow and arrow and it's pretty clear she knows how to use it, but I don't think she has any other weapons besides my pistol. And she won't be very comfortable using it. There's got to be a way we can overpower her. Quick, empty out your vests, let's see what we have to work with."

We did as she said, laying the utilities out on a board balanced over one of the stacks of gold bars.

"I don't think my compass is going to do much good," I said. "And unless I hit her on the head with the sextant, it's useless." I took my spyglass out and turned it over in my hands. "This, on the other hand..."

"What are you going to do with that thing?" Zander asked.

"Get some information."

Sukey grinned. "He's right."

"What do you mean?" Zander looked up from what he was doing.

"I can find out if she's coming back alone," I explained. "And I can try to figure out what's going on in that city. I'll watch and you two work on a plan."

Forty-three

I climbed up to the top of the stairs and lifted the trapdoor just enough that I could stick the spyglass out if I crouched down on the top stair. I focused it and switched on the listening device.

First I did a quick scan of the canyon floor to make sure Halla wasn't already approaching the mine. Then I refocused on the city.

At the highest magnification, I had a clear view of the cliff dwellings. There appeared to be five hundred or more apartment houses, with a large central section between them connected to the apartments by a series of bridges high in the air. I realized that I hadn't been thinking when I'd decided the dwellings had been built in the same style as the adobe cliff houses in other parts of the Southwest. These were much more ornate, with rounded turrets and towers carved out of the stone and elaborate carvings winding around the outside of the terraces and windows. In the very center was a large structure with columns and a long set of stone steps. With the ceiling open, all of the gold-veined stone shimmered in the late-afternoon light.

The more I looked at it, the more I realized how brilliant the design of the city was. The buildings and terraces were all tucked under the canyon walls in such a way that they wouldn't be seen from overhead and the ceiling mechanism would shield the entire canyon from observers if need be. The ceiling, I realized, could also be used to shield the canyon from the scorching summer sun but let in the rain, making it possible to grow fruits and vegetables. We had seen the terraced gardens and grazing livestock. They seemed to have everything they needed: water, food, protection.

I zeroed in on one of the terraces, hearing a low hum of voices through the spyglass's listening device. A crowd of people was milling around on the terrace; it seemed to be some sort of market: people stopped at stands, looking at vegetables and fruit and baskets and other things. They were all dressed like Halla, in dark, formal Victorian-style suits and dresses and black hats. I was still so amazed at the existence of the city that I hadn't thought about the people who lived in it. There were kids and old people and men and women who were Dad's age, and as I watched, I saw a couple of boys running across the market, a little dog following them. An old lady said something in a language I couldn't understand to a man at one of the stalls, and they laughed. I looked carefully for any sign of M.K., but there wasn't a small, tough-looking blond-haired girl to be seen anywhere. I tried to keep my panic down; we would find her and she would be all right. That's all there was to it.

I tipped the spyglass up a bit and looked around the perimeter of the central cliff structure, spotting guards posted at each corner. They were wearing what looked like plates of armor made of gold, and helmets decorated with multicolored bird feathers, the green and blue and yellow cascading over their shoulders. They were holding wooden bows like Halla's and were scanning the canyon below the cliff city. I had read about the many different groups of Native Americans who lived in this part of the Southwest, but I couldn't put my finger on who these people might be. Halla, with her high cheekbones and beautiful features, reminded me of a picture of a Mayan princess I'd once seen.

Behind me, Sukey and Zander were planning our attack. "We'll wait until she closes the trapdoor behind her and then I'll put the light out. I think this should do it." I heard a snap and then the mine was dark for a second before Sukey lit the torch again. "She'll be ready," she said. "I'm sure she'll have the bow out, so we'll have to act fast. Before it's dark, Zander will pick up the shovel and use it to disarm her. It'll have to be near enough that he can reach for it. And then Kit and I will knock her down and we can tie her hands behind her back with the retracting rope. Kit, can you see anything?"

"Yeah, I can see everything... It's incredible, you guys. The city is huge and it's full of people and animals and everything." I was still looking at the apartment buildings, trying to count how many there were.

"But what about Halla? Do you see her?" Sukey asked.

"No. At least I don't think so." I adjusted the spyglass so I could see the canyon and was about to tell them that she didn't seem to have left yet when I caught sight of her, way off to one side of the city, making her way across the canyon. I focused on her and the listening device picked up the faint sound of her feet on the rocks. She had the bow on her back and she also seemed to be wearing some kind of backpack. She was striding along purposefully, moving fast.

"There she is," I told the others. "She's on her way back. She's alone. I'd say she'll be here in five minutes."

"Okay. Everyone take your places. Kit, you stand next to me over here." Sukey seemed to be enjoying being in charge. I put the spyglass away and did as she said.

It seemed to take an awfully long time, all of us waiting, the mine so silent that I could hear our breathing, but finally we heard the sound of Halla searching for the trapdoor and we saw it start to open.

"I have food for you," she said from above. "Everybody put their hands up where I can see them." She appeared on the stairs, the bow out in front of her and the backpack on her back. I glanced at Sukey. She looked determined, her chin thrust out, her amber eyes fixed on Halla.

The door closed and out of the corner of my eye I saw Sukey move.

A second later, the mine was plunged into darkness.

Forty-four

It was hard to tell what was happening. I heard the clatter of something wooden—Halla's bow, I assumed—and then the sound of someone falling to the ground. Halla called out and I heard Sukey's voice cry out in pain and then Zander saying, "I've got her!" and Sukey's voice saying, "That's me, you idiot!" and then the sound of someone hitting the floor. I wasn't sure what to do, so I sort of launched myself toward where I thought they were, and when I felt the long fabric of Halla's dress, I tried to feel for her hands but kept getting knocked over by someone—Zander? Sukey?—who was also scrambling around on the ground.

"The light!" Zander called and I heard someone knock against the torchbox on the wall and suddenly the room was full of light again. My glasses had fallen off in the confusion and it took me a minute to find them and look around.

Zander, Sukey, and I were sprawled out on the floor and Halla, the bow back in her hands, the arrow in it pointed right at us, was across the room, aiming her weapon at us and glaring as though she really wanted to let it fly this time. The backpack had opened up in the scuffle, spilling out leather packages of meat and cheese and fruit.

"That was not a smart thing to do," she said after a minute.

"Not as far as we're concerned." Sukey sat up, rubbing her elbow, which must have gotten hurt in the scuffle. "You were going to kill us."

"I wasn't going to kill you," Halla said. "I found out about your sister. And I brought you food and water." She gestured toward the backpack. "See. You might as well. It's just going to go to waste otherwise."

"Where's M.K.? Is she okay?" Zander and I both jumped up, sitting back down when Halla tightened her grip on the bow.

"She's alive, anyway," Halla said, watching us carefully. "One of the *Keedow*'s guards found her. She had been attacked by the cat, but I heard someone say she'd defended herself with a knife and done more damage to the cat than it had done to her. They said she had a bad infection on her arm, but they treated it and she's going to be healthy again."

I felt relief wash over me. "That's our M.K.," Zander said. "Where is she?"

"They've got her in a locked room in the city," Halla told us. "I couldn't figure out a way to get to see her without making everyone suspicious. They saw your firewood and the plants you collected and they're convinced someone came with her. They're looking everywhere in the canyon. I'm not going to be able to keep you here very long." She pushed the food toward us with her foot. "Eat something. Whatever happens, you've got to have something to eat."

"She's right," I said, feeling a little guilty now. "It's been hours and hours since we ate. If we're going to find M.K., we're going to need energy."

"Don't they lure rats into traps with food?" Sukey muttered. "Cheese. Peanut butter. Isn't that how they get them to go in? It's probably poisoned."

Zander thought about that for a minute. "No. There wouldn't be any reason to poison it," he said, looking up at Halla. "Let's eat." I was so hungry I found it pretty easy to take the peach he offered me, along with a couple of swallows of water from a leather pouch, a slice of bread, and some cooked meat cut into strips. We sat down and devoured the meal and it wasn't long before Sukey came over and started eating, too.

"Thank you," I said finally, looking up at Halla, who was now watching us with an annoyed expression.

"You're lucky you're still alive, you know," Halla said after a minute. "What was your plan here, anyway?"

No one said anything so finally I told her. "The plan was that you were going to help us get M.K. and then show us how to get out of the canyon."

"And when you get to the other side, you'll tell everyone about the canyon, right? Without a thought as to what would happen to us when the rest of the world found out about us?"

We all looked at each other. We couldn't deny that's what we had been planning to do. But when she put it like that, it sounded pretty bad.

"Well," I said finally, "if it's true that only a few people know about you, it is a pretty amazing archaeological find."

"There are species of animals no one's ever seen before," Zander said. "I owe it to science to…" Halla rolled her eyes and he trailed off.

"And the gold," Zander went on. "Don't you know how much it's worth? I mean, this is an incredible place. People will want to see this…"

But as he said it, I could almost hear Dad's voice, railing against the governments that had looted the New Lands for resources. "*They don't care about the discovery. They only care about the money they can squeeze out of it!*" he'd ranted. "*And BNDL doesn't do a damned thing to stop it. It's criminal!*"

Zander looked worried and I knew he was thinking the same thing that I was. What *would* happen to the people in the canyon when everyone came to get the gold? When the Nackleys came? When Mr. Mountmorris got here? When ANDLC decided to extract all the gold?

None of us said anything and Halla watched us for a minute before saying, "How did you get here, anyway? No one's supposed to be able to get anywhere near the caverns."

"Because you kill everyone who gets anywhere close, right?" Sukey's voice was very quiet.

I was staring at all the gold, Dan Foley's gold, and thinking fast, remembering the thought I'd had when I'd first seen the city.

"No," I said after a minute. "Not everyone. They didn't kill Dad." I hesitated for a moment, trying to keep the thoughts clear in my head. "Dad didn't get killed. For some reason Dad didn't get killed. Dad came here and maybe he was looking for the treasure, but then he found *this*. He found the gold and the city. And he must not have told… he must not have told anyone. " I looked at Halla and lowered my voice. "He didn't want us to tell anyone. *That* was what Dad's secret map was about. That's why he hid it for us to find. That's why the man with the clockwork hand gave the book to me. Dad *did* want us to come here."

I sat there thinking for a minute, trying to get it all straight, and then I started talking more quickly, my words racing to keep up with my thoughts. "I think he wanted us to see this, to see your city, but I think that he didn't want us to tell anyone about it. He wanted us to keep it a secret the way he had."

"*He* didn't tell anyone," Zander added. "We would have known if he had. Raleigh would have known."

Halla and Sukey were watching us.

"He must have convinced them—" I looked at Halla— "must have convinced you, your people, that he wouldn't tell. And they must have let him go."

She nodded just a bit, a movement of her head so slight that it could have been a twitch. But I didn't think so. "What?" I asked her. "What do you know? Did you know him?"

"She couldn't have known him," Sukey said. "You said he was here twenty years ago. She's our age."

Halla just listened.

"What?" I asked her again. "What do you know?"

She looked from me to Zander, studying Zander for quite a long time before she said, "Tell me about your father."

"He was an Explorer and a mapmaker," I said. "He's gone now, dead, but we found a map of Drowned Man's Canyon. And we heard a story about treasure. So we came looking."

"We had no idea you were here," Sukey said. "Honestly. It was just about the treasure."

"Other people have come looking for the treasure," she said. "We can't understand why. It's just *aurobel*." She shrugged. "There's so much of it here."

"Well, outside the canyon it's worth a lot," Zander told her. "A lot."

She looked at Zander, studying him again for a long moment.

"What was your father's name?" she asked finally.

"Alexander West."

"What are your names?"

Zander looked confused. "I'm Zander. This is my brother, Kit, and our friend Sukey. Our sister's name is M.K."

"What was your... what's the word? Nickname. What's your nickname. That your father called you?"

We all looked at each other. "He called us 'the Expeditioners',"
I told her finally.

She watched us for a long time. I couldn't believe how beautiful
she was, like a princess or a mythical queen, standing there with her
bow, her black dress all around her, her hair hanging down around
her face from the scuffle, her eyes intelligent, wondering. When she
turned them to me, I felt as though she was trying to learn about
me by watching me, by staring at my face. My glasses were slipping
down on my nose and I pushed them up, embarrassed for some
reason.

"I have something to show you," Halla said finally. "There's
something you really have to see."

Forty-five

"What is it?" Zander asked.

"I think you should wait and see it for yourselves."

"She might be tricking us," Sukey said. "This might just be her way of turning us in to the guards."

Halla hesitated. "It's about your father." She nodded at Zander. "When I first saw you, I thought you looked, what's the word... familiar."

"But you couldn't have met him," I said, then grinned. "Unless you're a really young-looking thirty-five-year-old."

She smiled. "No... but I think you'll want to see this."

"Then how do you know what he looks like?"

"I have to show you. And I think we can find your sister. It's dark now. We can sneak into the city while everyone sleeps. The guards will have given up on finding you during the night. They figure the cats will get you if you're still out there."

Sukey didn't say anything. But Zander and I nodded at each other and then at her, and somehow, without saying a word, we all agreed.

"Follow me," Halla said. "Stay right behind me and do what I say. If I see the guards coming, we'll have to hide."

"All right," Zander said after a minute. We didn't have any choice. We'd decided to trust Halla. M.K.'s life might depend on it.

Sukey hesitated, but the rest of us got up and followed Halla up the stairs. The sun had sunk behind the canyon walls while we'd been down below and we climbed into the now-dark night, the stars overhead and distant flickering torches from the cliff city the only lights we could see.

"I can't risk lighting a torch and being seen," Halla whispered, "but I know the way. Just follow me and we'll be okay."

We started into the black emptiness of the canyon, the lights from the cliff city a distant goal.

Forty-six

It was strange, walking along in the dark behind her, not knowing what was ahead. I searched the sky for Pucci a couple of times, but if he was out there, I couldn't see him. We walked for fifteen minutes before we found ourselves looking up at the city from below.

"The guards are posted up on the top of the buildings there," Halla whispered, pointing to the central part of the city. "If we stay right against the walls, they can't see us."

"What's the city called?" Zander asked in a low voice.

Halla hesitated for a moment and then said, "Oh, you mean... Ha'aftep Canyon," and it struck me how strange it would have been if some kid had come up to me all of a sudden, while I was standing on the road outside our house, and said, "So, what country is this?"

"There was a council meeting in the main part of the *Keedow's* administration," Hala whispered. "It must have gone late. Once they're gone, we'll be able to get in."

"What's the '*Keedow*'?" I whispered. "You keep talking about that."

She hesitated for a minute. "He's in charge of the canyon. He's the one who decides whether people can build and what they can grow. Whether they can marry. He makes all the decisions about when the ceiling closes and everything."

"And about what happens to people who wander into the canyon?" Sukey asked.

"Yes, I suppose he does. The old *Keedow* believed that there were some people we could trust with our secret. But the new one…" She hesitated again. "Well, he doesn't think we can trust anyone." She stopped. We were now almost directly underneath the cliff structures. "The thing I want you to see is in a part of the council administration that's been locked for a long time now, but I discovered it one day when I was exploring."

Halla looked both ways and pushed on a section of the wall. We heard the grinding of gears, stone on stone, then a door slowly opened in the rock. I stopped to inspect the gear mechanism so I could tell M.K. about it. They looked like huge, stone clockwork gears, the carved surfaces clicking against each other as the wall moved. Beyond the doorway, we could see stairs carved into the golden interior of the wall. Halla went first, lighting her torch once the door was closed behind us. Zander and I found our lights and put them on. As we climbed the stairs we could see that the white and golden walls had been carved with beautiful designs, suns and moons and stars and trees and birds. I stopped and stared.

The symbols were the ones Dad had used in the code that had led us to the map.

"How was all this constructed, anyway?" I asked as we walked along.

"A lot of it was done by hand, in the early days, anyway. But now they have drills." Halla pointed to more of the decorative carvings in the wall. "And other, how do you say... technologies. These were done four hundred years ago, when our people retreated into the canyon and made the hidden city."

"And what about the ceiling. Gears?" M.K. would have had a field day, figuring out how it all worked.

"That's right. There are over seven hundred that make the ceiling open and close."

We climbed the stairs and waited at the top until she looked out to make sure that there was no one coming. When she ducked back in and gestured for us to follow, we crept slowly along the hallway and followed her through a stone door that swung out into an enormous hallway.

The hallway was also carved out of the marbled golden rock, and there was a railing along one side. When Sukey and I peeked over we were looking down into a huge open area. There were fifty or so people down there, including ten or more guards, holding bows and arrows like Halla's and wearing black uniforms decorated with the bright bird feathers. We immediately ducked back.

"Follow me," Halla hissed, leading us into a small closet and shutting the door behind us. It was full of stone buckets and receptacles, like some kind of cleaning-supply closet. "We're going to have to wait until they're gone. Stay here and don't move or make a sound. I'm going to see if I can find your sister. Someone said she was being kept in the *Keedow*'s quarters, so I'm going to check there first." She slowly opened the door, looked outside, and then went out, shutting it carefully behind her.

"How is she going to get us past all those guards?" Sukey whispered. "I don't like this. Even if we find M.K., it's going to be impossible to get out of here alive."

"So what do you suggest that we do?" Zander asked her. "I don't think we have any choice here."

"I can't believe I let you crazy Wests talk me into this. My mother doesn't even know where I am and now I'm never going to see her again." She turned away, pretending to be looking at the wall, but before she did, I could see that there were tears in her eyes. I felt a deep knot of guilt in my stomach and I reached out to touch her shoulder. Zander frowned.

Suddenly we heard voices outside, speaking in the same language I'd heard through my spyglass. It didn't make any sense to me, but I could tell that they were coming closer and I put a finger up to my lips to tell the others to be quiet.

Then we could hear voices just outside the closet. We looked desperately around but there was nowhere to hide. I grabbed a stone bucket and Zander and Sukey did the same.

The door opened.

Two guards stood outside the door, looking in surprise at the three children hiding in the closet. "*Tafmay!*" one of them said. The other one turned his head and opened his mouth as if to call out, but before he could, we heard a loud *thunk* and he fell to the ground, the metal pot that had hit him on the head clattering to the floor and rolling away. Another one came down on the head of the other guard and he fell down, too, his head smacking against the stone floor. They were both out cold.

We looked up in surprise.

Standing behind them, holding her knife out in front of her, was M.K.

"I figured *you'd* be coming to rescue *me*," she said with a big grin, "not the other way around."

Forty-seven

"But where have you been? How did you get out?" I asked her once we'd dragged the two guards into another closet and hidden ourselves again.

We couldn't stop hugging her and finally she got tired of it, pushing us away and rubbing at a patch of dirt on her cheek.

"This huge cat attacked me," she said. "I got a couple good jabs in it with my knife, but before I could get back to you, some of those guys saw me and captured me. They took me through these secret tunnels in the walls of the canyon and brought me back here. By then I wasn't feeling very well. I was really hot and my arm was throbbing and I was so hungry I was feeling sort of dizzy. They gave me food and water and—this is the weird part—this guy wearing these long robes and all these feathers came in and looked at my arm. I don't know what he said, but someone brought him these little rocks, kind of like crystals, and he put them on my arm. It got very hot, almost like he was burning me, and then all of a sudden it was better. Look." She pulled up her sleeve and showed us the wound. The skin that had been swollen and infected only a couple of hours ago was now smooth and healed. You could see where the gash had been, though, because the surface of her upper arm was now strangely shimmering, as though her skin had been embedded with gold glitter.

I looked at Zander. This *was* weird. "And you feel okay?" I asked.

"Yeah, fine. Anyway, they wouldn't tell me what they were going to do with me or anything and they just kept asking me if I was alone. I figured I'd better get out of there, so I used my knife to wedge open a sort of vent in the ceiling and pulled myself up. It came out right over there in the hallway. I was about to see if I could find another one of those tunnels when I saw you and that girl come up the stairs. Then I saw the guards."

Sukey looked worried. "How did you keep your knife?" She asked M.K.

"I hid it in my shoe after I got the cat." M.K. grinned. "They never even looked. Who is that girl, anyway? Did she capture you? And where's Pucci?"

Before we could answer, we heard two low taps on the door and Halla's voice saying, "It's me. She's escaped. They're all looking for her. I told them that I saw her escaping the city and running into the canyon, so that should buy us some time to find her. All the guards are heading out after her."

She opened the door and smiled when she saw M.K.

"And this must be her," Halla said. We introduced them and Halla said, "We don't have much time. Follow me and don't let anyone see you." We went out into the hall again and she opened another door in the wall, waited for us to follow her in, and shut it quickly.

"Okay, let's go." We followed the long hallway for a few minutes before she pressed on an intricate carving on the wall. It was a relief sculpture depicting a large group of people climbing a staircase to the cliff city. There were more of the hieroglyphs that Dad had used for the code.

"I'm trying to remember where it is," she said. "I discovered it kind of by accident." She must have pushed the right spot because all of a sudden we heard a click and a door swung open and we were looking into a small room. Halla used her torch to light another, larger torch mounted on the wall, and as the room was suddenly bathed in light, we could see what was inside.

"Look," Zander whispered. "Look, Kit, look."

The walls were covered with maps—maps of the world, of the United States, of Latin America, of Europe and Asia. There were old maps of Arizona and maps of the New Lands, and maps of Ha'aftep Canyon and of Drowned Man's Canyon. They had been created with some kind of natural ink in various shades of blue and red and brown. They were beautiful.

"Where did these come from?" I asked.

"They used to be hanging out in the great hall," she said, "for everyone to see and study. But the new *Keedow* decided that it was too dangerous to have them out there, that it might make people want to go to all these places. So he hid them here, with... well, you can see for yourselves."

We had been so focused on the maps that we hadn't noticed the large table in the middle of the room. It was carved out of some kind of brown stone that I hadn't seen in the canyon, and the surface, when I touched it, was warm and smooth. There was a large golden frame in a stand on the table. Around the frame were little objects, stones and gold coins and little statues.

And in the frame was a portrait of Dad.

Forty-eight

He was a young man in the portrait, perhaps in his early twenties, and he was looking out across the canyon with the unmistakable silhouette of the cliff city behind him. It was beautifully painted with vivid, natural inks, and it gave me the eerie feeling of standing in front of a dead man. If I'd been alone, I think I would have touched the painting to make sure it was real.

"He was a hero to a lot of the people," Halla told us. "My father knew him, and he told me that it was because he came here and he showed us that we didn't have to be afraid of everyone. He told us about the world outside the canyon. He taught us English, so we would be prepared in case we were discovered. He drew some of the maps. He said he would help to protect us. But the new *Keedow* says that we can't trust anyone outside of the canyon. So he put this back here." She looked at the picture and then glanced shyly at Zander.

"You looked familiar when I first saw you. It took me a little while to figure out who you looked like. For a minute I thought you *were* him, but when you started talking about your father, I figured it out."

I had so many questions for her and I was trying to think of what to ask first when Zander said, "But I don't understand. What did Dad want us to *do* once we got here?"

"I think he wanted you to see the city. And I think he wanted you to have this," Halla said, opening a drawer in the table underneath Dad's portrait. She took out a leather pouch and handed it to me.

"What—?"

"Open it," she said.

I opened the pouch and took out a large envelope.

My heart sped up.

"It's Dad's writing," I said. And it was, his beautiful, scrolling letters running back and forth across the paper.

I ran a finger over the letters for a long moment.

"What does it say?" M.K. was almost jumping up and down, her little face turned up in anticipation. Even Sukey was looking at me with excitement.

"'*The Expeditioners*'," I read. I flipped it over and found a red wax seal over the flap, embossed with the same symbol that I'd seen tattooed on the arm of the man with the clockwork hand. Then I looked up at Halla. "You knew this was here and you never opened it?"

"It's not addressed to me," she said.

My hands shaking, everyone's eyes focused on me, I slid a finger under the thick seal and opened it up, taking out a piece of thick paper. I unfolded it.

"'*To my dearest Expeditioners,*'" I read. "'*Well done. This is the next piece of the puzzle. With all my love, Dad.*'"

There was a long silence.

"That's it?" Zander asked finally. "He doesn't explain anything?"

"What's the next piece of the puzzle?" M.K. asked. "What does he mean?"

"It's another map." I turned the paper around so that they could see it. It was a very simple map drawn in green and red ink, with a few words at the bottom. "That's all he writes and… it's just another… map." My disappointment was so sharp I could taste it, hard and bitter and acrid, like poisonous leaves, and I realized that a part of me had been expecting to find Dad himself in the canyon, grinning and laughing, ready to gather us up in a hug and tell us everything was going to be okay. Staring at the map, at his words, I felt the loss of him all over again. It was all I could do not to start crying.

Halla looked confused. "Is it a map of the canyon?" she asked.

"I don't know. No, I don't think so. It says 'Girafalco's Trench' at the bottom." It looked strange and somehow familiar to me, but I couldn't figure out why. "I would need to spend some time with an atlas, calculating the contours and the elevations, to figure out where it is. Even then I might not be able to." I turned the envelope over and ran a finger over the surface of the wax seal. "At least we know one thing now. He was a member of the Mapmakers' Guild. He must have been."

Sukey looked scared then. "You can't let BNDL find out."

"Maybe there's another message hidden in the map," Zander said.

I took out the spyglass and was studying the map through it when I heard the door click. "Someone's coming," Halla whispered. As quickly as I could, I shoved the map and the spyglass into the map pocket of my vest.

We heard the heavy sweep of the door across the stone floor and we all wheeled around and found ourselves face to face with a tall man a few years older than Zander. He was dressed in a black suit and top hat decorated with the bright feathers that also decorated the guards' helmets, and there was something about the way he stood that made me think he was an important man.

"Hanno! What are you doing here?" Halla asked him. She looked scared.

"I had a hunch," he said. "When I heard that a child with blond hair had been found in the canyon, I had a little idea about who it might be. I thought this might be a good place to look."

Forty-nine

He turned to us and put out a hand. Not knowing what else to do, we each shook it in turn. "Welcome to Ha'aftep Canyon. You must be the children of the great Explorer Alexander West. My name is Hanno. And I am the *Keedow* of the city. I see you've already met my sister here."

"Your sister?" Sukey asked him. "You mean..." She looked at Halla. "You're some kind of princess or something?"

Halla looked embarrassed. "Well, I wouldn't put it like that. My brother is the *Keedow* and—"

"And our father was the *Keedow* before him," Hanno said. Now that I knew they were brother and sister, I could see the family resemblance. They had the same cheekbones, the same dark eyes. There was something regal about the two of them, about the way they stood and talked and gestured.

"How long have your people lived here?" I asked him. Now that we'd seen what Halla wanted us to see and I knew M.K. was safe, I had so many questions about the city that I couldn't ask them fast enough. "How did my dad find you?"

"We've been living here for four hundred years," Hanno said. "Our ancestors came north from central Mexico to escape religious persecution. They believed they had been visited by people from another world, people who had taught them... well, advanced engineering principles, secrets of healing the human body, supernatural knowledge, I guess you could say. But they were ridiculed for their beliefs and they decided to find a place to live farther north. Turns out that the Spanish who were waiting for them were much worse. They tried to enslave them, so they retreated to what is now called Drowned Man's Canyon and lived in the canyon walls. But they knew it was only a matter of time before they were found, so they began to work on the tunnel, creating an underground system of caverns where all of the people could hide if needed. One day, a young man working on the tunnels broke through and found Ha'aftep Canyon and the vein of *aurobel*. Gold. And here we are."

"Did you know our father?" Zander asked him.

"No, I was only a small child when he came." Hanno turned to Halla. "You've done well," he said. "The girl wouldn't talk when they had her imprisoned. I assume you've learned how they got here?"

Halla nodded. "He"—she nodded toward Dad's portrait—"gave them a map."

He looked at us. "I knew our father shouldn't have trusted him. Why isn't he here himself?"

"Because he's dead," I told him.

"Ah." He waited a long moment and then said, "Our father would be sorry. He liked him very much. Our father was too trusting." He turned to Halla. "I hate to say it, but we're going to have to dispatch your friends as soon as possible. The girl seems to be a bit of an escape artist and we can't risk them making it back to the other side and telling everyone about us."

"'Dispatch'?" Sukey asked in a quiet voice. "As in... kill?"

"We have very humane methods. You can understand, can't you? I just can't risk the destruction of our city, of our way of life."

"But you let our father live? Why can't you let us live, too?" I asked.

"My father had different ideas than I do," Hanno said with a frown. "And your presence here proves that your father never should have been allowed to return to the other side."

"But we wouldn't tell anyone. We wouldn't say a word." Even as I said the words, though, I knew that he was right to be afraid. We might not say anything, but the Nackleys were just outside the canyon and if they captured us, they might make their way to the canyon just as we had. As long as they thought the treasure was still out there, the city and its people weren't safe.

"No," he said. "Halla, take them and lock them up in the prison room until we can arrange the procedure."

"Halla?" Zander said, turning to her. "You don't agree with him, do you? You trust us not to say anything?"

"Sorry," she said, bringing her bow up and aiming it at him. "I knew all along that I'd have to turn you in. I wanted to see what was in the envelope." She looked at her brother. "Nothing. Nothing of interest to us, anyway."

I caught her eye. "Why didn't you just open it?" I asked her again.

She looked horrified. "I told you, it wasn't addressed to me, was it? Now come on, keep walking and do exactly as I say."

We followed her out of the room and down the hallway.

"You're not really going to let him kill us?" Zander asked her once we were in the hallway. A couple of guards had fallen into step at a respectful distance behind us.

"Sorry," she said with an embarrassed shrug, "but you can't really have thought I was going to let you go." We walked in silence for a while and finally came out into the main hallway. A bunch of the guards were standing there and seemed to be waiting for us.

One of them said something to Halla in the language I didn't understand and followed us along the hallway to a door where a couple of other guards were posted. One of them opened the door and Halla pushed us inside.

"Again, I'm really sorry," she said. And then she was gone, the door shutting with a loud thud, followed by the clicking of what must have been three or four strong locks.

Fifty

"*Of course we can trust her. Why would she kill us? But she's so nice...,*" Sukey said in a deep voice that I suppose was meant to mimic Zander's. "I can't believe I went along with your stupid plan. Now we're going to be dead and it will probably be Halla who will put an arrow through your heart."

"Actually," I pointed out, "he said they had humane methods so I don't think it's going to be an arrow—"

"I don't care *how* they do it!" Sukey said. "They're still going to *do* it."

"This is just like the room they had me locked in," M.K. said, after inspecting the perimeter, "except it has bars and there's no vent. I don't see any way out of this."

"Great," Sukey said in a broken voice. "What are we going to do now?"

No one had an answer for her.

For a long time, we all just sat there. I don't know how many hours went by, but eventually M.K. lay down with her head in my lap and Zander and Sukey stretched out on the floor, too, and somehow, in spite of the direness of our situation, we all fell asleep.

I woke up first and reached over to lift Sukey's wrist so I could see her watch. Her skin was cool, and underneath my fingers I could feel the steady, insistent pulsing of her blood. I wanted to hold her hand again, to hold her, and to tell her how sorry I was that we'd gotten her into this, but her eyes fluttered and she looked up at me in alarm.

"It's just me," I whispered. "I was just checking the time."

"I thought it was them," she whispered back. "I thought this was it."

We stared at each other for a couple of long moments before she looked away, and then Zander and M.K. woke up, too, and the four of us sat there in silence, no one knowing what to say. It was M.K. who finally spoke. "I think I kind of thought that Dad was going to be here," she said in a quiet voice. "When I saw that envelope, I felt like he was playing a trick on us."

I nodded. "I know what you mean. It was like they were telling us he was dead all over again."

"Why would he do that?" Zander asked. "Why would he leave us a map with that note, and no explanation of any of it? How are we supposed to know what to do with it?"

"Maybe," Sukey said, "it's like with the other map. Maybe this

329

is only part of it and maybe there's another part somewhere that you have to find."

"I think you're right," I said, sitting up suddenly. "When you think about it, we were the only ones who could have figured it out. No one else knew about the double map, no one else knew about the Expeditioners. He didn't tell us anything more, because he didn't want anyone else to be able to figure it out. It's useless as it is, but there's something else to this map, a clue that only we can solve.

"Dad never told us that he'd been kicked out of the Expedition Society. Why? He never told us about the secret map. Why? He never said anything about being part of the Mapmakers' Guild. Why? There's some sort of big secret here. I think there must be other places, other secret places that Dad knew about, that maybe other people from the Mapmakers' Guild knew about, too. And for some reason, he wanted us to know about them. It was a secret map that led us here. Maybe the new one will lead us somewhere else important."

"Where do you think it is, Kit?" M.K. asked.

I studied the map closely. "'*Girafalco's Trench*'," I read out loud. There was something about the map that seemed off, even without knowing the location. The whole thing looked strangely smooth and the contour lines were odd. It was almost like...

"Well," I said, "I'm not positive, but I think this is a bathymetric map."

"A bathy what?" Zander asked.

Sukey sat up. "I studied this in my cartography class. He means it's an underwater map. Of the ocean floor."

"It could be a lake or river, too." The more I looked at it, the more convinced I was that Dad had given us an underwater map. "But the fact that it says 'Girafalco's Trench' makes me think it's the ocean. Trenches are in oceans. See how smooth it looks? I've seen one of these before. Zander and M.K., do you remember that map that Dad had hanging in the study? Of the Hemelman Trench? That's what made me think of it."

I had started to get excited about the map, about collecting atlases and other maps and figuring it out once we were out of the canyon. And then I remembered. I wouldn't be figuring anything out. I wouldn't be getting out of here alive.

I sat back down, tucking the map back into my vest. I knew the others had read my mind because they sat back down, too, and we all stared blankly at the wall, trying not to think of what was about to happen.

And then we heard Halla's voice outside the door. "The *Keedow* wants them taken to the death chamber," Halla told the guards outside. "I'll do it. Can you open the door, please?"

The locks clicked and we looked up from where we sat on the floor to see her standing there in the doorway. "Come on," she said, not meeting our eyes. "Follow me."

You would think if you had just heard someone say they were taking you to the "death chamber" that you would do whatever you had to do to get free, but we were shocked, I think, and we followed, walking obediently along until she looked quickly in both directions and then leaned into the wall. There was a clicking of gears and a disguised section of wall swung out. "Quick," she said. "In there. Right now." Dumbfounded, we did as she said and a second later heard the wall click back into place behind us.

"All right," she said. "I'm going to get you out of here."

"You're not going to kill us?" I was disoriented now, not sure what was happening, and even more confused by the strange low light in the tunnel. There seemed to be some torches here and there, but otherwise it was completely dark and I wasn't sure if we were headed up or down.

"Of course not," she said. "I had to pretend so Hanno wouldn't know I'm helping you. Follow me." We ran through the darkness, following Halla, and I remembered what M.K. had said about hidden tunnels behind the canyon walls and underneath the ground.

"Okay," she said finally, leading the way to the top of a short staircase lit by a large torch. "Here we are. We're near the mine."

"Wait," I said, stopping. "Hold on a minute."

"What?" Sukey asked. "What's wrong, Kit?" They were all looking at me.

"We haven't been thinking straight," I told them. "We haven't been..." I turned to Halla. "Your brother is right. *We're* not going to tell anyone, but that may not... that may not be enough. There are fifty or so people out there. Before, they were just looking for the treasure, but now they're looking for us, too. All they'd have to do would be to look behind the waterfall and find the cave. With the IronSteeds, with their equipment, They could come down in a glider or a SteamAirship, break open the ceiling... they'd have no trouble getting here."

"Well," Halla said confidently, "they wouldn't get very far."

I adjusted my vest. "No, you don't understand. They have weapons, airships, all kinds of tools. And if something happened to them, more people like them would follow. They're working with BNDL. That's a… a government agency. They would never give up on the treasure… or whatever else they're hoping to find here. Our father knew about your people and the canyon, but I think he had other secrets, too, and these people will do anything to find out what they are."

For the second time since I'd met her, Halla looked worried.

"They're bad, these people," I told her. I paced around the narrow tunnel for a minute. "I have an idea, though. What if we made it seem like these men—the Nackleys, they're called—what if we made it seem like they'd found the treasure, only in Drowned Man's Canyon? What if we put some gold, some of the treasure, there, and we led them there so they would find it?" I was making it up as I went, but I knew it was a pretty good idea.

"They'd stop looking," Sukey said. "No one would ever come here looking for it again. You'd be safe forever!"

"That's pretty brilliant," Zander said, grinning at me. "I can't believe you thought of it."

"Thanks a lot." Somehow, Zander making fun of my intelligence was the most comforting thing I could have heard. I turned to Halla. "Would you mind if we take some of the gold?"

She thought for a minute. "If anyone finds out, I'll have to say you overpowered me and stole it. And you're going to need horses and saddlebags to carry it out. But I can get you some, I think."

Fifty-one

Twenty minutes later, we heard Halla whistling, and we came out of the tunnel into the darkness to find her standing there, leading four sturdy-looking mares and holding a torch.

"Pucci!" M.K. called when she saw him fly down to greet us.

"He was waiting for you by the mine," Halla told us. "I told him you were okay and I think he understood me."

Pucci landed on Zander's shoulder and nuzzled his cheek, making his happy little chuckling noise. And then, to everyone's surprise, he hopped over onto Sukey's shoulder and did the same.

She broke into a grin. "I'm happy to see you, too, Pucci," she told him, giving him a little scratch on his head.

"We can use the light to load these saddlebags," Halla told us. "The guards are out at the other end of the canyon. They won't be back for ten minutes."

We started bringing the gold up from the mine, piling the gold bars into the leather bags and then scattering the ingots and statues and jewelry on top. Even when we'd almost filled the bags, the mine was still full of gold.

As we worked, I thought of something and I looked up at Halla. "Your ancestors were the ones who nursed the conquistadores, the Spanish men who brought all this gold into the canyon."

"That's right," she said. "They buried them as far away from the canyon as they could, in case someone was looking for them."

"And what about Dan Foley? I've been wondering about him. Did he make it back here? Did he return to the treasure?"

"No," she said. "There was a flood. They say it was one of the biggest ever in the history of the canyon. He drowned in the caverns. My ancestors found his body and buried him here in the canyon. They weren't leaving as much by then. There were too many stories about us, too many people getting curious about where those stories came from, and they didn't want anyone finding the body and looking around too much."

I imagined a lonely grave, a wooden cross marking it. Poor Dan Foley. He'd found his golden treasure and he didn't even know it.

We kept loading, and when we were finished, we buckled the saddlebags in place. Halla led the way over to the solid rock wall next to the waterfall. As we watched, she pressed on a small piece of quartz embedded in the wall and a huge door swung open to reveal another large cavern that seemed to rise upward into the rock.

"It's a shortcut, to get you past the waterfall, and it meets up with the other tunnel before the gertoms," she said. "You'll be fine on the horses. The birds don't like them and the cats usually don't mess with them if there's more than one. Besides," she grinned and handed Sukey her pistol, "you've got this." Then she pointed to the knife, which was back on M.K.'s belt. "And that."

"Thank you," I said.

"Thank *you.*" She leaned over to kiss me on the cheek and I was glad that it was dark because I'm sure I blushed, though I would have loved to have seen Zander blush when she did the same to him. She kissed M.K. and Sukey, too, and we mounted the horses and waved to her. Pucci lighted on her shoulder for a moment before taking up his post on Zander's saddle.

"Goodbye and good luck," she called. "Maybe I'll come over to the other side someday and find you. If the *Keedow* ever lets me."

"You should do that," Zander and I said at the same time.

"West," Zander said. "That's *W-e-s-t.* We live on Oceania…"

"Oh for god's sake," Sukey muttered. "We better get going."

We waved again and as we started into the cavern, I turned around one last time and, in the dim light from my vest light, saw Halla standing against the black space of the canyon. Her expression was a mystery to me and when I turned around again, she was gone.

We rode for hours in silence, exhausted, not wanting to break the spell of everything we'd seen. I think I must have fallen asleep at some point, because when I woke up, we were almost back to the main part of the cavern. This tunnel traveled deep down into the rocks, and over my head I could hear the underground river running fast.

"I think we can make it," I told them. "If we can get out of the caverns without the Nackleys seeing us, then I think we can do this. The trick is to redirect them. We'll have to get back to the cave and pile all of this gold up, cover it with dirt and sticks, make it look like it's been there for a while. Then I think they'll believe that it's the real mine. The cave is high enough up in the canyon walls that it's possible it's never been found. Then we'll just have to figure out a way to make them think they've found it. And then they won't go looking for the people—"

"Not so fast," came a voice out of the darkness.

Fifty-two

We pulled our horses up and looked into the blackness ahead to find Tex, standing next to his horse and grinning at us like a cat who'd just caught a mouse.

"Get down off the horses," he said in a grim, low voice. "Get down now and you won't get hurt."

"What are you doing here?" Zander asked him.

"I could ask the same of you," he said. He raised his hand then and we could see he was holding a pistol.

"What do you want?" Zander asked. I knew he was stalling for time.

"I want to know what you saw," Tex growled. "Did you find the treasure? You were talking about gold. Tell me what you found. Tell me what you saw."

"We didn't find anything, you no-good crook!" M.K. spat on

the ground, near his horse's feet. I thought I saw Tex smile, but I couldn't be sure in the dark tunnel.

Zander whistled then and Pucci flew up in the air, squawking and flapping his wings, dive-bombing Tex's face, the metal talons out and ready to strike.

"Get that bird away!" he yelled, waving his arms, and the pistol, around wildly. "I'll shoot him, I swear I will."

"We've got to lead him away from the canyon," I whispered to the others. "We can't let him go any farther."

"So what are we waiting for?" Sukey asked. "Ride!"

At the exact same moment, we all dug our heels into our horses and all four took off as though they'd been stung. We careened through the cavern, the light from our vest lights bouncing off the walls here and there, the horses' hooves clattering on the stone. A couple of times, I felt my horse's hooves slide on the cavern floor and she almost lost her footing, just barely managing. I was aware of Zander and M.K. ahead of me and Sukey behind me, and of Tex's horse behind her, its hooves also slapping on the stone. It felt like a carnival ride, hurtling through the darkness.

We rode on.

It seemed like no time at all before we were back in the main part of the caverns, racing away from the underground river and then entering the part of the caverns inhabited by the slugs.

It was the slugs that brought us down.

As the rushing of the underground river dissipated and we entered the narrower section of the caverns where the slugs were,

I could see their glowing green light all over the floor, feel my horse scramble to keep her footing on the slimy surface, and I called out to warn the others.

But I was too late. As we came clattering to the end of the tunnel, we could hear the waterfall just outside and the lights on our vests bounced along the slug-covered walls. Zander and M.K. and I managed to stay astride our horses, but Sukey's horse slid and she went tumbling off. Her horse got back on its feet, but Sukey was lying on the ground, holding her knee.

"I'm sorry," she said, looking up at me.

I pulled my horse up to try to help her. "Here," I said, reaching down. "Grab my hand. We're almost to the end of the tunnel."

But Tex was already on top of us.

"Stop right there," he called out, pulling up his horse.

From the ground, Sukey managed to toss her pistol to Zander and his voice came out of the almost-darkness. "I'm not afraid to shoot."

He already had it out and pointed at Tex. There was just enough illumination from M.K.'s light that I could see his mouth fixed in a serious line, his eyes narrowed.

"Neither am I. So put that down," Tex said. "You wouldn't want it to go off by accident."

"It wouldn't be an accident," Zander said.

Pucci was perched on Zander's saddle and he made little worried sounds in the back of his throat, but he didn't try to attack Tex again.

Tex dismounted and reached down to pull Sukey to a standing

position, holding her in front of him with her arms pinned behind her back. "Well, we wouldn't want there to be any other *accidents*," he said. "Drop your weapon. I want to know what you know about this canyon."

I looked at Sukey. She was terrified, her amber eyes wide, though I could tell she was trying to seem brave by struggling against Tex's grip. She must have realized she didn't have a chance, because she finally gave up, standing quietly.

"Let her go!" M.K. cried out.

Tex and Zander held the weapons on each other, neither of them moving.

"Let them go," Sukey said. "You can do whatever you want with me, turn me over to BNDL, lock me up in a BNDL prison forever. I'm just a crazy Neo. No one'll care. Just leave them alone. They don't know anything."

"Get down off your horses," Tex said.

There was a long silence and finally Zander said, "Do it." We got down and Zander looked at Sukey and then back at Tex.

"Leave her alone, you big bully!" M.K. said, going for her knife.

"Hold her back," Zander whispered and I grabbed her, holding her while she struggled against my grip.

He and Tex just stood there opposite each other, neither one of them moving, the weapons locked on each other. I had the feeling it could go on forever, the two of them standing there, neither one willing to give up.

But after a couple of minutes, Zander dropped the pistol on the

ground and said, "Let her go," in a quiet voice. Tex let go of her and Sukey struggled away and came to stand next to us, glaring at Tex.

He scowled at us. "What did you mean when you said they'll never find the people? Did you see someone in the city in the canyon? Did you see the people?"

My heart sank. If he knew about the city and the fact that there were people there, it was only a matter of time before the Nackleys did, too.

There was a long silence and then I said to Tex, "You can't tell the Nackleys about the canyon. You can't. Do you know what will happen to these people? My father was an Explorer and he always said that Explorers had done more harm to the world than good. He always said—"

His face like a mask, just his eyes and mouth illuminated in the dark cavern, Tex grinned. I could hear laughter in his voice as he finished my sentence, "—that the world would be a lot better off if all the Explorers had just sat at home and smoked their pipes in their armchairs. He couldn't resist himself, though, could he?"

He laughed again. "Nope, my friend Alex could never resist a good adventure."

Fifty-three

We were speechless for a couple of long moments.

"You knew Dad?" I asked finally, when I'd found my voice.

"I did," Tex said, gruff again, as he put his pistol away.

"But you're working for the Nackleys," Zander said. "Aren't you?"

"I had to make sure that they didn't find the canyon. I knew Leo from the Academy, and when he told me he had new information about the treasure, I figured he must have gotten hold of one of Alexander's maps somehow. Now we've got to get out of here. They're all after you and we can't risk leading them into the caverns." He picked up a length of rope that had fallen on the ground and mounted his horse. "Follow me," he said. "We'll talk once we're back in Drowned Man's Canyon."

Not sure what else to do, we all mounted our horses and followed Tex back through the tunnel.

"We're going the wrong way," M.K. said. "Aren't we supposed to be heading back toward the waterfall?"

"Just follow me," Tex said in a gruff voice.

I was starting to get nervous, when he pulled his horse up and reached out to push on the wall of the tunnel. A door, carved into the rock like the ones in the secret canyon, opened and we followed him out into blindingly bright light. It was late morning now, already hot, the sun blazing overhead in a blue sky. Pucci seemed glad to be back in the open and he soared high above us, making happy circles in the sky.

"This is the door I saw you disappear into!" I told him. "The day they caught us and brought us to the camp."

"I thought someone followed me that day. There are hidden doors like this one all over the canyon. That's where we get all the stories about aliens and monsters sneaking out of the walls of the canyon. The people of the canyon would wear costumes when they had to come out to hunt or forage during droughts or when crops failed.

"Now," he continued, "your idea about the gold is a good one, but we've got to move fast. They've got scouts all over the canyon. I'll ride ahead and—"

But we weren't going to let him get away without telling us more about Dad.

"How did you know Dad?" Zander asked. I could hear that he was still suspicious of Tex. "I don't understand."

"I went to the Academy with Alexander and Leo Nackley and Raleigh McAdam," Tex said. "My last name is—"

And suddenly I realized that we had seen a picture of him, a younger version, without a beard.

"John Beauregard," I said. "You're John Beauregard?"

"That's right. I grew up in Texas and when I moved out here they started calling me by my childhood nickname, Tex. Your father found Ha'aftep Canyon and entrusted me with his secret."

"Was this when you came here with Raleigh and Leo Nackley?" I asked.

"No, they didn't have any luck on that trip. Alex came back a couple of years later and discovered it on his own. Then he brought me the next year, just before he married your mom. Raleigh was spending all of his time in the North Polar Sea by then or he would have been with us. We no longer trusted Nackley, so we didn't ask him along. Your father believed that we'd been close to finding Dan Foley's mine on that first trip. He studied the maps and had an idea about the waterfall. Turned out he was right."

"So he found the canyon and the people and the two of you agreed not to tell anyone?" Zander asked.

"They didn't just agree not to tell anyone," I said. "They agreed to protect the people and the canyon."

Tex hesitated. "That's right. And I'm assuming you somehow found the secret map. But that's a story for another day. We've got to get out of here before anyone sees us."

But there was so much more I wanted to know. "Wait, how long have you been out here?" I asked. "Dad never talked about you. Did he know you live here?"

"He knew." Tex paused, then said, "There's a lot that you kids don't know about your father. It would be too dangerous for you to know."

"What?" Sukey asked him. "What would be too dangerous?"

"Are you a member of the Mapmakers' Guild?" I asked him.

He paused for a moment. Then his face sagged and he said, "I told you, it's just too dangerous."

Suddenly I was mad: at Tex for being so cagey, at the Nackleys, at Dad for getting us into this. "I'm tired of everyone saying this thing is too dangerous!" I shouted at him. "You don't think we're already in danger? We're carrying a couple hundred million Allied Dollars' worth of gold, and I'm carrying two maps now, and there are a whole bunch of people right over there who would kill us to get them. We're wanted by the police and BNDL for assaulting those agents. What is going on here? What did Dad know? Why did he leave a map for us in the secret canyon? What does he expect us to do with it?"

Tex whipped around, almost falling off his horse. "He left a map for you in the canyon? Of what?"

"You didn't know?"

He shook his head.

It was M.K. who asked the question that was on all our minds. "Those government guys said he did something illegal, that he took money from some bad guys in Munopia. They said he broke laws. Is that true?"

Tex finally stopped, turning his horse around so he could look at us. "Your dad was a great man," he said. "Everything your dad did, there was a good reason for it. Just remember that."

It was what Sukey had said as we were hiking through the caverns, and when I turned to look at her, she raised her eyebrows. "Yeah, you don't have to listen to me next time," she said with a little smile. "Clearly I have no idea what I'm talking about."

Tex hesitated again. "We have a lot to talk about, but I think you'll agree that now is not the time. Let's wait until we're all safely out of here. As I said, I think the plan's a good one. But you're going to need my help. It's a circus at the camp. Leo's got a newspaper reporter out there, ready to report his find. I don't know what Foley and Mountmorris will do when they see you." He looked serious for a moment. "They're very, very powerful men, you know. They'll do anything to protect what they see as ANDLC or BNDL property. And they have the full support of the government. Don't ever forget that."

He took a flask out of his saddlebag, unscrewing the cap and taking a long swig. "Now, let's get up there and fabricate an archaeological wonder of the world. They'll be riding through with the reporter later this morning. I think I can get them to go up there and take a look." He turned his horse in the direction of the cave, and rode off into the early morning light, the rest of us following along behind.

Fifty-four

The stolen horses had taken off, but Sukey's backpack was still in the cave and it didn't look like anyone had been there while we'd been gone. Pucci hopped around, pecking at the ground and tilting his head as though he was remembering that we'd been here before. Tex dismounted and checked it out. "It'll do," he said. "Let's unload it into that corner and then cover it up as best we can. It has to look like it's been here for over a hundred years, getting dusty, leaves and sticks and debris blown over it."

We did as he said, piling up the bars and then scattering the rest of the items around on the ground and covering them with dirt and rocks. We left a few pieces of gold showing through.

"What do you think?" Sukey asked.

I studied it. "I don't know. Obviously, it's not a mine. An expert would be able to tell that it hasn't been here very long, but

I'm guessing the Nackleys will be willing to overlook that. This is probably millions of dollars of gold. Think how many airships they can build with this."

"You're right," Tex said. "In any case, they ought to be able to figure out that it's Dan Foley's treasure. Hopefully that will be enough to keep them from looking for it anymore." He mounted his horse and took the Ha'aftep Canyon horses' bridles in his hand. "I'm going to take them back to the tunnel so they can make their way back to the canyon. You all sit tight. I've got to figure out how to get you back to Azure Canyon. But we've got time. The Nackleys shouldn't be coming through for an hour or so."

He started to ride away, then turned back and called to us, "Remember, we have to protect the maps at all costs. It's what your dad would have wanted." And then he was gone.

"How are we going to get home," M.K. asked, "if he can even get us back to Azure Canyon?"

"We'll have to hike out," Sukey said. "But then my glider's waiting for us up there."

"We may not have a home to go back to," I pointed out. "If they don't throw us in jail, they'll probably send us off to some orphanage or military school somewhere. We'll end up like poor Pucci."

Sukey looked worried. "But maybe they'll send you to the Academy."

"Hah! Wouldn't that be nice?" I rolled my eyes.

"Or maybe we could live with Raleigh," M.K. said hopefully.

Zander stood up. "Did you just hear something?"

I listened for a moment. "No... at least, I don't think so. Maybe it's Tex."

"Pucci?" Pucci flew up into the air and did a quick circle, calling down a warning.

"It's not Tex," Zander said. "It sounded like..." And then we could all hear it, a loud clanking and stomping that echoed around the canyon.

"IronSteeds!" Sukey jumped up. "Come on, we've got to get out of here." She grabbed her backpack and we threw the last couple of sticks over the gold.

But as we ran out of the cave, someone in the party saw us and raised the alarm. They blew an air horn and we heard Leo Nackley's voice come over a megaphone, "It's the West children! Up in the rocks! Someone detain them!"

"What do we do?" I whispered.

Zander looked panicked. We were high up in the rocks and unless we could figure out how to fly in the next ten minutes, there was no way to get past them. "I don't know. Maybe get them to look in the cave and then try to get away once they find the gold?"

"I've got my pistol," Sukey whispered.

Zander reached out and put a hand on her arm. "Unfortunately, they've got more," he said. "Don't pull it on them, Sukey. Please."

She nodded and we all watched as a group of six agents rushed up the path toward us, Leo and Lazlo Nackley behind them. There was nothing we could do. The agents fanned out to prevent us from escaping and the Nackleys approached us.

"Get back to camp and tell Mr. Foley we've found the children!" someone yelled as we stood there, just waiting for them. Pucci, who had been sitting on a rock jutting out over the canyon, rose into the air and took off in the direction of the waterfall, probably to alert Tex. I scanned the crowd below and recognized Dolly Frost, the reporter for the *Times*, and Jec Banton, along with Agents Wolff and DeRosa and more of the BNDL agents from the camp. Everyone was looking up at us, waiting to see what was going to happen.

"What are you doing up there?" Leo Nackley demanded. "Where have you been all this time? You're in big trouble, you know."

Lazlo stood behind him, his back very straight, his eyes steady on us. He had a suspicious look that put me on my guard.

"Come on! Where have you been?" Leo Nackley's face was bright red and there was a thin line of sweat running down one cheek.

At that moment, Zander did something brilliant. I was watching his face as he said, "Nothing. Nothing at all," and saw how his left eye twitched, just a little, and he gave a little glance back toward the cave.

"What?" Leo Nackley demanded. Then he lowered his voice. "Did you find something in that cave?"

"No, no. Don't go… There's nothing there. Nothing there at all," Zander stammered. We all stood there, trying to look guilty.

"Go look in the cave, Lazlo," Leo Nackley said in a low voice before turning around and saying to the agents, "Detain these children."

"But…," Lazlo Nackley started before doing as his father had told him.

The agents stepped forward. "Discreetly!" Leo Nackley hissed, glancing down nervously at the reporter. Agent DeRosa stood next to me, making it clear that I wasn't to move a muscle.

Lazlo glanced at us again, then made his way into the cave and we all stood there anxiously, waiting. A few minutes later, he came out and waved his father over.

"What is it?" I heard Leo Nackley ask.

"Well, it's… gold, all right," Lazlo said in a low voice. "But I don't know. It doesn't look quite right."

I felt my stomach sink, but then Leo Nackley went in to take a look himself and when he came out, he was grinning from ear to ear.

"My boy has found it!" he announced. "He's found the treasure of Drowned Man's Canyon!"

Things started to happen very fast then. "Get all these people out of here!" Leo Nackley shouted to someone and the agents hustled us along the path to a spot up above the cave. They made us sit down on a bit of rock jutting out from the wall of the canyon, probably to dissuade us from trying to escape, and we watched as the drama unfolded below. Leo Nackley said to the agents, "Mr. Foley and Mr. Mountmorris want to talk to them. Keep an eye on them until they arrive. I've got to go talk to that reporter. If she tries to take any pictures, make up something to get the camera away."

Then he gave us a thoughtful little smile and headed back down toward the cave, where we could hear everything he said to the reporter, Dolly Frost, as she jotted notes down on a notepad. "This is it, the fabled golden treasure of Drowned Man's Canyon. This is

very close to an area that Lazlo has already identified as an excellent possibility for the old mine. We are working under the assumption that Dan Foley moved the gold from the mine to this ancient cliff dwelling. Lazlo, tell Miss Frost how you identified the cave as a likely site for the gold."

Lazlo, embarrassed, mumbled something about seeing the gold glinting in the sun.

"But I thought your father said the gold had been hidden inside the cave for more than a hundred years," Dolly Frost asked suspiciously. "How could you have seen it glinting in the sun?"

"It must have been the angle," Lazlo said after a long moment. "It's low on the horizon."

"And how much do you believe the gold is worth?" Dolly Frost asked him.

Lazlo looked up at us then and I met his eyes for a minute. There was something on his face that I couldn't read, and then he looked away and said, "I'm sure there are experts calculating its worth right now, Miss Frost. All I'm concerned about is the archaeological value of the find and knowing that my country and its allies will be made stronger and more secure with this gold."

And then the BNDL agents were stringing orange rope around the cave and hanging up huge signs that proclaimed By Order of the Bureau of Newly Discovered Lands. U.S. Federal Government Property—Trespassers Prosecuted to the Full Extent of the Law.

"I'm thirsty," M.K. whispered to me.

"Me, too," I told her. The sun was very, very bright and there wasn't a bit of shade where we sat on the rocks.

"Could you at least get us something to drink?" Sukey asked Agent Wolff. "It's really hot out here."

Down below, Leo Nackley was telling the reporter that Lazlo's find was the greatest since the discovery of the Giant Ruby of Tipitopo. "We'll be taking it out of the canyon over the next couple of days," he said. "We'll wait until we're back home to do a thorough examination. It must be protected from the elements and... thieves."

"Shut up!" Agent Wolff barked at Sukey. "You're supposed to sit here and be quiet."

"But—"

"No, no. Agent Wolff," a deep voice said behind us, "by all means, give the children some water. Then we're going to search them and have a little talk. They got away from me once. They're not going to do it again."

We looked up to see Francis Foley and Mr. Mountmorris standing behind her.

Fifty-five

All I could think of was Tex's voice saying, "We have to protect the maps at all costs."

I tried to escape.

Turning away from Zander and the others, I darted away from the agent who was guarding me, trying to run around the other agents and head higher up the path. I had the idea that I might be able to climb up the rocks, find a route up there to another one of the caves where I could destroy the maps, to keep them from ever being found. They would catch me eventually. I knew that. But maybe I could stop them from getting the maps.

It wasn't a bad plan. I made it about two hundred yards up the wall of the canyon by sheer will, scrambling and looking for footholds and handholds while they shouted at me from below. I could see a small cave up ahead and I thought I could make it, but then my foot slipped on the rock and I went down hard, rolling twenty feet on hard ground.

Everything spun for a moment. My head throbbed.

I heard Sukey call my name and then I looked up and saw the agents rushing toward me. Drops of sweat stung my eyes. My glasses had fallen off and everything was a little blurry, but I could see Francis Foley's sharp, predatory eyes. He was angry now. I could see it. It transformed his face, made it duller and more dangerous, the face of someone who would do anything to get what he wanted.

"Don't bother trying to get away," he said in a low voice. "We will always catch you."

Behind him, Mr. Mountmorris was a green blur.

I scrambled in the dirt for my glasses. I put them on and, in a panicked, heart-thumping moment, saw the end of the pistol that Foley was pointing at me. And then I heard the sharp *crack* that echoed off the walls of the canyon.

I was sure that I'd been shot. I even closed my eyes, but then I looked up to see Tex standing there, pointing his own pistol up into the air.

"What's going on here?" he asked.

Francis Foley kept his weapon out in front of him. "Mr. Tex," he said in a low, even voice, "we're doing just fine, but thank you for your concern. These children have been trespassing on an archaeological site now controlled by BNDL. We're detaining them until we can place them in responsible care. But thank you for checking."

Tex was still holding his pistol and when I looked up at Francis Foley, he seemed wary of the grizzled cowboy.

I met Tex's eyes and he gave a tiny nod, as if to say, "It'll be okay." I don't know if Foley saw it or not, but he kept his own weapon up and he said, "Please wait down below, Mr. Tex. This is none of your business."

Tex stepped forward and pointed his pistol at Foley.

"Leave them alone, Foley," Tex said in a low voice. "You don't need them. You found the gold. Besides, you said yourself there was nothing on the map. Let them go and we won't tell anyone that the Nackleys didn't find it themselves."

"I don't know why you care, Mr. Tex," Foley said. "But I suggest you do as I say." Foley barked at the agent who was holding me. "The map! Find it now!"

"No," Tex said.

To this day, I'm still not entirely sure what happened next, whether Tex moved first or Foley did. I heard a shot and then another, and then, as we watched in horror, Tex's arms windmilled as though he was trying to get his balance, and his pistol fell to the ground. He was standing at the very edge of the path and he stumbled once, then twice, struggling to keep his footing. Far below him was the floor of the canyon, jagged rocks lining the bottom of the wall.

"Good god, Francis!" Mr. Mountmorris said.

"He tried to shoot me," Foley yelled down to the group below. "He wanted the gold for himself!"

"That's not—" Sukey started to call out, but the agents jumped on her, covering her mouth, and we all watched as Tex, a red stain spreading across the front of his shirt, lost his balance and fell over the edge of the path, landing on the ground below us. I think I must have closed my eyes as he fell, because the next thing I remember is looking down to see him lying there, a dark spot against the pale ground.

He wasn't moving at all. His eyes were blank, staring up at the sky, at the bright sun and the clouds drifting toward the east, toward Ha'aftep Canyon and the people there who didn't know their protector was gone.

Fifty-six

And then all hell broke loose.

Suddenly it seemed like the canyon was full of people and IronSteeds. I heard Foley snarl at Agent Wolff, "Get them out of here. Do not let them get away."

"Mr. Foley? Mr. Mountmorris?" We all turned around to see Dolly Frost below us, making her way up the path toward Zander, Sukey, and M.K. "What's going on here?" she called up. "Who are these children? Who is the man who was killed back there?"

"Get them out of here before that damned woman gets to them," Foley hissed. He looked furious, his sharky eyes small in his red face.

"Mr. Foley, Mr. Foley," Dolly Frost was calling out.

"Get this one out of here, too," Foley said, nodding to me.

I didn't have much time. I looked up and saw Zander, the spitting image of Dad, struggling with Agent DeRosa, and M.K., who would

have come to my aid with her little knife if she could have gotten away from Agent Wolff. And Sukey. Sukey was trying to get free, calling my name, and I remembered how it had felt to hold her, to keep her safe and warm for just a minute, even though everything had fallen apart.

"What is going on here?" Dolly Frost was asking.

She had almost reached us. I knew this was it. I thought of Dad and I reached up, grabbing Foley's jacket and pulling him down so he could hear me. Mr. Mountmorris was behind him and I said to them, "Listen to me. Listen hard. There isn't much time. You know as well as I do that Lazlo Nackley didn't find that gold. You know as well as I do that we used my dad's map to find it. Now, we're willing to let the Nackleys take the credit. But you have to let us go. You and BNDL got what you wanted. The gold. You can use it to buy airships and send Explorers all over the world. So let us go. Sukey Neville, too. Promise me nothing will happen to us and we'll forget about everything we just saw. If that reporter wasn't here, you might get away with it. But she is. And I don't care how much power you have, you might be able to claim you killed Tex in self-defense, but you can't explain away a dead reporter. There are too many people here."

I was breathing hard, my head throbbing where I'd hit it on a rock.

"Mr. Foley, I demand an answer," Dolly Frost was saying.

He stared at me for another long moment and then he looked at Mr. Mountmorris, who nodded, holding my gaze for a minute.

I stood up, my legs shaking. "I'll talk to you," I called down to her. "I saw everything."

"What happened?" she asked. "Who shot that man? Why are you children here?" She wasn't much older than we were, tall with blond hair, wearing beige Explorer's leggings and a vest with lots of pockets. The vest looked brand-new. "Mr. Foley, there's a dead man down there and I demand to know what's going on."

Foley turned away and reached out a hand to help her climb up to where we were. "Oh, these children are... they were just camping down here and we had a... a misunderstanding. You know, it's very important for BNDL to secure any potential find, for the safety of everyone involved, of course. There's been a lot of concern for their safety and I just wanted to make sure they were quite all right. Very unfortunate, the accident with Mr. Tex. I'm sorry they had to see that. But we'll make sure they get home safely. I'm going to accompany them myself."

Dolly Frost still looked skeptical. She looked right at me. "Is that true?" she asked. "Was that man trying to take the gold? Did he shoot at Mr. Foley? Mr. Nackley is claiming that his son is the rightful discoverer of the treasure of Drowned Man's Canyon. But you seem to have been here first. Did you find the treasure before the Nackleys got there? Did you see the gold?"

"Oh no," I told her. "Lazlo Nackley's the one who found it. We were just hiking past. We never saw the gold. And Mr. Foley's right. That man was working for Mr. Nackley, but he must have wanted the gold for himself. I saw him trying to take it."

"And who are you? What's your name?"

She had the notepad out and she was writing down everything I said.

"Christopher West," I told her. "My father was the great Explorer of the Realm Alexander West."

I looked up at Mr. Mountmorris. I was so tired, I could barely form the words. "And now, if you don't mind, we'd like to go home."

Fifty-seven

Mr. Mountmorris came to see us on a still, hot day in August that smelled like the end of summer.

It had been a strange couple of months, full of nightmares in which I relived Tex's death over and over again, and other dreams in which Halla spoke to me in exotic languages I didn't understand, or giant cougars leaped at me from behind boulders. Every day, alongside stories about Simeria and aggression by the Indorustan Empire, the newspapers had reported new details of the Nackleys' find, and if any of the archaeological experts they'd called in had any doubts, they weren't saying so publicly. I had gotten tired of seeing Lazlo's smug face staring out at me from the morning paper with the headlines calling him a "National Hero" and "Brave Boy Explorer." There hadn't been anything about Tex's death; they'd managed to keep it quiet.

When we went out to the market now, I always had the feeling that someone was watching us. Once, I'd turned quickly and caught sight of a figure ducking into an alleyway, but no one had tried to contact us, and though we'd turned the house upside down looking, we hadn't found another map.

In July, Raleigh had come for a visit and never left. He loved the beach and he would go out every morning to walk on his IronLegs, still getting the feel of his new body. He'd gotten better and better on them and he could be found most evenings puttering about the kitchen, making us dinner, telling us stories about Dad, Pucci watching him from his perch on a curtain rod and sneaking bites of meat or salad when Raleigh wasn't looking.

Now it was August and Sukey had come out from the city for the day for a picnic. She'd be leaving for the Academy soon and we knew it would be a while before she'd be able to visit. She'd brought some lunch: Fazian beef sandwiches she'd lifted from the Expedition Society and Deloian cocoa cake that had been in Delilah's Explorer's rations that week. Raleigh had baked bread and we had plums from the plum tree in our yard.

We'd been sitting on a blanket on the beach, eating and looking at a photograph of our parents that I'd found up in the attic. I'd brought it down to show Sukey because she wanted to know what Nika had looked like. I still couldn't think of her as Mom or Mother. I could barely remember far enough back to when I'd called her that, but Raleigh's stories had stuck in my mind and I thought of her now as Nika, intelligent, beautiful, frozen in time. The photograph was a wedding portrait, printed at one of the government-approved photography studios, and it showed them hand in hand, standing in a field in their fancy clothes, Dad in a gray morning suit and Nika in a long, lacy white dress with a high neck and short sleeves. Raleigh had cried when I showed it to him, but he'd told us more stories, about how they'd met at the Expedition Society and how he had been the best man at their wedding. He'd told me about how he thought her father had been a Muller Machine engineer, and that was how she knew so much about them, but he didn't know for sure.

"You look so much like her, Kit," Sukey told me, running a finger over Nika's dark hair, cut in bangs like M.K.'s in the picture. I'd been staring at it ever since I'd found it, at Dad's happy smile and Nika's level, contented gaze.

Sukey put it down, folding her hands together behind her head and stretching back out on the sand. We all stared at the sky for a long time and then she said, "I just keep thinking about Tex, lying there on the ground. It doesn't seem right that they got away with killing him when he was just protecting us."

"He was protecting me," I pointed out. "But mostly he was protecting the maps."

"But we have to tell someone," Sukey said. "We have to tell someone the truth. They can't just... murder people."

"You know we can't," I told her, as gently as I could. "This is the only way to protect the canyon."

"He's right," Zander said. "I bet if we could ask Tex, it's what he'd want us to do."

"How's it going with the map?" Sukey asked me.

"Nothing yet," I told her grumpily. "I haven't found any references to Girafalco's Trench anywhere. But even if I do figure it out, I don't know what we can do about it."

Zander was tossing little pieces of ham to Pucci, who was perched on the end of his foot. "We can go there," he said. "Raleigh will give us money. There's obviously something there that Dad wants us to see. That the Mapmakers' Guild wants us to see. And there's the man with the clockwork hand. We're going to track down the man with the clockwork hand."

I stared at him. "Zander. They would never let us go."

"*Never*," Pucci squawked.

"And I'll be back at the Academy," Sukey said sadly. "I don't know when I'll get to see you."

"I wish we could go with you," M.K. said. She had ripped the sleeves off an old T-shirt of mine and I could see the shimmery, glittering skin on her arm. Whenever it started seeming like Ha'aftep Canyon and everything that had happened there had been a dream, I had only to look at M.K.'s arm to know it had been real.

"So do I. Maybe you can come visit."

"What are we going to do, ask Francis Foley for permission?" I asked them. I hated the way they were pretending it was even a possibility. I felt sick at the thought of not seeing Sukey again for months, and it seemed like forever until Christmas vacation. I couldn't even look at her. "You don't understand. I bought us some time, but they know something's up. I'm sure we're being watched.

Foley isn't going to leave us alone. Even if I could figure out the other map, we'd never get there without them following us."

"*Never say never,*" Pucci squawked.

We all turned to look at him.

"I'll say it again, that bird is weird," Sukey said.

We were all silent for a long time. It was one of those hot summer afternoons where you lose all track of time, the air perfectly still, all of us drifting in and out of sleep. I looked over my shoulder at the house and, through the windows, caught sight of Raleigh moving around in the kitchen. Then I turned back to watch Sukey. She was wearing a summer dress, a funny Neo thing made of shiny green fabric, and the green made her hair look brighter than ever. She had a new light in her right ear, a pale amber one, and I liked the way it almost matched her eyes. She caught me staring at her and I closed my eyes and pretended I was sleeping.

At first I thought I was imagining the sound of the engine, the steady *chug chug* of it over the water, but Pucci gave his warning call and when I opened my eyes I saw the huge silver form of an airship.

It was the *Grygia*. We all watched as it came closer and closer and then, thanks to some new technology I hadn't heard about, hovered in the air over the beach. There wasn't a landing platform on the beach, but a set of stairs unfurled from the door of the gondola. We all watched as Jec Banton, holding a folded green umbrella, came down them, then waited on the sand next to the wreck of an abandoned boat. He was wearing his red jumpsuit, only he'd removed the sleeves. His hair still looked like a lethal weapon.

"Where's the map?" Zander whispered to me. "Did you hide it?"

I nodded. I'd found a perfect place for the bathymetric map and Dad's note to us, a floorboard in the attic that could be tipped up to reveal a little hiding spot below. We'd burned the maps of Ha'aftep Canyon as soon as we'd returned home. But my heart was still beating nervously as we watched Mr. Mountmorris, dressed for the weather in a thin green-and-white-striped suit and a white plastic sun hat, come slowly down the stairs.

It seemed like it took forever for them to walk across the sand to us, but when they got there, Mr. Mountmorris gestured and Jec Banton shook open the umbrella, which turned out to be a folding chair. It was a beautiful thing, with thin but sturdy wooden legs and an intricately carved seat, like something Dad might have made.

Pucci hopped over and pecked at the chair, then looked suspiciously up at Mr. Mountmorris, who sat down and studied us for a minute.

"How are you getting along, children?" he asked finally.

"You mean, have we recovered from seeing a man murdered?" M.K. asked, her little face set in a scowl.

Mr. Mountmorris's blue eyes flashed. "He was impeding a BNDL operation. Mr. Foley was very much justified." He seemed to be forcing himself to remain calm and he took a deep breath before saying, "I feel that perhaps you are angry with me."

"You lied to us," I told him. "You didn't tell us that you worked for BNDL."

"*BNDL,*" Pucci squawked.

371

"And you lied to me," he said, glancing at Pucci in a puzzled way. "But that's not what we're here to talk about."

"Why are you here?" Zander asked him.

Mr. Mountmorris rearranged the strands of white hair stretched across his scalp. "I've been thinking about your dilemma. Despite the trouble you caused, you did ultimately... aid, shall we say, in the recovery of the gold from Drowned Man's Canyon. Since the death of your father, you are, sadly, without an adult presence to guide you"— he nodded to Sukey— "in the way that Miss Neville has her mother to guide *her*. In these... difficult times, that is most unfortunate."

Jec Banton nodded sympathetically.

Mr. Mountmorris went on. "You showed great... initiative in locating your father's map and so forth, and despite what you may believe about those of us charged with protecting the New Lands and resources of the world, initiative does not go unrewarded." Mr. Mountmorris reached up to wipe his forehead with the green silk handkerchief he always seemed to carry. "As you know, I have many contacts at the Academy for the Exploratory Sciences and we have found three places there for you, if you agree to take them. What do you think?"

"Why?" I asked him. "Why do you want to help us out? So we won't tell anyone about Tex?"

Jec Banton shook his head as though we'd said something unpleasant.

"Oh no," Mr. Mountmorris said quickly. "I think we trust that you won't mention that unfortunate situation. In truth, I believe we

372

could benefit from your particular talents. If you agree to certain conditions, that is."

"What conditions?" I asked.

"That you abide by all the rules and regulations of the Academy. They like to keep things running like clockwork there, you know. They're very particular about the rules."

"That's it?" I was wary, waiting for the catch. He was buying us off and I wondered what the price was going to be.

He smiled. "That's it. Mr. Banton has all the necessary paperwork, which he'll leave with you. Let me remind you that you have now entered very elite company. The Academy received 2,371 applications this year for twenty places in the incoming class. Now, if there aren't any more questions, I'll say good day."

Jec Banton handed M.K. a brown envelope. "Hail President Hildreth!" he said, and we all raised our hands to our foreheads.

They had already turned to go when I called after them, "What about Dad?"

It took Mr. Mountmorris a long moment to turn around, and when he did, he looked tired to me, as though his offer had cost him a lot. "What about him?"

"Are you going to put his picture back up at the Expedition Society? Are you going to tell everyone he wasn't a crook?"

"That," Mr. Mountmorris said in a quiet voice, "is completely out of my hands." They walked back across the yard and someone in the *Grygia* dropped the stairs down again.

"Is he serious?" Zander asked me.

Sukey had jumped up and she was twirling M.K. around. "This is so exciting. I can introduce you to everyone and show you around. I can't believe you're coming with me! M.K., you're going to be able to use the Academy workshop. You can build a steam engine. You can help me work on a better engine for the glider!"

Pucci gave a loud and happy squawk.

"You can come, too, Pucci," Sukey said. "Lots of students bring animals with them."

"It's great," M.K. said, smiling. "But why is he helping us?"

"They want to keep an eye on us," I told her. "This way they'll be able to watch us, make sure no one's trying to contact us. We won't be able to make a move without an agent there."

"But it's what we always wanted," Zander said. "Becoming Explorers. Traveling. We might be able to go to Fazia."

I wasn't sure. "They'll own us," I told him. "It's bribery, pure and simple."

Pucci alighted on his shoulder, chattering happily to himself. Zander smiled, his blue eyes sad for a minute, and then he shrugged. "What choice do we have?"

"Come on, Kit," M.K. said. "We have to go tell Raleigh! Let's start packing. Sukey, you can tell us what we need to take."

"They'll give you uniforms," Sukey said. "But you should bring regular clothes and any gear you want to have." She was grinning and I couldn't help smiling back at her. At least we wouldn't have to say goodbye.

I thought about what Mr. Mountmorris had said, about the

Academy running like clockwork, and suddenly I knew it had been a little secret joke he'd meant for me, just to make sure that he knew I'd lied to them. None of the agents had ever mentioned the Explorer's clockwork hand. But he knew I knew and he was reminding me that he held my whole future in his hands.

I watched as the stairs were pulled up and the *Grygia* began to rise into the hot blue sky.

"I have to tell Delilah," Sukey was saying, her eyes shining, her cheeks flushed, and her freckles standing out against her skin. "Maybe she can fly us all up there. Zander, wait until you see the Training Grounds. And there are tons of atlases in the Academy library, Kit. I bet you'll find the location of that map." She took my hand. "Come on." Her skin was warm and soft against mine. When she squeezed my hand, I felt a hot thrill run through my arm and up across my shoulders.

As I turned to follow her, I gave the airship one last glance. It rose slowly, majestically, and I saw Mr. Mountmorris's face in the window. The airship got farther and farther away and finally disappeared over the water, followed by a tail of dark smoke that was the only sign they'd been there at all.

But I could have sworn that he'd smiled at me, a small, grim smile that had disappeared almost instantaneously, like a frog's tongue snapping out to catch a fly.

Or maybe it was just a trick of the light.

Acknowledgments

Huge thanks go to Esmond Harmsworth for his truly tireless support of this book; to Brian McMullen for his ideas, care, and skillful shepherding of it; and to Alyson Sinclair and all of the talented folks at McSweeney's. Vendela Vida and Dave Eggers are owed a big thank you for their friendship and support. I am so grateful to Katherine Roy for her beautiful artwork and for the many ways in which she brought my characters and their world to life. I am grateful too for my inspiring students (past and present) and colleagues at the Center for Cartoon Studies, who always teach me something. Same goes for Joni Cole and all the writers at The Writers Center of White River Junction. Thank you to my insightful early readers, Noah Glenshaw, Jacob Glenshaw, Jamison Dunne, Griffin McAlinden, Lisa Christie, Rachel Gross, Tom Taylor, and Vicki Kuskowski. I owe an enormous debt of gratitude to Amanda Ann Palmer, for her unflappability, her most excellent kid-wrangling, and her friendship. And huge thanks to Sue and David Taylor, for many things, but especially for reading to us, taking us on adventures, and for being the most fabulous grandparents.

And so many, many thanks to Matt Dunne, for everything.

About the author

S. S. TAYLOR has been fascinated by maps ever since age 10, when she discovered an error on a map of her neighborhood and wondered if it was *really* a mistake. She has a strong interest in books of all kinds, old libraries, expeditions, mysterious situations, long-hidden secrets, missing explorers, and traveling to known and unknown places. Visit her at www.SSTaylorBooks.com.

About the illustrator

KATHERINE ROY is an artist and author living in New York City. She loves adventure, history, and science, and is currently writing and illustrating a book about great white sharks. *The Expeditioners* is the first novel she has illustrated. See more of her work at www. katherineroy.com.

THE EXPEDITIONERS